ELEPHANT MOUNTAIN

How many young women decide to leave their husband-to-be at the altar and run off to join the Peace Corps? After graduating from college in 1971, 21-year-old Laurel Bittelson finds she has a burning desire not for marriage, but to pursue 1960's style "relevance" in her life. Although she'd never been further from her Boston home than Vermont, she leaves fiancé, friends, family, and her music behind to live and teach in Uganda, East Africa. What she has no way of knowing is that her life will be changed forever, as she falls in love with an African man in a country heading into chaos under the brutal Ugandan dictator, Idi Amin Dada. For Laurel, in so many ways, there would be no going back.

ELEPHANT MOUNTAIN

A Novel

Linda Johnston Muhlhausen

Published by **BLAST PRESS**
324B Matawan Avenue
Cliffwood, NJ 07721
gregglory@aol.com
gregglory.com/blastpress

This is a work of fiction. Names, characters and events are either the products of the author's imagination or used in a fictitious manner.

"General Idi Amin has seized power from President Milton Obote, the man who led Uganda to independence in 1962. The general led a military coup while the president was out of the country attending the Commonwealth conference in Singapore."

BBC World News, 25 January 1971

"The people finally realized that certain branches of the military had been charged with killing their own countrymen. In September and October of 1972, large-scale disappearances took place. The government continued to give the same insufficient answers, and by then the people comprehended the full horror of Amin's regime."

Thomas Melady and Margaret Melady
Idi Amin Dada / Hitler in Africa

"The dead are literally innumerable: all their names will never be known, their numbers never counted."

Henry Kyemba, *A State of Blood*

ACKNOWLEDGEMENTS

This novel is dedicated to the country of Uganda, where I was privileged to serve as a U.S. Action Corps (a.k.a. Peace Corps) volunteer teacher in 1971-72; to its people, their present and future prosperity.

Though most place names in the novel are real, and it is set within the historical framework of the reign of terror of former Ugandan President Idi Amin Dada, the characters and specific events in the story are fictional. The character of Ellen Webster is a fictional tribute to the late Dian Fossey, a real-life "gorilla woman." U.S. Department of State telegrams are excerpted verbatim from the actual documents, but parenthetical notations are mine.

I would like to thank Ms. Amy Reytar of the National Archives, College Park, Maryland, for assistance with my research into State Department documents; the Ugandan Embassy in New York City for providing a text of the Ugandan national anthem; my parents, George and Caroline Johnston, for their acceptance and support of my Ugandan odyssey and the anxiety it caused them; and my husband at the time, Carl Muhlhausen, for sharing the journey. I also owe a debt of gratitude to current and past members of Monmouth County Fiction Writer's Guild for their guidance, support and patient reading, and to Gregg G. Brown, publisher of Blast Press, for his dedication to this project.

Lastly, sincere gratitude to former U.S. Ambassador to Uganda (1972-73) the late Thomas Melady for his care and persistence in helping to implement the safe evacuation of

Peace Corps volunteers from a country in chaos, despite considerable risk to himself and his family.

A portion of profits from the sale of this novel will be donated to the African Wildlife Foundation, www.awf.org

I

DEGREES OF FREEDOM

II

THINGS FALL APART

III

ELEPHANT MOUNTAIN

IV

FINDING GRACE

I

Degrees of Freedom

"…he who has conquered his own coward spirit
has conquered the whole world."

Thomas Hughes
Tom Brown's Schooldays

1

Public Transportation

Laurel tried not to look at the old man standing in the aisle with a pathetic half-dead chicken under his arm. He had been smiling and winking at her ever since the bus groaned into motion this morning, a full two hours behind schedule. The man had the kind of face photographers love to shoot in rural Africa to suggest the nobility of a hard life etched in the deep lines and weathered brown skin – but what no photo would capture was his sheer brass, she thought, musical terms being the way she usually made sense of things; the persistent trumpeting of a young man in an aged body.

Three mind-blowing months ago, she was supposed to get married, the date imprinted in gold on invitations and cocktail napkins: June 5, 1971. The church and reception were booked, plane tickets and resort package purchased by his parents for a guiltily bourgeois two-week honeymoon in Aruba.

Now, she was about as far from being married as a person could get, bumping along with another Peace Corps volunteer in a recommissioned school bus down a narrow dark ribbon of asphalt in Uganda, East Africa.

The bus was a garden-variety school bus, painted blue and pressed into commercial service. Seats had filled quickly and a few people, like the old man with the chicken, were left standing. She felt a little guilty about leaving him standing like that, but she had learned that, as in most places, there were expectations among Ugandans about how people should act according to their status. As a white female visitor, her priority seating was a given. There would be shock if she tried to give up her seat, and disapproval if the man accepted it – to say nothing of how pissed her future housemate Carolyn would be at having to sit next to the man and his chicken, which in itself might have been worth it. Anyway, as the bus filled with the smells of body odor and a kind of organic funk from the bundles and baskets people had crammed in with them, she could see the man was enjoying his commanding view, and like it or not, she and Carolyn were the main attraction.

The weeks of teacher training in Kampala had been more about acculturation, in Peace Corps speak, than actual teaching; figuring out how to relate to this totally new environment. And there was a lot to get used to. The crazy horn-blaring taxis, the relentless beat of African pop music from bars. Smells of exhaust mixing with perfume from the flowers that spilled over every scrap of earth in corners and alleyways. Jostling crowds of people at the market on Nakivubo Road; vendors calling out at any white face, *Madam look, best mango cheap price;* taxi drivers waving and shouting, competing to get the fare.

It took some getting used to, all right, like the cockroaches big as your thumb in the dorm rooms at Makerere University, or petty theft of clothes left to dry outside or in bathrooms. She had heard there were armed gangs of thieves known as *kondos* that might strike restaurants and hotels, but had not encountered any and wondered if white people were given a pass on high-profile crime, like they were on so many other things. Then her purse was snatched right on the college campus by a well-dressed young African man, and she realized whites were assumed to be wealthy and would of course be targets just as much or more than anyone else. The volunteers were not wealthy by American standards, but here in Uganda their money, traveler's checks, clothes, watches, cassette players and clock radios were beyond the reach of many people and could be turned to easy cash. Wise up, she told herself. She had to pay attention, avoid being lulled into a false security by people's friendliness.

Laurel had never been out of the U.S. before, in fact the farthest she had been from Massachusetts was to Vermont, for skiing. Her parents did not like to travel. *Better to stay home, where we are safe,* her mother would say. Her poor beautiful mother, who had suffered as a child in Poland during World War II but never talked about it. Laurel thought maybe this was the reason why she felt she needed an adventure after college, to prove to herself that she could break out of that envelope of fear, and why she had done it so soon after the wedding debacle, so she wouldn't have time to worry herself out of leaving. Coming to Africa had been terrifying but exhilarating, and she had been able to regulate herself to stay in tune. Overall, the whole volunteer training experience turned out to be kind of a blast. She was already missing it, the way she had missed home during those first weeks – the way she still missed home, if she let herself think about it.

She would not write to her mother about the dead man they had seen lying in the scrub grass in the center of a traffic circle in the Kampala downtown. She had never seen a dead person before, but you could tell right away. His brown skin looked dull and ashy in the sunshine, and gravity had taken hold of his body the way a fallen tree sinks into the ground. Their student guide quickly shepherded them away. *Do not worry, soon an ambulance from Mulago will come to collect him.* At least there would be an ambulance and a hospital, but the disharmony, not knowing how or why the man had died, or who he was, had shaken her.

She would also not write about the party at the home of the American ambassador, where the volunteers had lined up to be greeted by the new Ugandan president, General Idi Amin Dada. He did not address them in English, just stuck out his hand at each person while laughing with his entourage at some inside joke. President for Life Idi Amin Dada. A large, loud man, imposing in the full regalia of his army uniform – how she had quickly moved away from his dry, hot hand and bulging bloodshot eyes.

But she would write home about the wonders, things both new and amazing. There had been that huge red ball of sun coming up on the horizon when the volunteer group first landed at the tiny airport in Entebbe, and every day since then the rhapsody, as she termed it, of improvising life in Kampala. New sights, sounds, smells, colors. Friendly, smiling people greeting her on the streets as if she were royalty, endlessly entertained by her red hair and freckles. The welcome reception, the Makerere student chorus that sang for them, *We are the Shining Stars,* their voices untrained but pure, their composition consonant, smooth, cutting through her jet lag with a sweet natural harmony that calmed and made anything seem possible. After all the dissonance still ringing in her head from back home, the *how could you do it,* meaning, walk away from Alan, and why on earth did she want to go to Africa of all places, that half hour had been just what the doctor ordered.

As the bus bore south from the capital, the central plains of Uganda opened out before her like an alien planet. There were so many shades of green, from the pale celery of elephant grass to the dark emerald blankets of tea and coffee. She imagined she was on a boat moving through a green sea, that the scattered homesteads were islands, the occasional flowering bush or tree a flock of brightly plumed birds arrayed on a rock, like musical notes ready to fly off her fingers in all their brilliant colors. A boat tunneling through the bottom half of the world, to the unknown destination in the southwest corner of the country: a school named Butawanga.

<u>2</u>

Do you take this man?

Laurel waits in a little parlor room in the church with maid of honor Tessa and the two bridesmaids, in her long white dress and veil, mid-heel white satin shoes that are too wide but that is okay they said because her feet are likely to swell by the end of the day. The gold watch glowing on her left wrist, Alan's gift so she wouldn't be late for the ceremony. Alan who lives in the concrete world and doesn't go around with his head filled with music. Alan who lives in a world of broken people who need fixing. He wants to fix people and that is why he will make a good doctor. He wants to fix Laurel, and she knows she needs it and she has already quit smoking and lost some weight and now has this gold watch with diamonds on the face so she can stop being late to everything, this gift he bought for her though he knows she doesn't like to own gold and diamonds and other symbols of conspicuous consumption.

This man who had seemed like such a miracle because he was willing to love her and take care of her. Dr. and Mrs. Alan Kemp. Laurel Bittelson Kemp. A new identity, and she would not have to be her deficient self any more. *Regulate*, she tells herself, a piano-tuning term used since childhood to temper herself in times of stress.

Standing here in this fusty church room in her wedding dress singing quietly to herself from a Beatles' song, the lyric about happiness being a warm gun, over and over like a mantra, playing with key, rhythm, inflection, so she can keep herself from thinking. Tessa's hand lightly on her arm, the sweet smell of her bouquet; Mama's glowing face, the still-blonde hair in a chignon. *You look beautiful, Laurel.* Laurel almost believes it. Her own burnt-orange hair done up in stiff curls piled under headpiece and veil, liquid foundation and powder to even out tone and cover freckles, padded bra to fill out the beaded bodice. Like an ad in a magazine, the kind of magazine she never looks at.

Now Mama is seated in the sanctuary with Alan's family and all the other guests, waiting. Papa squeezes her hand, waits by the door to walk her down the aisle and give her away. Tradition. Organ music swells up over the murmur of voices from inside, where about fifty people wait for this man and this woman to be joined together in the bonds of holy matrimony, forever, 'til death . . . 'til death. . . *regulate, regulate, oh fuck* –

"Tess. I need to see Alan. Now."

"Oh? Well, then I'll get him." She shoots a question from her eyes that Laurel cannot answer. The two bridesmaids are busy chatting with each other. One is Alan's younger sister, the other a friend of Laurel's from the B.U. music department. A violinist, with the telltale pink welt under her jawbone.

A minute later Tessa is back. "Too late. He's up at the altar. The church guy said they're ready to start."

"No, you have to get him, Tess, just go up there now and get him!"

Her father turns to face her, puts his hands gently on her arms. He doesn't speak, but his gray-blue eyes hold her with wide alarm. The door opens and the first swelling chords of the wedding march come in. Too late, too late for talking. "Papa, I can't do it."

9

His lips part, he gasps. She can see his crooked, decaying teeth. He is too fond of sweets, her father. "Are you sure?"

She unfastens the watch, lays it on a shelf below a mirror, pulls off her veil, gathers up her long skirts. "Yes." It sounds like someone else's voice.

"Well, that's it then." Papa wrings his hands. "I'll go in and tell them."

Her bridesmaids see that something is wrong and crowd her with alarm in their high-pitched whispers. Tessa stands like a statue, eyes wide. Laurel turns and walks out through the carpeted foyer.

She does not look back.

Even in the clopping white satin heels, it only takes a minute to run out of the church and around the corner to the sandwich board sign she knew would be there, having seen it before like a talisman: U.S. Action Corps Recruitment Center. A basement entrance, down the steps panting with her white dress bunched up under one arm and smiling, smiling.

They'll never find me here.

<u>3</u>

What if I die in Africa?

It was her first public pit latrine, in the garden behind a shadowy bar at a stop in the town of Kabale. The smell of it came up like a humid fart, but after seven hours and probably two more to go, it was this or bust.

Some passengers were getting off here, including the chicken man. He bowed to the two white girls and drawled, *Wa-zung-u*, that ubiquitous generic Swahili word for white people. When Laurel smiled in return, Carolyn elbowed her in the ribs and said, *Better stop smiling or he'll be asking you to marry him. That chicken will be your bride price.* Laurel told her to shut up, that people here were just being friendly to foreigners, but still she was relieved when the man walked away with the limp animal under his arm.

Continuing passengers got out of the bus long enough to stretch their legs and relieve themselves, the men and most of the women avoiding the latrine for the bushes. Some of the women here could pee standing up in their long *basuti* dresses, just by spreading their legs a bit and tilting the pelvis. Evidently there was no underwear to get in the way. It would not be possible in a knee-length dress, with the pulling down of panties not to mention the whole privacy thing, so squatting in the latrine was the only option. She took a deep breath and held it, went in with the roll of toilet paper from her backpack and was out again by the time she needed to gulp air – voice training paying off in this at least.

Getting back on the bus required a reshuffling and re-greeting process, shaking hands with or nodding to everyone on the way down the aisle. A few young men who had not been on the bus before climbed up to sit on the roof among tied-down bunches of green matoke bananas, and Laurel wondered why things like that, that would have seemed impossible back in Boston, now hardly made an impression.

Outside town, the road changed from a narrow band of asphalt to hard-packed dirt, studded with stones. Carolyn settled back, taking up more than her half of the seat.

"Talk about a one-horse town. At least Gregg and Kevin are posted here in Kabale, you know? It's the closest town to where we're going."

So, Carolyn was already planning on seeing Gregg. They had been pretty cozy during training. Well, that was her business, as long as it didn't end up causing trouble at their school. A school near the town of Kisoro. The boonies, all right, where people were no doubt traditional and conservative.

"You know," said Laurel, "I thought Gregg was out of line back in Kampala, the way he talked about things he had no business talking about."

"You mean, like, if maybe some of us were sent here by the CIA because big daddy Amin is sucking up to Qaddafy, the Islamic socialist?"

"But where did he even get an idea like that? I mean, look at our group, Carolyn. We're all just out of college, and most of them are just looking to have a good time." Like you, she thought. "Not exactly spy material."

Carolyn looked at her sideways. "Hey, you never know. The best spies would be the least likely ones."

"I just think we need to remember where we are. Haven't you noticed that no one talks about politics here, not even the college kids we met at Makerere? I think there's a reason for that."

"And haven't you noticed that no one speaks English on this bus? You worry too much, Laurel. We're Americans, no one's going to arrest us for talking."

"I'd rather not test that theory. Gregg should just keep his mouth shut."

Carolyn sniffed, slouched down and closed her eyes. "Okay, so Gregg can be an asshole. But you got to admit he's sexy."

Laurel didn't answer. She hadn't really thought about whether Gregg, or any of them, was sexy. Maybe she would never look at a man that way again and that would be fine, maybe better than fine. In freshman year before she met Alan she had gone through a free love phase, as she thought of it now. She remembered wanting to try sex, to experience that forbidden adult activity. She got a prescription for the contraceptive pill from the university health service, then set about pursuing any guy with a guitar slung over his shoulder. Not the ones in her department studying serious music, but the would-be rock band members, because they seemed so – what, relaxed? Sure of themselves? What had she been looking for, anyway, to buy into all the stupid childish counterculture delusions like her best friend Tessa? But the Pill made her feel bloated and gave her headaches and the sexual revolution was not revolutionary, just men trying to have as much sex as they could get, without strings attached. She looked back on her two fumbling encounters as mistakes that did not bear repeating. No, feeding some inferior musician's ego was not her idea of a good time, and the sex act itself was highly overrated. Mystery solved. Experiment over. Finis.

Then, when a tall good-looking pre-med student named Alan actually noticed her, he had felt like a miracle of solidity. Sex with Alan had developed slowly, and when it did, he knew more about her own anatomy than she did. And at first, she had responded in a way she had not known before.

Now, all that was left behind like so much excess baggage. When she got back home after Peace Corps, she would be free to do what she really wanted to do without having to justify herself to a man. And what she really wanted to do was compose music, though it was a long-shot dream. For now, it was the rattling of the bus, the heat, the roaring engine and grinding gears, and the way Carolyn's head was resting on her shoulder.

The landscape became a flat stretch of grasslands carved into rolling, rounded hills, the road winding along the contours. Before long, the hills deepened, the road a single lane cut in against the sides of sheer cliffs. The bus labored to climb what was now a very steep grade, bumping over rocks or skidding over loose gravel. There were no guardrails to keep them from swaying off the road and plummeting down to the valley floor – and it was a long, long way down.

Laurel took hold of the metal bar of the seat in front of her, now vacant. Sweat bloomed from her forehead and underarms. She could not tear her eyes away from the terrifying drama of the view. This is it, she thought. We'll go over, and I'll die here in Africa in this stinking bus and no one will find us for days. With one hand, she grabbed her backpack and squeezed. There, she could feel the rectangular box containing her recorder, a soprano made of pearwood, still with her,

14

waiting for her to breathe life into it. *Regulate, regulate.*

She couldn't believe Carolyn could stay asleep at a time like this. She had half a mind to wake her just to have someone to share her fear. The remaining passengers were dozing or talking quietly, some laughing, with no trace of concern in their voices. What was the matter with these people? The word *ignorant* burrowed like a chigger under her skin, but she shook it off in alarm. How she had bristled when, back in the States, the Peace Corps psychologist, a black woman with her hair styled in a big "Afro" had said, *All whites are prejudiced.* You don't know me, Laurel had replied, but the woman's words had remained branded in her brain. What if she was right? Racist. Like syphilis, some horrible social disease no one wants to admit they have –

As the bus rocked toward certain destruction, she closed her eyes and imagined playing her piano, the satin feel of ivory keys against the nubs of her fingers. If only she could feel it again, even for a minute, that perfect union of touch and sound, the rapture that was like love, left behind as suddenly as she had left Alan. But she was too scared to call up more than scattered phrases, a line or two, of the music that had been her life.

Running away was what everyone thought. Her mother, Alan, Alan's parents. Running away from commitment, from responsibility. But the idea of joining Peace Corps had been taking root inside her and growing more insistent as the American reality got more and more hard-edged. Vietnam, the draft, the police beating anti-war demonstrators at the Chicago Democratic Convention and the Ohio National Guard killing protesters at Kent State, Afro-Americans fighting for their civil rights, the military-industrial-imperialist complex, the U.S. as the world's bully. A kind of frustrated panic had been growing in her that Alan did not share, that it was time to react, to do something positive and real. To regulate. Joining Peace Corps felt right, as a way to show people in other countries that Americans were basically good people. It was not running away, it was running toward – she believed that with all her being – except at this moment she would have given anything to be transported off this deathtrap of a bus, back to the safety of her parent's home in Concord, Massachusetts, U.S.A.

<u>4</u>

Letter to Tessa

August 22, 1971

Jambo, Tess!

I know, two whole months and this my first letter, mea culpa, but it's all been crazy busy and I did send you the postcard with the crested crane from the National Museum, hope you got. P.C. training in Kampala is already over and by the time you get this, my roommate Carolyn and I will be at our school. The crash course in teacher and language training was fairly laid back. I don't have a clear idea of what to do when I get there. I'm worried about screwing up.

Makerere students hang out in the Kampala bars, not my usual scene you're thinking, but when in Rome. They drink beer and dance to loud African pop music which gives me an atonal headache. The African guys mostly want to get good jobs in Kampala after graduation, like in a bank or big company, and make enough to buy clothes and watches and help support their parents and extended families – they seem so much older than us as far as responsibility goes. AND – no stupid come-on lines, no rap about politics. I didn't even have to answer for Nixon and Vietnam, not yet anyway. One volunteer asked a student about how Ugandans felt about their new president. The student said everyone was very happy, but there was something cautious in his voice. Amin's only been president for 7 months, but they expect him to make life better than it was under the previous president Obote. I'm not so sure.

I saw him once. He's a scary guy.

Carolyn and I are assigned to the same school. She's big, bold and brassy. She flirts with all the male volunteers and staff. Yes, I asked – she's Taurus. No, I didn't get day and time of birth, so just fill me in on the basic Taurian (?) traits.

Last week I saw a dead man lying in the dirt in the middle of a traffic circle, with cars and trucks speeding around. There were 6 of us volunteers plus Joseph our student guide. No one suggested doing anything. We followed Joseph like a flock of sheep back to campus. Later I was ashamed for not doing something. I know Alan would have, if he were here. But I can't measure myself by Alan any more.

Damn airmail letter, writing small but already out of space. Wish you could see Wandegeya, where bats fly out of trees by hundreds at sunset, artist's delight. Cockroaches big as thumb, choral group of Makerere students called "Kampala Shining Stars." Harmony pure, like angels.

Love you & please write! L.

5

Outer Limits

A little after 7 p.m., the bus finally ground to a stop at the intersection of two black roads.

Laurel snapped out of her lethargy and looked out the window for some sign that this was their stop. The driver turned in his seat and waved at her, then the remaining few passengers started gesturing and chanting, Boot-Wang-A, Boot-Wang-A. She grabbed the straps of her backpack and got up.

Carolyn got up and shouted to the driver, as if he was hard of hearing. "But where's the school?"

The driver stood now, too, pointed out the open door and shouted back at her. "Boot-wang-a."

"This must be the place, Carolyn." Laurel stepped out into a brace of clean, cold air, Carolyn grumbling behind her. No one else got off. Those who were left were going on to the last stop, Kisoro.

After a reshuffling of bags and parcels, their duffels were unloaded from the roof by the two remaining men who had hitched a ride on top of the luggage.

The bus lumbered away with its black cloud, and all she could see in the gathering dusk was the dirt road disappearing into thick trees and bushes. Carolyn turned in a circle and threw up her arms. "What the fuck are we supposed to do now?"

"Well, the driver pointed down this road."

"But how do we know how far it is? It could be miles to

the school. This is so fucked up."

Fucked up is right. After almost 10 hours and the terror of the cliff-hanging road, she was exhausted, and suddenly chilly in the sleeveless shirtdress she had found in the bins back home at Filene's basement in an eleventh-hour shopping trip. All she had worn in college were bell-bottom jeans and tee shirts, but in Uganda most women wore dresses with length below the knee, which had not been all that easy to find among the miniskirts.

Let the music guide you and the notes will follow, her old piano teacher had said. Mr. Heywood, the one who had lasted the longest before Mama fired him.

"Fucked up or not, let's go." She shivered in air that felt like October in Massachusetts. She pulled a cardigan out of her duffel, put it on, shouldered her backpack, grabbed the duffel and started walking. Carolyn extracted a nylon windbreaker from her large, army-surplus- looking duffel, and fell in next to her.

"I'm just glad to have my feet on terra firma."

"What are you talking about?"

"You were asleep the whole time so you missed it. Out of Kabale we were on a one-lane dirt road on the side of a very steep cliff. No guardrail, swaying every time we hit a rock, and with the way it was top-loaded it was pretty hairy. A thrill a minute."

Carolyn's breath made white clouds in the air. "You're exaggerating."

"No, I'm not. Every time we skidded around a hairpin curve I thought, just my luck, we're going over and I'm going to die in Africa, before I even get to do what I came here to do."

"So why didn't you wake me up? Like they say, misery loves company."

Laurel knew why, because Carolyn would not have taken it seriously. "And I couldn't understand why no one else was worried."

Carolyn snuffed. "That's because being worried doesn't keep the bus from going over. Better to be asleep in a situation like that."

Laurel stared at this dark-haired woman she hardly knew. "Are you always so fucking sensible?"

"Yeah, but right now, I'd just like to know how much further we have to walk."

"At least you woke up for the bamboo forest and those black and white monkeys." The road had finally turned away from the sheer cliffs and through walls of thick, tall bamboo, a cathedral of green, the air turned cool and moist.

"Colobus. That was pretty cool." Carolyn looked around. "But where the fuck are we?"

Laurel shifted her duffel to her other hand and sniffled. This really was beginning to seem like some stupid screw up. "I don't know, but we might as well keep walking. Unless you have a better idea?" She fought a growing sense of unease. They had been walking for about 10 minutes, with only the occasional top of a thatched roof poking out from bushy trees. The air was laced with the smell of wood smoke, but there were no people to be seen, and no sound other than their own footsteps crunching on dark ashy soil, magnified in the still air. "I mean, the school has to be here somewhere, right? The driver said, 'Boot-wang-a'."

"Okay, but let's remember, this is Africa. The school might be ten miles away for all we know. Or maybe there was some trail we missed somewhere" –

"Hey, that looks like a clearing up ahead." Relief flooded

in. "I'll bet that's it. Has to be."

They came into a large clearing that opened out into a rectangle with two rows of identical concrete buildings, a big Quonset-shaped structure, some dusty playing fields, and around the perimeter a scattering of cottages. Earth, buildings, and sky were so uniformly gray and the thick clouds slung so low, it felt like the inside of a tent. Laurel stopped, put down her duffel.

"This place looks like a prison camp." Carolyn raised her voice against the silence like a naughty child in church. "Or, like, something from the Outer Limits – don't adjust your television, we control the picture – I mean, where is everyone?"

Laurel knew that people like Carolyn were always looking for the worst and finding it. Her mother was like that. But then, her mother had reason to expect the worst from the world.

"Maybe they didn't know we were coming. I mean, we're teachers, not royalty, Carolyn." Still, it reminded her of walking onto a stage for a dress rehearsal in front of a hall full of empty seats. As a child, she had imagined an atomic bomb had exploded nearby and killed all the people so she did not need to rehearse, after all.

They walked down the dirt road that circled the inside of the compound. The concrete houses were most likely faculty housing, but they looked deserted. There were no curtains in windows, nothing planted in dusty yards. The soil here was black, ashy. Around Kampala, it was red.

"Maybe it's not really the school. Maybe it's an army camp and we'll both be raped and murdered, and then Peace Corps will have a lot of explaining to do."

Well maybe, but — "That's ridiculous, Carolyn. If it was an Army camp they would have stopped us by now." *You don't know how much evil is in the world.* Her mother's words. *Stay home, where you are safe.* "Let's keep going, maybe we'll find a house that looks lived in."

Where the road curved around there was a cottage-style house that appeared much older than the concrete ones. It had a garden path with a decayed wooden trellis that looked held up by its thick lattice of vine. The wood door had a black iron knocker, and over it a small engraved plaque: Headmaster.

<u>6</u>

Butawanga

Laurel knocked at the headmaster's door. No one answered.

Carolyn dropped her bag and heaved a sigh. "Doesn't anyone give a shit around here?" She stepped into the garden and looked in a side window. "There's someone in there!"

Fine, just fine, whoever it was would see Carolyn's big face staring in. Sure enough, the door opened and an old man with sunken cheeks and bulging, watery eyes blinked out at them as if witnessing a Martian landing.

"Mr. Senwangama?" It was the headmaster's name, the one they had been given.

Without a word, the man went back inside.

Carolyn sniffed. "If that's the headmaster, we're in trouble."

"Whoever he is, he wasn't expecting us."

Another man, short and plump, pulled the door fully open. "So, you have arrived already?" He had round, deep brown eyes.

"Well, yes, I mean – are you Mr. Senwangama?"

"But we thought you would be coming on Thursday."

"Peace Corps told us Tuesday – that's today," Carolyn said. "Somebody got it wrong."

In an awkward moment of silence, Laurel almost thought he would send them away, but then the man smiled and ran a

24

hand over his sparse graying hair.

"Well, no matter, no matter. You are most welcome. I am James Senwangama, the headmaster. Please to come in, you are just in time for supper."

Supper. All she had eaten today was some greasy fried dough called *mandazi* from a street vendor when the bus had stopped in Mbarara town.

The headmaster brought them into a small room, furnished with four chairs upholstered in faded fabric and a small table set with a cloth and tea service. Another African man seated in one of the chairs stood up when they came in. He was neatly dressed in dark slacks, white shirt and navy blue blazer.

"This is Mr. Ngira, one of our teachers." Mis-ta In-gee-ra; the East African accent was like British English but slower, with a musical lilt. "He is one of the first to return from the summer holidays."

So, most of the other teachers were not there yet; that was why the place looked so deserted.

Mr. Ngira pumped Carolyn's hand, then hers, with a strong, firm grip that was not the way Ugandans usually shook hands, light and barely touching. She realized this must be what he thought of as a proper Muzungu handshake.

The headmaster motioned them to the table with outstretched arms, a priest blessing his flock. "So, that is all right then, let us sit down." On the table, two plates with traces of food on them flanked a small platter with one sandwich left on it. The old man who had first opened the door came in with two clean plates, then disappeared. Carolyn took the remaining sandwich. How embarrassing, Laurel thought. With two unexpected guests there would not be enough food, but then the old man came back with another platter of sandwiches.

The headmaster smiled at him. "My servant does not hear or speak. But, he is a good servant. He knows my ways very well." The man did not change his dour expression. "We are growing old together."

Mr. Ngira laughed too loudly and said, "Your age is proportional to your wisdom, Headmaster."

Your classic suck-up, she thought.

The sandwich was corned beef, butter, white bread quartered with the crusts cut off, and it tasted really good. She wanted to stop talking and devour it, but Carolyn was busily eating and someone needed to make conversation. "What subject do you teach, Mr. Ngira?"

"I teach Science and Maths to the upper forms." Perched on the edge of his chair, his slacks pulled across his thighs. *Maths*; it was so British, reminding her of her English father, who still had an accent. *Toe-mah-toe.*

"When necessary I also take on some English classes, as do the other teachers. We all must pitch in when needed." He looked at Carolyn. "And you are to teach Maths as well, Miss Maxwell?"

Carolyn leaned back in her chair, cleaning her teeth with her tongue. She was dressed in a black A-line skirt and white schoolgirl blouse that pulled across her large breasts. "Yes. My degree was in Economics, but I guess they didn't think that would be very useful here."

Laurel looked down at her sandwich. Tact was not going to be Carolyn's strong point.

Mr. Ngira fingered his clean-shaven chin, as if he had a beard to stroke. "Do not worry, Miss Maxwell. Our Mr. Saliwa has History and Economics well in hand."

She wondered if he actually meant it as a put-down. Carolyn didn't seem to notice.

Mr. Ngira picked up his cup, sipped, and replaced it very carefully on the saucer, as if worried it might break. When all was secure, he glanced up and caught Laurel watching. When she smiled, he looked away.

In the light of a gas lamp the room was bright enough. There was a sofa upholstered in the same green printed fabric as the chairs they were sitting on. The style was English country cottage, comfy and warm, and who would have thought to find this here in tropical Africa! Against the walls were bookshelves and a heavy-looking breakfront, its top cluttered with books and papers. Sandwiches, hot milky tea, the smiles of the two men and the melody of their accents. It felt good.

"Yes," Mr. Senwangama said, "and – Miss Bittelson, is it? – has come to us to teach English Language and Literature."

"I was a Music Performance major, actually." True, but maybe not the best recommendation for this job. "But English was always one of my stronger subjects, and I'm really looking forward to teaching here, Mr. Senwangama." It was not exactly a lie about the English, since she had maintained a strong B grade. Writing papers had seemed so much harder than writing a sonata for piano, though her grades in music composition had actually been no better.

If the headmaster thought anything about her remark, he did not let on. "Teachers will receive a curriculum in the next several days. We begin our classes on Monday next, eh, Mr. Ngira?"

So, they would have almost a week to get ready. That was a relief.

Carolyn smiled. "Thank you for the food, Mr. Senwangama.

It was delicious. Can we see our house now?"

May we, but what was the hurry? She was still enjoying a last bite and a gulp of tea, but now the two men had stood up, the headmaster short with a rounded paunch and glossy black skin, Mr. Ngira taller, with brown skin. When she got up, her napkin fell to the floor and he bent to pick it up. His elbow caught the table, rattling the dishes. "Well, I am certainly very clumsy." He laughed self-consciously. He was nervous, maybe even more nervous than she was.

Outside, the headmaster hailed two students who were also early arrivals. They hefted the girls' duffel bags onto the tops of their heads. Laurel said she would carry her backpack, not wanting to risk damage to that little wooden flute that was to be her only means of making music. Also inside the pack were a half-roll of toilet paper, some paperbacks, a notebook, blank airmail letters, ballpoint pens and pencils. In her trunk, to be shipped to the school after their arrival, was her cassette player and twenty-four carefully selected cassette tapes, seventeen of them classical, including opera, the rest a mix of rock, folk, and two movie soundtracks, *West Side Story* and *2001: A Space Odyssey*. And six blank tapes to record any music she might come across; well, five-and-a-half now, since on her first night in Africa she had recorded the songs of the Makerere University chorus, the Kampala Shining Stars. They were college kids, as she had been until a few months ago – the voices untrained yet melded into a perfect natural harmony, full of hope, resonating with the liminal message: *yes, you have come, you are here, and new things will open to you* – she still carried their sound and its message in her mind, but she felt better having it on tape, too, to hear it with her ears whenever she needed.

As the students walked ahead down the path to the houses, Laurel studied them. Their white short-sleeved shirts and khaki shorts did not seem warm enough for weather like this. Tall, thin, long-limbed, black skinned; they walked quickly, talking and laughing. She couldn't hear if they were speaking English with each other, though they had with the headmaster. This is what they would be like, then. Her students. The students she had practice-taught in Kampala had been younger, in newer-looking uniforms, and many were Indian and Pakistani. These two were somewhere between boy and man.

It was almost eight o'clock. The near-darkness of the compound was like murky water. Mr. Senwangama set a leisurely pace down the road toward one row of concrete houses. He talked about the school, which was founded by the nearby Catholic mission in 1959 but was now run by the Ugandan government. They currently had a student body of 358 boys in the four grades or "forms." The new concrete faculty houses had been constructed by the World Bank, along with student classrooms, dorms and dining hall. "We are looking to the future here," Mr. Senwangama said, sounding proud, paternal. Laurel liked him. You could tell he cared about his school. And he was trying to make them feel welcome after sort of a rocky start. Whatever bureaucratic snafu had been responsible for the arrival day's confusion, it seemed forgotten.

She could also hear parts of the conversation between Mr. Ngira and Carolyn, walking a few steps behind. "Economics is very interesting indeed. I had one course of it in college," he said.

"Did you go to college in England?" Carolyn asked.

"No, not in England." The hearty laugh again. "In fact I have never left Uganda. I studied at Makerere, at the National Teacher's College."

"I went to college in Maryland, a very old private college, practically Ivy League—"

Some Ivy League, it was an all-girls' Catholic college, Laurel was thinking when the headmaster pointed out some thin wires overhead. "Any moment now – yes, there we are." There was the groan of a large machine coming to life, a steady whirring sound and scattered points of light flickering on. "Between terms we have electricity at eight o'clock P.M., for two hours. During term when the boys have their studies, it will be seven o'clock until ten o'clock. In the event you wish to stay awake later than that, you will have a gas lamp." They stopped in front of one of the concrete houses.

Mr. Ngira raised his hand in a salute. "Cheerio then, ladies. Perhaps tomorrow you will see the volcanoes." He turned away and walked with long strides down the dark road. Laurel stared blankly after him, having registered the clear timbre of his voice but not his meaning, until she remembered that there was supposed to be a range of volcanic mountains nearby. That was why the soil was so black.

"What a clown." Carolyn said, nodding toward Mr. Ngira's retreating form. Laurel was glad Mr. Senwangama did not show any sign that he had heard as he opened the door for them and stood, smiling. They followed up the single front step to the small concrete porch. He shook their hands again, said to let him know if anything was needed, and like a man with more important things on his mind left them there before the open door. Right now, Laurel just wanted to pee, brush her teeth, get out of this grimy dress and into her warm sleeping bag. She hoped there might be clean water inside, though an outdoor pump and outhouse were more likely.

She thought about the two students, their school uniforms, bouncing walk, balanced duffels, hand gestures. Soon, there would be full classes of them. Mr. Senwangama probably wondered if these Wazungu women were up to any real job, much less teaching adolescent boys. And he would be right to wonder, she thought. Mr. Ngira had a nice-looking face, but he was clearly as uneasy with her as she was with him. After having perked up from food and tea she was again very tired, and aware of feeling dense, disoriented, landed in some weird alternate world.

There was her duffel just inside the door. Carolyn had already picked up hers and gone inside. Over her fatigue, Laurel felt an inexplicable thrill. She turned to look back at the muscular sky. Volcanoes, she thought – just imagine. Then she walked into her new home.

7

Under the weather

The concrete house was bright and cold in the light of the gas lamp, the generator having shut down with a whining decrescendo at 10 pm. Laurel sat at the dining table in the large front room in her nightgown and sweater, writing letters on blue airmail paper, her sleeping bag gathered around like a shawl. Carolyn was in the bathroom, taking a bath by candlelight.

It was late Friday night, the fourth night after their arrival. She had spent the last few days trying to stay warm and find out what was expected of her. Mr. Senwangama said the rainy season was unusually long this year, but the bad weather should be clearing out soon. Small comfort, since a cold virus had taken root in her sinuses and was now in full bloom, making her too miserable to sleep.

She sat and stared blankly at the arc of lamp light on the gray concrete walls, the small flattened moon created on the white ceiling board. The room was furnished with the table and four chairs, a sofa and two cushioned chairs. Jalousie windows reflected the light like a wall of mirrors. The house had clearly been designed for coolness in hot climates. Even with the window slats shut tight, there was plenty of space for air to get in. She and Carolyn had stuffed old Peace Corps memos in gaps to keep out the cold wind. Still, the school must have been glad to get these houses; the modern kitchen with propane stove, bathroom with hot and cold running water and flush toilet, and two bedrooms, more than compensated for the chilliness. Even with the misery of her cold, Laurel could not believe her luck. The houses here were better equipped than she had ever anticipated. It crossed her mind that this undercut the challenge of the African adventure, but she convinced herself it was enough of a challenge just being a stranger in a totally new country, without coping with a leaky roof and an outhouse or who knew what else.

Lighting the lamp had been a trial of coordination: applying a lighted match to the saturated wick at the first hiss of air, the sudden whump of ignition, the damping down to a steady white glow. Even now that she had the process down pat, she always tried to clear her mind before starting, certain that one misstep in the litany of flame and fuel would have deadly consequences. *I practice Zen lantern lighting,* she wrote to Tessa, finishing a letter she had tried to start on the bus. She had met Tessa when they were both sophomores at Boston University. They had moved off campus to share an apartment in suburban Somerville for their junior and senior years.

I'd give anything for a tissue, not to mention a glass of orange juice. Laurel missed Tessa's sympathetic ear, sometimes too sympathetic, a weakness that had led to the constant parade of hippie freaks crashing in their apartment during college. *Carolyn is already making moves on this English guy Gordon who teaches Science here, old, at least 35. I told you in my last letter she's Taurus. Is nymphomania part of the profile?*

Laurel didn't think there was much to astrology, but she knew her friend would give her a full analysis when she wrote back, and receiving her advice would help bridge the physical distance between them.

Writing to her parents, she was more upbeat. No mention of her cold or Carolyn's behavior, just that Butawanga was a modern school at 6,000 feet elevation with a bracing climate, so could they please send a wool sweater and rain parka?

Laurel folded each letter into a neat square. The postage was prepaid, so all she had to do was hand them to the man who operated the small school store. When he collected a sufficient quantity of mail, it would be put on a bus back to Kampala. She could imagine the letters handled, processed, crushed with hundreds of others bound for the States. It was somehow hard to believe that they would ever find their way across a country, a continent, and an ocean, into her parents' white wood mailbox in Concord, or Tessa's long-fingered, perpetually paint-stained artist's hands.

Tomorrow, Saturday, Laurel and Carolyn were going to the general store in Kisoro with Gordon Coopersmith, the British expatriate teacher. He had stopped by yesterday to introduce himself, his white face at the door surprisingly out of context.

Gordon had taught science at Butawanga for five years. He spoke with a proper-sounding English accent peppered with the occasional profanity for which he swiftly apologized, which Laurel found unexpectedly charming. Tonight they had eaten dinner at his house, one of the older, cozier houses like the headmaster's, built in colonial days. Mr. Ngira, *please just call me Ngira,* was also there; apparently, he and Gordon were great friends. Dinner was some kind of chewy meat pie that Gordon was very proud of having taught his houseboy to cook. Their own "houseboy" was just learning how to work the stove and as far as she knew had no training in cooking.

Laurel had objected to having a houseboy until Gordon

34

explained that it would be expected. Cash-paying jobs like this were scarce and coveted among the local people. They were informed that the headmaster had already selected someone for them, and sure enough yesterday a very tall, soft-spoken teenager knocked on their door. Seventeen-year-old Caspar had gone only as far as Primary school, but he had a good working knowledge of English. She could think of nothing for him to do that first day, so he sat on their back step until it was time to go home.

This morning, another young man came to their door. He informed them, with Caspar translating, that he was to be their *shamba* boy. *I guess we're expected to have a garden*, she had mused out loud. *Don't look at me*, Carolyn had said, *I'm from Baltimore.*

His name was Sabinyo. He was shorter and younger than Caspar, had not been to school at all and spoke little English. Here, children could only attend school if their parents were able to pay their fees each term. Sabinyo, Laurel assumed, had not been as fortunate as Caspar. As soon as Laurel stepped into the backyard to talk to her new employees, shafts of sunlight hit the ground where the wind had opened tunnels in the clouds. Over her right shoulder, the top of a mountain was outlined against patches of blue sky, like no mountain she had ever seen before. It looked like an immense conical pile of steel slag, gray and menacing and looming very near. "Holy shit," she said, hoping the profanity that had slipped out would not register with Caspar. "Is that a volcano?"

"Yes, Madam," Caspar answered. "In fact, it is one of the Virunga volcanoes."

Sabinyo, looking at her as if she had just confirmed his low expectation of her intelligence, said the name, "Muhabura."

While they discussed the boundaries of the prospective garden, Laurel could not keep from glancing at the huge brooding presence that had been there all this time, unseen behind dark veils of cloud.

* * *

Laurel pulled off a section from a roll of toilet paper and blew her nose. Monday would be the first day of classes, the stack of books on the table a mute challenge: *Tom Brown's School Days, Things Fall Apart, Romeo and Juliet, Standard English Grammar, Book 4*. Literature every day, grammar three times a week. Homework, compositions, grades to assign. Four classes a day, a total of 76 students. All those names, all those faces. Students here took school seriously because their families were paying for it, often at great sacrifice. Teachers were expected to prepare them for the all-important exams that determined whether they could go on to the next level. It was a heavy responsibility. Teacher training in Kampala had been compressed into a few weeks, and it was short on specifics. How to plan for a whole term of lessons? When to assign tests, how to grade? *Smile more,* the Peace Corps teacher trainer had said. But she couldn't help feeling that all the smiling in the world would not make up for the incompetence of someone as unprepared as she was.

The dormitories had reopened and students were returning, walking in from all directions wearing the "schoolboy" uniform of white shirts and tan khaki shorts. Some were young boys, others as tall and mature as men. They passed by on the school road, bundles of belongings slung over a shoulder or balanced on the head, staring through the window at her. And it wasn't just the students. The dirt road through the school that passed by the teacher houses was used by people of all ages on their way to and from Kisoro. Sometimes, someone passing by would stop and stare for what felt like a long time, which she found annoying. When one skinny old man stood there watching like she was some kind of TV show, she went to the window and tried to wave him away. He didn't react, just kept standing there. She went into the bedroom to get away from the prying eyes, but when she came back, he was still there. Really, couldn't these people understand privacy? She kept her back to him and did not make eye contact and finally, he left. Somewhere in her fog of congestion she felt uneasy about her reaction. *These people?*

It was almost midnight when Carolyn came in to the living room, dressed in her robe with a thick white towel wrapped around her hair, heading for the kitchen. She had brought towels from home. Smart, Laurel thought. The ones issued by Peace Corps were thin and rough.

"I'm making tea, you want some?"

"Thanks, that would be nice, Carolyn."

Carolyn threw some of the wrinkled black tea leaves into the pot.

"Sometimes I don't know whether to make tea with this stuff, or smoke it." She added the boiling water, let it steep and settle, poured out two cups of strong murky brew and brought them to the table. This reminded Laurel of all the times she had sat with Tessa in the little kitchen in their Somerville apartment, drinking some herbal brew made from God-only-knew what.

"Have you noticed how people stop on the road outside and just stare in like we were some kind of TV show?" Laurel sneezed into her toilet paper. "It's so rude."

"I don't let it bother me anymore."

Of course not, because you're an exhibitionist. "Well, I like my privacy."

"It bothered me the first time somebody did it, so I went to the window and stuck out my tongue and made an ugly face, which scared the shit out of him. He looked like he'd seen a ghost." She snorted. "And in his mind, I guess he had."

Laurel groaned. Her eyes burned. "Wow, way to go, Carolyn. At least now they'll probably avoid us like the plague."

"Nah, actually after he got over the surprise, he laughed. I laughed back, and he went on his way. I decided, being white, I'm probably the best entertainment they've seen in a long time. So, let them look."

So, Carolyn had been more generous, in her way. Who was this girl? She sneezed, reached for the roll of toilet paper.

Carolyn winced. "You are one sick chick. I never get sick."

"How lucky for you." She had had enough of Carolyn's constant one-upmanship, trying to impress Gordon at dinner. She took a sip of tea and pushed the cup away. "No offense, but tea without lemon makes me want to puke." Her mother always kept fresh lemons on hand.

"Better get used to it. Citrus doesn't grow around here, it's too cold."

Laurel stifled an urge to tell her to shut up. But it wasn't Carolyn's fault, all of this. "Never mind, at least it's hot."

"That's the spirit. We have to make do with what we've got, right? Like me, making do with Gordon until the boys get out here."

Gregg and Kevin were posted in Kabale, the town that marked the start of the cliff-hanging Kisoro Road. "You don't seriously think they'll try that road on motorbikes?"

Carolyn gave a sly glance from under her heavy eyebrows. "I have a good idea they'll be over first chance they get. Until then, an older man might be cool for a change."

Laurel felt the sudden claustrophobic panic of things closing in around her, things she could not control. Like Carolyn. Or like before a piano recital, knowing that no matter how hard she tried it would go wrong. Like the dinner with the Kemp family, when Alan's mother had told her, *soon you'll be one of us, Laurel, a card-carrying Kemp,* as if it were some exclusive club she was joining. Now, she was really feeling over her head about teaching here. She was a music major, not all that great in English when you came down to it.

Watch your negative thinking, she could hear Tessa now. *Self-doubt is an Aries hang up.* Good old Tessa, believing the answers to life's problems could be found in the alignment of planets and stars. Sweet, but deluded, in a different way from Alan, who thought he could unravel the mysteries of human beings in the pages of his anatomy textbooks.

But Tessa and Alan were thousands of miles away now, and she had two days to get over this cold and get her act together in time for the start of classes on Monday.

She had to clear her throat of a gargle of phlegm. "I'm nervous about all of this."

"Nervous about what, for God's sake?"

"You know – teaching. I don't know if I can actually do it." She was aware that she was whining but unable to stop herself. "I mean, I know I'll be deficient at this, like with everything else in my life. Playing piano. Love. And now this."

"Deficient?" Carolyn snorted. "The way I figure it, these people are lucky to have us. I plan to put in my time and do a decent job, but hey, I'm also going to have as much fun as I can – which looks like it won't be easy in this place. I suggest you lighten up and do the same." She got up and took her empty cup to the kitchen.

Laurel bit her lip and sniffed. She was damned if she would let Carolyn see her cry.

<u>8</u>

Mama

He is making her do Eusebius again. Adagio, funny rhythm, and her mind is wandering. Of Schumann's *Carnaval* characters she much prefers the acrobatics of Florestan. In the bright October sunshine outside the bay window a boy from down the street is riding his bike with no hands, faster than she would ever dare to ride, and she is at the piano trying to find Eusebius, trying so hard because Mama is in the wing chair nearby and she will be angry again.

"Laurel is musical, Mrs. Bittelson, a natural ability, but she lacks control and concentration. Her mind rushes ahead, she gallops where she should canter, and so inevitably she stumbles."

"She is just nine years old. Control will come."

Laurel hears the stiffness in her mother's voice and wonders if Mr. Heywood hears it, too.

"Yes, yes, she is young, but I have worked with many serious players even younger than she. There always must be first an obedience to the music. In a way, I think she creates her own version of the composer's work. When she makes mistakes, she does not always recognize them as such. Whatever she plays, however she plays it, seems all right to her. I have never encountered a student quite like this—"

Listening, Laurel squirms inside, because while it is a relief to have the truth out in the open, she knows it will upset her mother. Laurel likes Mr. Heywood. He has fuzzy eyebrows that move up and down with the music like dancing caterpillars. He is only trying to teach her to play properly, so she won't always mess up at recitals and have to listen to everyone say, *do better, try harder*. But can't he see her mother's cloudy face, her eyes gray instead of blue? Can't he tell it's time to shut up?

"As you know, my father was one of the best concert pianists in Poland. If he were alive today, would you dare to stand there and tell him his granddaughter will never play?"

No one talks. Laurel holds her breath. She knows her grandparents were killed in The War. In 1941 her then-fifteen-year-old mother and her mother's younger brother had been sent to England to stay with their aunt. That is all she knows. Her mother doesn't like to talk about it, except to say that that was how she was in England and met Arthur Bittelson when she was nineteen, right after the war finally ended.

"Please, Mrs. Bittelson, don't misunderstand me. I have the greatest respect for your father's artistry, but I would say the same to him. Laurel has a natural ability, and she takes great delight in the music. She will be a good player, more than adequate."

Here Mr. Heywood glances at Laurel and smiles, but the caterpillars have surrendered into a flat line across the bridge of his nose. "But if you expect a solo career for her, with competitions and so on, you must find another teacher."

Later, just before dinner, her mother emerges from her room, where she spent the afternoon after Mr. Heywood left. Laurel feels angry at being left alone, but cries as soon as her mother hugs her. Why is it always so hard to please, when that is all she wants to do? She tries to do well at her lessons, but the notes are like slippery goldfish swimming inside her head,

42

confounding her by darting in unexpected directions. No matter how long and hard she practices, the mistakes are always waiting to take control of her fingers. Then, she feels so angry at herself she can hardly stand it.

Laurel closes her eyes as her mother's firm hands brush over her hair, always trying to tame those flyaway red curls.

"Don't worry, Laurelka. He has a primitive mind, that Heywood. What does he know?"

The last thing she should ever do is raise her voice to her mother, but she wants to be allowed to go outside after school and learn to ride her bike with no hands, even if she falls. She wants to have a television in the living room like all the other kids. She wants her mother to love her even though she is not a good pianist, and even her mother's beautiful, sad face can't stop the words.

"Mama, can't you see? He knows everything! I can't play like you want me to. I never can!"

Her next piano teacher is Mr. Rose, not his real name, which is Polish and too hard for Americans to pronounce. She never sees Mr. Heywood again.

9

White Fathers

The mission hill rose high behind the school, the plain wooden cross on the peak of the chapel roof showering grace on the countryside below. It was built by the French Catholic order of the White Fathers in the 1890s, of wood beams and whitewashed plaster.

Mr. Senwangama's Peugeot purred easily up the wet dirt road, the headmaster in front with his driver, Laurel and Carolyn in the back. Today was like all the others, dark and chill with misting rain from a blanket of clouds so thick there was no trace visible of the mountain giants behind them. It was four o'clock on Sunday afternoon. Tea with the priests would be a welcome distraction, at least for a few hours, from worrying about the start of classes tomorrow.

The three priests met them at the door of the rectory, where trees ablaze with orange flowers shaded an understory of creamy white and yellow lilies. Father Phillip was a portly, white-haired Irishman dressed in brown slacks and tweed jacket, contrasting with the long white cassocks of the other two. Father Lawrence was a tall balding man who stood by the door like a sentry, arms bent so that each hand tucked inside the opposite sleeve of his robe. He was French, in his forties, and was in charge of the mission's small infirmary. Then there was Father Matthew: glossy waves of black hair, a stray lock curling onto his forehead, blue eyes and long dark eyelashes, set off to advantage by flowing white vestments. He looked to be in his late twenties, and he was American. And he was sexy, Laurel thought, despite her no-men resolve; go figure that he would be a priest.

The parlor had a low table set for tea and surrounded by upholstered chairs, a stone fireplace and massive wooden mantle displaying small statues and pictures in ornate frames. One wall was covered with bookshelves stuffed with books. The electric lamps were not on yet, but candles in wall sconces warmed with a golden glow.

When everyone was seated, the priests chatted cordially with Mr. Senwangama, who wore a dark blue jacket over his white shirt and tie instead of his everyday V-neck cardigan sweater. Laurel gathered that the headmaster had attended religious services at the mission this morning, as he probably did every Sunday. Ties between the school and the mission were still strong, and she understood that most of the Ugandans around here were Catholics.

When Father Phillip asked the inevitable, *and why have two young American ladies come all this way to Africa,* Carolyn offered up motives of idealism, service, and Christian charity. Oh really, Laurel thought, but Carolyn's answer was evidently sufficient for them both, because Father Phillip's question to her was *and who gave you your lovely red hair.*

Laurel raised her hand to her head, a reflex she couldn't help whenever attention was drawn to her hair. Was he being sarcastic? At a time when the style was very long and straight, hers stuck out sideways, and the longer it got, the more it stuck out, so it never touched her shoulders. Clown hair. In high school she had tried ironing, or gelling it down with Dippity-do, but it had ended up looking as stiff as a corn broom. It was another way that she did not fit in. And now here was this priest, complimenting her.

"Well, thank you. I get the hair from my father." She did not bother to explain that her father's hair was always thin, that the fullness came from her mother.

When the conversation turned to teaching, Father Phillip made it clear he did not want to talk to Carolyn about mathematics. "But literature, now, that's another story." His eyes zeroed-in on Laurel. "I suppose they'll have you trotting out that stalwart son of the Brown's, for starters."

It took her a moment to decipher this. "Oh, yes, *Tom Brown's Schooldays*. It's on the curriculum."

Father Phillip laughed. "The glory days of the English public school." His masterful Irish brogue and reverberating tenor had everyone's attention now. "A world apart from the African boarding school, eh, James?"

Mr. Senwangama smiled. "Perhaps on the surface, Father. But, it is a story of morality and faith which our boys will benefit to understand."

"Well said, Headmaster." Father Phillip looked back to Laurel. "Still, I hope the version you've got doesn't require them to wade through language like, and I quote, 'the most reckless young scapegrace amongst the fags.' What do you make of such a phrase, m'girl?"

Laurel was embarrassed not to have a ready answer. "I don't remember reading that."

"Then they must have given you a modernized version. Just as well," Father Phillip said, exchanging a glance with Father Lawrence.

"Unless we're talking about the *other* meaning," Carolyn chimed in, "a fag is a cigarette, right? That's what Gordon calls them, anyway."

There was a moment of suspended silence before Father Phillip smiled. "You're right, Carolyn m'dear, and our friend Mr. Coopersmith is very fond of his fags. But in the time Hughes was writing of, a fag was a young schoolboy made to endure the predations of older boys."

For once, Laurel was glad for Carolyn's big mouth. But really, had Father Phillip memorized the entire book, and was he intending to catechize her on every passage? If he knew so much, why didn't he come down the hill and teach?

"Some of the language is just as strange to me as it will be to my students," she said. "But I agree with Mr. Senwangama about the lessons in the story, and that's what I hope to get across." She didn't care if she sounded snippy. "Anyway, I have a good dictionary, so I'll be learning along with them — staying a few steps ahead, of course."

Father Phillip gave a noncommittal laugh and changed the topic to Chinua Achebe's view of colonialism. Laurel had to admit she had not yet read *Things Fall Apart,* since they would not get to it until later in the term. Last would be *Romeo and Juliet*, which she had read in high school but needed to reread a lot more carefully. She was sure the priest would know it chapter and verse. Luckily, Father Lawrence entered the conversation, wanting to discuss "the music" with her, before Father Phillip could sink his teeth into Shakespeare. Laurel listened gratefully as Father Lawrence expounded on Bach and Couperin in his high-pitched whine of a voice. Father Phillip lost interest and began talking to Mr. Senwangama. Carolyn was intent on the beautiful Father Matthew.

Something about the way Carolyn sat, framed against the sepia tones of the bookcase, her head thrown back, dark hair loose and splayed behind her shoulders, reminded Laurel of a painting she had seen in one of Tessa's art books, of a sensual Circe offering her enchanted cup to Ulysses. Father Matthew looked as wary and trapped as the lost mariner of the painting. Laurel took a voyeuristic pleasure in watching the priest squirm.

Mr. Senwangama did his best to keep the conversation lively, but after an hour, tea cold and biscuits wilted, the priests had discharged an obligation and were clearly impatient to have them gone. She understood that there would be no repeat invitations. She had done her best to impress but felt young, inexperienced, uncultured. Other than being white, she thought, they really had very little in common.

* * *

Laurel was making one last cup of tea before bed, to soothe her still-congested nose. Carolyn sat at the table applying pink polish to her fingernails under the light from the lamp. It had been a strange day.

"The priests were obviously impressed with your little speech about why you joined Peace Corps, Carolyn. I was impressed, too."

"Why. You think you're the only goody-two-shoes around here?"

Laurel stared, bleary-eyed. "Carolyn, how about we make a deal. I'll stop asking you to regulate if you stop calling me goody-two-shoes."

"Yeah, fine, it's a deal. But do you think you're the only one who joined up to save the world?"

"I never said I wanted to save the world."

Carolyn tossed her head back. "You don't have to. It's,

like, fucking obvious."

Laurel blinked, trying to figure out how to take this. "Like I said, I wanted to get away from my privileged lifestyle for a while, see how people live in less developed countries. What I didn't say was how sick I was of Vietnam dragging on and civil rights protesters killed and students shot at Kent State and all the flag-waving by America the bully."

"Yeah, well, and I left out the part about wanting to get as far away as possible from my parents." Carolyn capped the polish bottle and sighed.

"Alan said, when I first started talking about Peace Corps and that maybe we could both join, he said, 'why would I want to waste my time slumming it in some foreign country where I don't belong?'"

"Well, so he's an asshole, though I'd be willing to overlook a lot more than his politics to marry into family money. But anyway, it has nothing to do with belonging. We'll never belong. I'm here to fill a need in a place where, let's face it, there's a hell of a lot of need."

When she put her mind to it, Laurel thought, Carolyn got to the truth of things. Not belonging was a given. It was why she felt so unreal, like she would wake up from this strange dream any minute and find herself in her Somerville apartment with Tessa and the morning street noise coming in through the window. "Any regrets?"

Carolyn blew on her pearly pink nails. "Nah, not really, except this place is bor-ing, with a capital B. Could you believe those priests? Were they, like, for real?"

Laurel laughed. "The way Father Phillip looked at me, I thought there must be snot sticking out of my nose."

"He reminded me way too much of my father – likes to

49

hear himself talk, always right, always trying to put other people down." Carolyn grimaced. "Dad's not a priest, but he might as well be. That's how I ended up in a Catholic girl's high school, because Daddy thinks American public schools are going straight to hell – and he should know, he's a high school teacher."

Laurel took a moment to process this. "Maybe he's right. I felt like such an ignoramus next to Father Phillip. I mean, I thought I was pretty well-educated. Now I feel even more deficient than usual."

"Don't let it get to you. Father Phillip is a pompous blowhard. And the skinny one, Father Lawrence, with that voice like he's got his balls twisted – I thought I would die from trying not to laugh."

Laurel chuckled. "He could sing castrato, for sure." She was immediately ashamed of her remark. After all, Father Lawrence had rescued her from the conversational jaws of Father Phillip. "But he was nice, and he knows a lot about music." It had felt good, the flowering of conversation out of parched earth. "So, last but not least, what did you think of Father Matthew?"

"Fuckin' weird. It was like pulling teeth to get him to speak to me. Just yes, no, I don't know, and something he quoted about a gate. Freaked me out."

"I didn't think any man could freak you out, Carolyn. But I have to say he's good looking, for a priest."

Carolyn guffawed. "Yeah, but in his case it doesn't matter. He doesn't dig chicks."

It took a moment for this to register. "Homosexual? What makes you think so?"

"Now it's called gay, like in gay liberation? It was obvious.

I gave him both barrels, and there was no interest. Zero."

"He is a priest, Carolyn. And anyway, what I saw was more like heavy artillery. You looked like you were out to suck his blood, or turn him into a swine. I half expected him to grab a cross to protect himself."

Her roommate's face told her she had gone too far. Carolyn thought herself irresistible to men. It was a point of pride with her.

Carolyn tossed her luxurious hair, freshly washed, glossy as a raven in the lamplight. "No way, I was sweet as sugar. He's a fag, all right, and I don't mean the kind you smoke or whatever that English schoolboy shit was all about."

Laurel laughed. "There go my priest fantasies. What a drag."

"Like I said, bor-ing."

"And I thought going up to the mission would take my mind off teaching. Instead it made me feel worse. Father Phillip might be pompous, but he knows a lot more about literature than I do." Laurel sighed. "Believe me, Carolyn, I have no illusions about saving the world. I'll be lucky to save myself from always fucking up."

"Of course he knows more, he's like, ancient. Chill out, it's just high school. African high school. "

"Aren't you nervous at all?"

"I was a *Maths* minor in college." Carolyn picked up one of the textbooks she had left stacked on the table and flipped through the pages. "I mean, we're talking algebra here, like ninth grade, you know?"

"Maybe I am getting too up-tight."

"Shit," Carolyn said, stopping on a page in the textbook, "what the hell kind of equations are these? Maybe I will do a quick review, just to refresh my memory."

Laurel could not pass up the chance to gloat. "Well, I'm as ready as I'll ever be, so I'm off to bed. Don't stay up too late, school starts at 7:30 tomorrow, 7:30 sharp, like Ngira says." Ngira was so proper, yet always that hint of humor beneath the surface. Thank goodness for him and Gordon, the only ones so far she had been able to go to for teaching advice. Once or twice she had asked one of the other teachers about how they graded or how much homework to assign, and they had been polite but reticent, laughing uneasily as if she were testing them; now she confined her serious questions to Gordon and Ngira.

Carolyn settled down on the sofa with books and pencil. "Ugh, yeah, I know. Don't rub it in."

Laurel lit a candle, held in a simple tin holder, and left the pool of lantern light. Somehow the thought of Carolyn's last-minute preparations made her feel less alone. She washed up and went to her bedroom, picked up her recorder and played: "Shenandoah," "The Minstrel Boy," "Amazing Grace," meandering along the familiar melodies, inhaling the sweet nutty smell of the flute, entering a timeless space where not even the relentless countdown to tomorrow could touch her.

<u>10</u>

Father Matthew's Journal

Matthew put down his pen and looked at the kitchen garden through his small window. Rows of sturdy cabbages, potato and onion, delicate vines of pea and lima bean splayed over trellises, swelling from the rich earth under Mtembo's loving touch. An eager neophyte, Mtembo had embraced the Christian faith with an open heart, according to his good and generous nature. Matthew knew that to hold such power over these simple people was a heavy responsibility. God expected his priests to safeguard all the souls so willingly entrusted to them, like Mtembo – and his pretty sister.

From his room, Matthew could also see the limbs of apple and peach trees etched against the dark sky. So much innocent beauty was almost unbearable. He turned back to his journal, the strokes of black ink a weapon blazing through the landscape of his sin, testing the depths of decay like a tongue probes a sore tooth.

Kisoro, 5 September, 1971

Why doesn't Paul write to me? He hasn't answered one of my letters. Is this his idea of a kindness? I am perishing from loneliness, banished as I am from the spiritual comfort that only he can give. If only I could speak to him, beg him as my Father confessor to show me how to be strong. Phillip and Lawrence have no inkling of my spiritual suicide, and I could never confide in them. They would send me away, and I would never see Rabelais again.

I understand now why Paul sent me here. This Eden where men and women live simple lives of the flesh has tested my determination to seek salvation in a chaste life. After those first few months of transgression I was succeeding, applying all my energies to the physical labor of good works, repairing roads and houses. I buried carnal thought and safely channeled my energy into a deep regard for the people.

Now all that has changed. I have fallen abysmally, not in action but in my heart, which Paul would say comes to the same. But of course he must have known all along what I was only beginning to admit: my greatest temptation would not come from a woman.

Matthew put a hand to his temple. Today those two American girls had made him physically ill. They were young and ignorant, insufferable in their different ways, the redhead arrogant and shrewish, the dark one acting like a whore, flirting with him.

Woman, he thought, was the strangest of God's creatures, corrupt by nature and at the same time the purified vessel of new life. When he first arrived he had considered African women to be degraded by their innocent compliance. Still, he had taken advantage of it, going through the bestial motions to relieve himself of physical need and afterward loathing his weakness, all the while preaching abstinence from the pulpit. The women here saw through the guise of priest to the weak man beneath and sought him out, smiling and giggling behind their hands. Were they expecting affection in return? Salvation? Money and material gifts, more likely. He noticed that they steered clear of him after one or two sexual encounters. After several months he swore he would put an end to his debauched secret activity, and he did. The last straw had been Mtembo's sister, an innocent virgin who abandoned herself to him with religious zeal – it made him sick with shame even to think about it. It was all a filthy indulgence, like smoking or drinking or masturbation, nothing that could not be ended through strength of will, and nothing at all to do with love.

Back home in Chicago, in the year before he entered seminary, there was a girl he met at the record store where he worked. They liked the same music, and he would call her as soon as the latest Presley, Everly Brothers, or Ray Charles 45s came into the store. They came together for several months of rather formal dating before the inevitable happened – she wanted to make love. He thought he wanted it, too, but found he had to force himself to kiss her, or touch her where he knew he was expected to. The first few times, he brought himself to climax fast and hard, with a violence that shocked him and made her look at him with big, questioning eyes. Soon there was no completion for him, and he was relieved to feel her desire melt away under his indifference.

You don't know how to love, she had said when she broke up with him. He realized she was right, that he had been taking affection from her yet giving nothing in return. He recognized this as a kind of abuse that brought back anguished memories of a father who withheld love from his wife and child, blaming them for his failures. Growing up, Matthew had understood that his mother was like a flowering plant deprived of light and water. As he grew into manhood, he found he could no longer bear to watch her prematurely age and wither, or listen to his father's drunken self-deceptions. Matthew escaped to seminary, and the year after he was ordained his mother died of breast cancer at age forty-nine. After that, he decided he was done with love. It had nothing to offer him.

It was only after ordination, living in that run-down Bronx parish, that I began to discover what human love could mean. Father Paul was everything I aspired to be. In that neighborhood languishing in poverty and prejudice, he showed me how people found dignity through the close spiritual guidance of the Church. He showed me by example how to serve God.

I can see him now, his pale round face, brown eyes, the soft small hands that belied an iron will. "We are salesmen," he said on the day I arrived. "This church is our showroom, and we must bring in the customers." We went everywhere, invited or not, welcome or not, into the streets, stores, bars, people's homes. "The streets are where you'll cut your teeth, little priest" – odd the way he called me that, even though I was a head taller. He was so patient, helping me don the vestments and practice Mass, hearing my confession, giving me Holy Communion. Never had this sacrament felt so healing and intimate as it did from those hands. The Body, the Blood, the Passion of Christ flowed into me along with a full sensual awareness of a life that was pure in spirit.

Yes, sensual, for God has made us sensual beings. That was sensuality in its most sanctified form. But it has been true since the fall of Adam that the baser instincts are stronger. Did Paul guess how I struggled with my impure thoughts and fantasies?

Did he struggle as I did?

I understand. I see it all now. He knew my lustful nature would turn our friendship to sin, sooner or later, and did the only possible thing. He sent me away. I thought I would die from the pain. Now I know it was the only thing he could have done.

Omnia vincit Amor – if Virgil lived today he would be in for a shock. A love like mine conquers nothing. Love between men – yes, let me write it, let it live at least on this page – is persecuted and condemned. Even if I were not a priest, the teachings of my church are abundantly clear on this point. Paul was right not to allow me to question theological doctrine, even in our most private moments. That way lies madness, he said. Yet I do question, God help me, unlike Phillip and Lawrence, who are too long in the habit of accepting the dictates of the Church as if they were from God Himself – well, if I add blasphemy to my other sins, what can it matter now?

If I should express sexual love for another man, my church turns its back on me. Does God turn his back on me, too?

In all our talks about philosophy, Rabelais has never suspected that his presence runs like an electric current through me. The gesture he makes when he is in thought, his fine smooth skin, the strength of his handshake, are almost too much to bear. I know he does not love me, yet I continue to hope. I am ever the rational, self-disciplined clergyman with him, because this is what he values and what draws him back to me.

The boundary between friendship and love is fluid. If I watch and wait long enough, living for those moments when I can grasp his hand or look into his eyes, he may come to seek the kind of intimacy that would make me feel truly blessed.

Closeted in his room, Matthew fought against his quickening heartbeat and the insistent stirring of desire. He cried out with a low animal groan of anger and despair and forced himself to resume writing.

I have failed the test that God has sent me. I can no longer pretend to be His instrument. "Strait is the gate, and narrow is the way, which leadeth unto life, and few there be that find it." So much of the gospel of St. Matthew speaks through the ages directly to me. If I ever had the way, I have lost it. What's worse, I do not repent the crooked path I have chosen. I must leave the Church.

But what would I do as a layman? I might be employed at Butawanga as a teacher, as dedicated as Rabelais in teaching his beloved Mathematics. I would have a daily association with him, but my persona of priest would be gone and he would no longer seek my counsel on spiritual matters. Worse, infinitely worse, the restraint which my religious vocation exerts upon me would be gone. I would make my desires known too soon and he would recoil, and I would lose all hope of him. And what of those girls there at the school right now like some two-headed Eve beckoning to Adam – no, seeing their power over him would cause me even more anxiety.

I see no choice but to continue in this impossible position, trying to serve my Church in self-imposed exile from the healing light of God. I only know that I must have Rabelais and would rather remain an apostate posing as priest, cut off from any hope of divine love and forgiveness, than to forswear the exquisite torment of his presence.

"Wide is the gate, and broad is the way, that leadeth to destruction"— I must write to Paul again, and again, until he answers. I can't believe he would forsake me completely in my hour of need. He's the only one I can trust to advise me. Damn the slowness of the mail here. I know he'll answer. If he can't or won't, then I am truly lost.

Lost. The word weighed on his mind like a death sentence. The real name of the African man he called Rabelais, whose image was with him all his waking and dreaming hours, formed in his mind. He battered his head with his hands, pulled his hair until tears came to his eyes. He threw himself face down on his cot until in his agony his body found a rhythm that finally brought release as the barely formed word Ngira died on his lips.

<u>11</u>

Lightning Balls

Kisoro was about 15 minutes of bumping along a rocky dirt road in Gordon's rusty Saab. It was a tiny town, just one road with a few plain shops and raised wooden sidewalks. Today they pulled up in an open field just outside town, where people with baskets of vegetables to sell laid them out on blankets, which doubled as seating for the sellers. Only a few customers moved through the displays. Market day here was so different from busy, colorful, sunny Kampala. Gray day, gray buildings, black road, brown, gray, and black clothing; one woman's dingy yellow headscarf and an orange cap on a young man stood out, along with displays of yams, green and red peppers, and cabbages the size of basketballs. There was a comfortable intimacy in the talk, laughter, gesturing of the buyers and sellers. Not that Laurel understood what was said – Peace Corps, in a bureaucratic screw up, had tutored them in a language that was not commonly spoken in this region. So far she had picked up a few words of the local Kinyarwanda, like the all-important greeting and response *Mulaho*, *Mulahoneza,* and even this basic knowledge seemed to delight the people she met here in town. Since the students spoke different regional languages, English was the norm at the school.

At the market, people's eyes widened and conversation halted, vendors called out greetings and customers stepped back to watch the Wazungu approach. Gordon helped them negotiate for vegetables in a mixture of Swahili and Kinyarwanda. You have to bargain, he explained, otherwise they think you're just stupid. Other market-goers watched from the sidelines, clucking when a price was too high, murmuring approval when a good price was reached. This kind of shopping took time, but it was also a social event, more fun than just picking up things from shelves or bins in a big store.

A young boy stood with a goat tethered on a rope that he yanked each time the animal moved or bleated. Carolyn and Gordon discussed buying the goat and sharing the meat. Laurel watched the animal, its unfocused yellow eyes cast down, the rhythmic shuddering of its muscles. She could feel its fear. "Carolyn. There is no way I'm buying that animal to kill it."

"Well, we don't have to kill it. Caspar will do it."

"I don't want to see it in our yard."

"What the hell are we supposed to do for meat?"

"I don't know. Do without it," she said with the force of new conviction. After all, Tessa had been a vegetarian all through college.

Carolyn shot an exasperated look at Gordon, who replied with a wink. Carolyn shrugged and walked away from the goat. "Fine, have it your way."

They walked further down the street and bought a rug made from thickly woven rushes for the living room floor. They watched the tailor, who sat outside his shop working a treadle sewing machine, and it occurred to Laurel that they could have curtains made for privacy. She would bring window measurements next time they came to town. As they headed into the general store, or *duka,* Laurel saw Gordon down the street, handing cash to the goatherd. She fought the urge to march over and take the goat away. What would she do with it, how would she care for it? And Gordon would just find another in its place. Of course, she was being childish; this was how people got meat. But she understood how it felt to be scared and helpless like that goat, and if she had a choice, she decided, she would not be eating meat any more.

In the duka, there was an unexpected bonanza of merchandise that helped her forget her frustration at the goat business. She and Carolyn bought a teakettle, teapot, frying pan, staple foods like flour and butter, imported canned foods, kitchen towels, soap, toothpaste, tampons and sanitary napkins, cleaning supplies. They each bought a thick wool blanket, since the Peace Corps issue blankets were as woefully thin as the towels. It was an expensive day, almost 700 Ugandan shillings, roughly 100 U.S. dollars, split between them. Mr. Gupta, the Asian owner of the duka, spoke English, and made her feel as catered to as the mink-clad clientele of a fancy Boston Back Bay boutique.

* * *

That night they were again invited to dinner at Gordon's house, a warm refuge in this cold, rainy place. Ngira was there too and was much more relaxed than he had been that first day at the Headmaster's house. Gordon liked to tell stories about his Kampala days, lubricated by cocktails of Waragi and Schweppes Bitter Lemon. The Ugandan gin and bitter soda felt good on her sore throat, so good she didn't even mind Gordon going on about this English guy Kenneth he met like seven years ago, when he first came to Uganda. Anyway, it gave her an excuse to sit back and not have to talk and just watch Gordon and Ngira play off each other.

"A real die-hard old colonialist, was Kenneth."

Like you are now, Laurel thought.

"He was already in his 50s, and I was freshly arrived as a lad of 28. Your age now, Ngira. *When I was a lad I sailed to sea —*"

"Please, spare us the Gilbert and Sullivan, and get on with it," Ngira said.

"I stayed with Kenneth for several weeks while casting about for what I could do to escape return to dear old moldering, geriatric England. Of course, one had to do more than Kenneth, holed up like a spider in his African idyll, waiting to catch the occasional traveler or university student in his conversational web. How's that for metaphor, then?"

"It is most poetical, but is there also a story to be found here?"

"Of course there's a story, if you would have a bit of patience, Ngira." Gordon closed his eyes and seemed momentarily lost to that other time. "We were sitting on the verandah of his cottage on Bombo Road, drinking that damned *nguli* his houseboy brews up – why the man can't spring to a decent whiskey or gin eludes me – watching the sunset, when these two young Germans turn up, a male and a female, traveling about on their *Wanderjahr.*"

Gordon told how Kenneth had brought the young woman to tears by going on about how all Germans were Nazis at heart, until her young man threw a punch that Gordon intercepted, taking the blow.

"The poor old sod can't manage to let go of the war, you see. He was a pilot in the RAF, and bloody lucky to be around to tell about it."

The War. That bloody war, as her father liked to say. "My grandparents died at Treblinka."

Suddenly, silence.

"Wow, Laurel. Do the words 'wet blanket' mean anything to you?"

"Sorry, Carolyn. I don't know why that came out. Maybe it's the gin."

"Bloody hell," Gordon said. "But I didn't figure you for Jewish."

"I'm not. They weren't. My grandfather was a concert musician – a pianist – and they used to invite friends to their home, other musicians and intellectuals, I guess, and probably some were Jewish, but they all talked against the Nazi movement. My mother says they were humanists, and that made them enemies of the regime."

Laurel felt stupid for exposing her family's distant tragedy in the middle of a party. Everything stood still for a long moment, until Gordon got up and produced another bottle, Beefeater's this time, which he proudly displayed.

"Time for another round, some real gin this time."

"Yes, time for another little drinkie," Carolyn agreed. Gordon looked at her adoringly, his blue eyes like pools at the bottom of craters in the craggy landscape of his face.

He's practically panting after her, Laurel thought, but then Carolyn's flirting would be hard for a single man out in the African bush to resist. There was also something like a twinge of jealousy – to be desired like that, even if it was too much, too soon, and why couldn't Carolyn at least wait until they were more established at the school, and was she actually planning to have sex with this middle-aged man?

"No more drinks for me, Gordon, and no reflection on the quality of your liquor," Laurel said. "It's late and I've got a cold. Thanks for the hospitality."

Ngira insisted on walking her home. Of course, Laurel thought, it would be awkward for him to stay there as the third wheel to Carolyn and Gordon.

The generator was off, so it was pitch dark outside. There was rumbling in the distance from a storm that had just blown through, and the ground steamed and glistened with melting hailstones. The cold air snapped with ozone.

"What a terrible thing for your family," Ngira said. The hail – actual ice – crunched under their feet before disappearing. "And for you, not to know your grandparents."

"But I don't know why I just blurted it out like that. I've never really talked about it before, outside my family."

"We do not always choose the truth, but sometimes it chooses us."

"When I was a kid I used to tell people that my grandparents were living in Florida. Sometimes I think I actually believed it."

Ngira's breath made ghostly clouds in the cool air. "Here, too, there are many bad things people would rather forget. There has long been killing between Tutsi and Hutu in Rwanda. In fact, some of our students and teachers are Tutsi refugees. In this country, Obote persecuted the Baganda people. I am afraid it is too much in human nature to abuse power, and to hate."

They were standing in the road outside her house. In the heavy silent darkness Laurel was glad for Ngira's company. "And Amin? How will he use his power?"

Before Ngira could respond there was an explosive crack. A bright light split the darkness and whizzed by her head and she stood there stunned, hair statically charged and bristling for the seconds before Ngira pulled her down to the ground.

Another bright ball zigzagged through the air above their heads as if seeking them and then was gone, like a goblin of fire.

She looked up at the black sky. "Oh my God, what was that?"

He helped her up. "Lightning balls. Sometimes they follow in the wake of a storm, like the flick of the tail follows a dragon."

"That was wild. I wouldn't want to be struck by one. Thanks for pulling me down."

He smiled. "They are gone now." He waited in the road until she had opened her door. "And to answer your question about the new president, I do not know how he will be. But the philosopher Rabelais once wrote, the appetite grows by eating. That is always the danger."

"Yes, I see." She wasn't really sure that she did. "Good night, Ngira."

Inside, she watched him walk away, swallowed up by darkness.

12

Fourth Form

> *Oh Uganda, may God uphold thee,*
> *We lay our future in thy hand,*
> *United free for liberty*
> *Together we'll always stand.*

Singing the first stanza of the Ugandan National Anthem had been an ice-breaker, all that stood between Laurel and the convoluted structures of English grammar. After five weeks it was still a welcome ritual, the rich fabric of their voices, the strong individual strands: John Munyangaba flirtatious, Thomas Kinabua assertive, high-pitched, John Ntunzyma cheerful, bright; the collective sound of the bright optimism of her students. She was Miss Bittelson, but the "el" sound was hard for them to pronounce, so it sounded like "Bitta-son." Most often, she was Madam.

Today, in first period class, she wrote two sentences on the board:

I <u>can</u> go.

I <u>may</u> go.

"What is the difference in meaning between these two sentences?" John Ntunzyma was always the first hand. "Yes, John?"

"Can is to be able to go. May is to be permitted to go."

"Yes, that's exactly right. John can go to the school store, but he may not go during class. Yes, Thomas?"

"But, Madam, who must give the permission?"

"It doesn't matter, Thomas, anyone can give permission." Laurel walked to his desk. "Thomas, may I borrow your grammar book?"

He giggled, then handed her the book.

"Thank you, Thomas. But how would you answer me – using can, or may?"

"Oh, yes, Madam, you can borrow my book." Seeing Laurel's expression, he added, "because now you are able to borrow it." He was so certain he was right, her heart went out to him.

"Well, that does seem to make sense, but when permission is involved we would use may." She was losing them in this silly distinction. She walked to the back of the class, where a big boy known only as Kizuma sat slumped in his chair, fighting sleep. She picked up the grammar text from his desk, watched his eyes slowly focus on her.

"I can take Kizuma's grammar book without asking, but to be polite I should ask if I may borrow it."

She put it down.

"If you want to borrow Kizuma's book, what should you say? Patrick?"

"I would say, Kizuma, may I borrow your book? You will not be reading it, anyway."

Some of the boys tittered.

"All right, Patrick, that comment was against our rules of citizenship in this class." It was not very often that she had to worry about misbehavior in any of her classes. "But your answer is correct. So, Kizuma, may I borrow your book?"

She felt bad about putting him on the spot, but he was the

slowest student in the class, and it was often the only way to get his attention.

"But then, how can I do the homework, Madam?"

The rest of the class moaned like a Greek chorus.

"I don't really want to borrow your book, Kizuma. We are trying to show the difference between can and may. Have you been listening?"

"Oh, in fact no, Madam."

Hisses and groans from the other boys.

"Class, quiet please. Kizuma, you used the word can correctly when you asked 'how can I do the homework.'"

The boy smirked triumphantly at his classmates. Laurel was starting to sweat.

"But to answer my question you would say, yes, Madam, you may borrow my book." It was time to get out of this impossible lesson, leaving the added complication of may as "might" for another day. She wrote the grammar assignment on the board. "You can do this page for homework, please."

Surely, Father Phillip would not have bungled the grammar lesson.

Her students had been shy those first weeks, clearly unsure of what to expect from this red-haired American female. If they noticed her lack of confidence, they did not show it. These boys, as all her classes, were depending on her to give them the tools they needed to pass the O-level exams to qualify for the advanced level of high school.

Whatever they really thought of her youth and inexperience, they were always polite and respectful. Just as all the male teachers were "Sir," she was "Madam."

In each class she was greeted with brown faces, shirts in shades of white, long legs sticking out from their schoolboy shorts and crammed under too-small desks. The boys varied in age and size, some having started school later, or having missed a year when there was not enough money to afford the fees. With few exceptions they were all serious students, each inspired with an individual desire to succeed as undeniable as the drumming of rain every afternoon on the classroom's tin roof.

"Now, let's get on to that stalwart son of the Browns."

Stalwart means strong and brave, she had explained on the very first day. Now that they were reading about the struggles of poor Tom Brown, the introduction was always good for a laugh.

Aries is a sun sign, Tessa had said, *which means you're hot when you set your mind to something.* She could do this, she would do it. English was her native language, for God's sake. Damn it, she was not going to let these boys down.

* * *

Laurel sat on her stoop watching the sun expand and lower in a painted sky. The cloud cover had finally yielded to blue sky and sun in mid-October, and it was now her habit to sit outside in the mild evening air. She couldn't see the mountains from her steps but knew they were there behind her, their sharp geometry outlined in purple; they looked closer as the sun dropped, so that sometimes, in the depths of night, she imagined them moving to engulf the valley before morning.

The first time she had brought out her recorder and played into the clean quiet air, she quickly drew a small crowd: a few students, some of the other teachers' small children, villagers who had been passing along the school road. Everyone stood still and listened, flashing oblique smiles, sometimes a quiet

70

giggling. A female Wazungu sitting on the steps outside her house making music for no special reason; that was not a sight they saw every day.

Sometimes she played familiar hymns or folk songs, whatever she had by memory, "Shenandoah," "Jesu, Joy of Man's Desiring," "Stairway to Heaven." Steven Foster, J.S. Bach, Led Zeppelin, it was all music, like fruit on a celestial tree, ripe for the plucking. She improvised melodies, challenging herself never to repeat the same phrase, trying on different rhythmical patterns, forgetting what she had played as soon as it left her lips and disappeared in the cool, damp air.

Now her playing did not attract as much attention, although passersby might still stop to listen. Sometimes a student or two would come around to try his hand at the instrument. John Ntunzyma often brought a bamboo flute and harmonized with her, and they exchanged simple tunes. She liked these times, almost as much as when Ngira stopped by.

The hearty greeting, the casual smile. "Hi ho, Laurel! Are you busy?"

"Yes, I'm watching the cabbages grow." This was their little joke, and they had not yet tired of it.

"But perhaps, like the pot that never boils, cabbages will not grow when they are watched."

"I'd better stop watching, then."

They laughed.

"And how did the day go for you?"

"It was good, except that my fourth class really botched up their homework essays on Romeo and Juliet."

Ngira chuckled. "Ah yes, Shakespeare is difficult. When I think of what you are up against, I remind myself how glad I am to be teaching Maths."

"John Munyangaba asked me why 'this fellow Shakespeare' couldn't just say what he meant. Thomas came to my rescue by telling him that it's like a potato plant: the words are the leaves, and the meaning is the fruit, which must be dug out. Sometimes I think I should let him teach the class." She hoped Ngira didn't mind being her sounding board. He always made her feel better. "Oh, and I've decided to start tutoring Kizuma. I told him to meet me at the library tomorrow at homework time."

Ngira was looking at the patch of carnations that Laurel had planted along the side of the house, grown spindly from reaching for the sun. "Eh, your little flowers attract some very large bugs."

"I thought they were birds!"

"Don't worry, they are harmless."

"Good. They come around every afternoon, but I don't think they know what to make of my strange flowers."

Neither spoke for a moment. Ngira scratched his chin. "I think the Head might not like it, this business with Kizuma. Have you asked him?"

"No. Why, do you think he'll object?"

"It is only that it will seem like favoritism. The other students will say, Heh, we have paid the same fees, but she is helping Kizuma to get ahead of us."

Laurel couldn't help laughing. "But he's so far behind!"

Ngira shrugged.

"In the U.S. if a student needs extra help, he gets it. That's the theory, anyway."

"Yes. But which of our students would not be glad of some extra help in preparing for exams? Here, if you have some brains and work hard, you make it. Those who are working hard do not like special treatment for those who are not."

Laurel felt her face constrict. "I can't believe this. You mean we should just stand by and watch him fail?"

Ngira folded his arms over his chest and exhaled. "No, perhaps not. In any case, you have already started the ball rolling. Shall we go and speak to the old boy?"

As they walked toward the Headmaster's house, the mountains thundered into view. "Every time I see those volcanoes it's like I'm seeing them for the first time. They take my breath away."

Ngira stopped and looked toward the horizon. "Back where I come from, we have the Ruwenzori. There is some snow on top, and when the moon is just behind the peaks, this lights up the snow so that the mountains shine like the moon. The Greek Herodotus saw this and gave them the name, Mountains of the Moon." He smiled at her. "Perhaps you will see it sometime."

They walked without speaking the rest of the way to Mr. Senwangama's house.

13

Letter to Tessa

October 17

Dear Tess,

Your letter only took three weeks to get here and it was like a precious gift from another world. I'm thrilled they're showing two of your oils at Fischer Gallery. I remember "Huit Clos," so deep and meditative, and "Clitter" (you slut!) is bold and beautiful. I'm sure they'll both sell. You're off and running, Tess, the sky's the limit! Wish I could be there for the opening.

Sorry about bitching so much in my last letter. I had just arrived at Butawanga, feeling homesick and sorry for myself, worrying about Carolyn. We're the only single females at an all-boys school, and respect is essential. If she screws up, she could bring me down with her.

Gordon and one of the African teachers, named Ngira, have been helping me figure things out, but I still have some hairy moments. The first composition assignment I collected from my students was appalling. "Flajamen (for Flashman) he is not knowing he can kill Tom." I'm really sweating this kind of thing because some of them are simply "not knowing" how to write in English. Language is like music when you think about it. There's the sounds that you hear, and the written notes that represent the sounds. You can learn a song by ear without ever having to see the notes on the page. Most of these kids are so much better understanding spoken English than reading or writing it. It's composition, I have to help them work on the notes on the page. I spend a lot of time writing corrections in their homework books, hoping they'll get the idea of how sentences make sense. One of them in particular needs a lot of remedial help, and I'm going to give it to him.

I miss my piano. I even miss Alan in some freaky vestigial way, like a bad appendix, ha, but piano was as essential as food. Alan never was.

I wish you could see how incredible it is here, everything in tempo rubato, stretched and expanded – the mountains (volcanoes!), air, sun, the sounds, the quiet – nature actually exists, people live accordingly, the whole place is vibrating to some deep earthy pitch and I'm just beginning to hear it. The headmaster and the other teachers have been very nice once they got used to the idea of us. There's also this mission with white priests, but shit, space, more next time. Comera, it means "be strong," my new mantra.

L.

[Excerpt from State Department records]

Washington, undated

Memorandum from the President's
Assistant for National Security Affairs Henry
Kissinger, to President Nixon

SUBJECT

Appointments with you for Foreign
Chiefs of State coming to the 26th UN General
Assembly (Sept. – Dec., 1971).

6. President Amin – Uganda. Neither
State nor I recommend this appointment. Amin
took power in a military coup several months
ago and so far, at least, has stirred up a
great deal of difficulty with his neighbors.
Finally, two American citizens apparently
were recently killed by Amin's undisciplined
troops and it is inappropriate for you to
agree to receive him while the matter is
still in flux. I recommend that we inform
Ugandan authorities that your schedule will
not permit a meeting this fall.

[Nixon] No, I will see him for 20
minutes.

II

Things Fall Apart

"Okonkwo remembered that tragic year with a cold shiver throughout the rest of his life....
He knew that he was a fierce fighter, but that year had been enough to break the heart of a lion."

Chinua Achebe, *Things Fall Apart*

14

The Boys

Today was the first Saturday of the month-long Christmas holiday, the day promising to be as clear and warm as all December days had been. Laurel was lazing in bed after the cool night, wrapped in the blanket that still smelled softly of spices from Gupta's store, when the roar and splutter of machinery outside catapulted her to the window. There were two motorbikes, and Gregg and Kevin beating clouds of dust out of their jeans and shirts. She pulled on her navy-blue bell bottoms and a tee-shirt, and went out with Carolyn to meet them.

Carolyn was in her bright tie-dye tee and blue jeans. "Well, it took you guys long enough to make it out here."

"Are you kidding?" Gregg spat on the ground. "This is, like, the end of nowhere!"

"No shit, man – and that road. Two hours to go 40 miles." Kevin's voice was shaky.

There was an awkward moment when no one seemed to know what to say next.

"You could have called first," Laurel said, sounding serious enough to give them a moment's pause before they got the joke. There were no phones at Butawanga.

* * *

The two boys dumped their dusty backpacks on the floor

81

and took turns washing up in the bathroom. Carolyn and Laurel started the water for tea. "What, no beer?" Gregg said as they put out the tea cups. His dark hair had grown longer, and spikes of it licked over his ears. He looked good, Laurel thought, tanned and trim. Kevin was still a bit pudgy, red-faced, but somehow taller than Laurel remembered. She had not been impressed with either of them during training, but she was glad to see them, the invasion of earthy smells and male noise more exciting than she liked to admit.

They all sat down to eat, spreading peanut butter on toast made in the oven's broiler. The boys were planning to stay over at least one night, since the road would be impossible to navigate after dark. They would roll out their sleeping bags on the straw mat in the living room. So they said; but from the looks Carolyn was giving Gregg, Laurel thought, he would be in Carolyn's bedroom that night. Well, that was her business. Still, it would be hard not to fantasize having one of them in her own bed that night. She tried not to think of falling asleep with Alan's arms around her after sex, how comfortable and comforting it had been.

Gregg and Kevin talked about traveling to Kampala and then to the Kenya coast over the vacation. They suggested that Carolyn and Laurel go to Kampala by bus and meet them there, and then they could all travel together. *Cool*, Carolyn said. *Yes, cool,* Laurel agreed, glad to have a definite plan of action for the holiday. The social life in the city would be a welcome change from the quiet isolation of Butawanga. Term was over. Tom Brown, Okonkwo, Romeo, all behind her. Some of her students had done very well on their final term grades, and all of them passed, even Kizuma.

Now, she deserved some fun, and damn it she was going

to have it. Traveling with other volunteers would be a chance to see other parts of this foreign and still fascinating place, and to be with Americans her own age. Being with Gordon and Ngira, or chatting with the other teachers at the morning tea break, was stimulating and carried the excitement of new discovery, but sometimes you needed to relax with people who shared your background. No matter how different the other volunteers were, they were still Americans.

Conversation ranged from teaching experiences to news of events in Uganda and the U.S. At their school in Kabale's rolling green hills, Gregg and Kevin could get Radio Uganda and BBC broadcasts most of the time. Here at Butawanga, Gordon's radio picked up BBC World Service only, as he liked to say, when the wind was right. There were some reports about Amin purging his opposition in Kampala, Gregg said, usual Third World dictator shit, nothing to worry about.

Gregg was teaching Chemistry and Physics, Kevin was teaching English, *not exactly my thing, but it beats being blown up in some rice paddy in Vietnam*. They talked about wanting to burn their draft cards, but neither of them had been ready to go to jail or run to Canada. When their college deferments had ended at graduation they were entered in the lottery system, where draft order was assigned according to a random selection of birthdates. Gregg's number was a fairly safe 209, but he had decided to join the Peace Corps anyway. Kevin had drawn a 34 and joined to avoid the draft for two years. "This Peace Corps gig probably saved my life," he said.

Gregg got up and announced, "Hey, it's vacation – time to lighten up, right, Kev?" He rummaged in his backpack and pulled out a bulging plastic bag. "Feast your eyes on this, ladies. It's the mother lode."

Carolyn grunted. "What is it, your dirty underwear?"

"Fuck no, it's weed. Grass. *Bhanja.* Marijuana. Almost a kilo of the stuff. Do you know what a stash like this would cost in the States?" He lifted the bag, grinning like a child with his sack of Halloween trick-or-treat candy. "One day this African guy shows up at our door with a pillowcase full. It grows wild here, and the natives know where to find it to sell to us Wazungu – dirt cheap. This is our third batch. There's like two fucking pounds of it – enough for vacation, right, Kev?"

"Let's see, two joints each a day, three a day on weekends – sounds about right to me." Kevin looked very pleased. Laurel did not know what to say. Tessa had smoked pot whenever one of her itinerant lovers had some, but Laurel had decided she didn't need another bad habit on top of smoking cigarettes. And she did not care to sit around the apartment giggling and losing control of her body and mind – same reason she had never liked alcohol. So Tessa smoked weed, Laurel smoked cigarettes, and then, a few months before the wedding date, Laurel did not smoke anything. She had been surprised how easy it was to quit cigarettes once she put her mind to it. Freedom from that addiction was like a revelation, and she felt stupid for ever having started.

But pot, here at Butawanga?

"Come on, guys, pot is illegal in Uganda too, remember? Put it away, please, and don't even think about smoking."

"You see what I have to live with?" Carolyn said, drawing the shape of a square in the air with her fingers. "Come on, Laurel, who's gonna know?"

"Anyone might come around – Caspar, Mr. Senwangama – you can call me a square, Carolyn, I don't care. I'm not taking stupid chances."

"Oh, come on, Laurel," Kevin said. "The school is, like, deserted."

Gregg took out a packet of papers, extracted one and laid it out on the table, began filling it with hefty pinches of the dried herb, humming the melody of Jefferson Airplane's "White Rabbit." Everyone watched, mesmerized, as he licked and sealed the paper around a bulging marijuana cigarette. "A perfect B-52." He put a lit match to one end of the joint until it caught fire, then blew out the flame. "Who wants the first hit from this bomber – Laurel?"

"No, thanks."

Gregg held out the joint. "Come on, Laurie. Let us turn you on."

"Just try some, see if you dig it," Kevin said.

Carolyn sighed. "For God's sake, somebody take a toke."

They had a point about the school being deserted. And Tessa said it was a pleasant high, not anesthetic like alcohol. She often wondered if she had been at least mildly stoned from the second-hand smoke in the apartment, so why after all was she being so uptight? Because one of the Peace Corps rules was no drug use of any kind. But Peace Corps was 10 hours away in Kampala. Now, there was only Gregg's steady hand, a tendril of acrid-smelling smoke, and three pairs of eyes.

* * *

Laurel stood on the road outside her house wondering where to go. It was two in the afternoon and the school was very quiet. A few remaining groups of students lingered near the dormitory buildings, but no teachers were visible. Many had already left for the holiday.

She rotated slowly, arms outstretched, feeling the warm air

flow over her, inhaling its clean moist just-washed smell. She stopped to smile at the sharp line of the volcanoes against the bright blue afternoon sky, softened by dabs of cottony cloud. The mountains, the school compound, were all so familiar now. It struck her how much she had come to like this place, the students and teachers, the headmaster, even though she still missed her parents and Tessa and sometimes even Alan, especially now that it was almost Christmas, missed them so terribly in fact that she suddenly felt like crying. Feeling so lonely out here on the road, but not wanting to go back into that house full of people getting stoned, with Gregg telling her, hold it out a little, suck in the smoke through your lips –

She had taken a few hits from the bomber, the sensation of smoke in her throat seductively familiar, yet there was a bitter taste and dulling vibe that she didn't like. A high-pitched noise in her head brought back Alan's warning about destruction of brain cells. *What the hell am I doing?* "I'm out of here," she said, and no one had tried to stop her this time.

She walked briskly down the school road, hoping to shake off a stuffy feeling in her ears. There was Gordon's house, but if she got involved with him he would expect to come over and meet their houseguests. Ngira would be less inquisitive, but his concrete house looked empty. Alone, then, with her mental music –

"Hi ho, Laurel! Were you looking for me?"

Ngira's booming voice and sudden presence made her startle and blush, as if she had been caught peering into his window. She giggled. "Oh my God, where did you come from?"

"I went to Saturday Mass up at the mission. You did not see me, coming down the road?"

"No, I didn't. I was playing Brahms, the Second Piano Concerto."

He smiled. "Ah, I see. Then in fact, you were too busy to notice me."

He said it so naturally that she laughed, and he laughed too. They started walking back down the road.

"Some day when you are free, perhaps you would like to come to Mass? And Carolyn too, of course."

Laurel did not want to think about Carolyn, the way she had draped herself over Gregg saying *I am so fucking stoned*, over and over. "I'm not Catholic." Why did her voice sound so far off?

"Neither am I, not exactly. Where I come from it was Church of Uganda. They ran the primary school where I was educated, a mission very much like this one. Here the Mass is not so different, and anyway I think the same God smiles over all of my country."

The same God smiles over all of my country. What a beautiful thing to say. "Wow, that is so deep."

Ngira looked at her sideways.

"I mean, do you go to Mass every day?"

"No, only sometimes, on Sundays. But tomorrow I will not be going. I am going with Gordon to climb Mount Sabinyo."

"My shamba boy is named Sabinyo."

Ngira fingered his chin. "It is the middle volcano. It means father of the teeth. Perhaps he took the name because he has rather large teeth."

"Oh, my God, he does!" They both laughed. Ngira had such a nice laugh. But Laurel was aware of acting silly. She couldn't stop smiling. Oh shit, she thought, I must be a little

87

stoned after all. Pull yourself together, before he notices. She wondered if he could smell the smoke on her, the way Alan always claimed he could smell the cigarette smoke on her clothes even when she hadn't lit up for hours.

She tamped down her voice. "I would like to go to the service sometime, if you feel like having company."

"I would like that very much indeed," Ngira said. As they approached Laurel's house the two motorbikes were just visible around the back corner. The curtains, bless them, were closed across the living room windows.

"You have visitors?" Ngira asked.

"Yes, two Peace Corps from Kabale. They're resting, but I wasn't tired and it's such a lovely afternoon I thought I'd take a walk in the hills around the school."

Ngira of course was obliged to offer to walk with her. Poor man, she thought, already tired from walking up to the mission and back. But she did not want to walk up on the hills alone. She took a deep breath of clean air before falling in step behind him.

* * *

The path was studded with rocks that hurt her sandaled feet. It was quiet on the hillside, except for the occasional distant grunt of cow or bleat of goat. A steady breeze traversed the slope, bending the wispy grass and carrying smells of earth and dung. She looked back at the house with the curtains drawn and the two motorcycles hugging the wall. By the time they got back, the smoking would be over and hopefully they would think of opening the windows to air things out. Maybe then she could at least invite Ngira in for some tea to make up for dragging him all over the countryside.

They walked uphill, Laurel picking her way through the rocks. Most of the vegetation on these foothills had been grazed away. From the top they had a view of an incredibly blue lake rimmed by trees, and further on there was a rolling expanse of emerald green, a tea plantation owned by Belgians, Ngira said. Clouds were suspended halfway up the tallest volcano, leaving only its rocky cone visible.

Ngira followed her gaze. "At the top of Muhabura, there can be something like snow, when the hail lies on the ground and does not melt."

"Do you like going up there?"

"Sometimes I like it very much. Not at first, even when Gordon and I went to the little one, Gahinga. For one thing I was not in very good shape. And then I thought, what a crazy Wazungu thing to do, there are wild animals and such up here." He looked toward the peaks. "But then, I ignored my fear. I began to like the challenge."

They started walking back down the hill.

"Up there I have seen antelope, sometimes elephant. Once on Gahinga we even saw some gorillas."

"Wow, fantastic."

"They were sitting in the sun, chewing leaves. We watched them for a moment, then went away as quietly as we could. Luckily they did not find us out."

Did he say smoking leaves? "Were they dangerous?"

"I don't know. They are very powerful animals. But there is a lady, over there in Rwanda, who lives with them. She is American. Perhaps you have heard of her?"

Laurel had read something before ever contemplating the Peace Corps, about a woman studying gorillas in Africa. "I don't remember her name, but I think I read about her in

89

National Geographic."

"People say she is crazy. They say she likes gorillas but hates African people. She shoots their cattle and frightens their children. They call her a white witch."

"How awful. Do you think it's true?"

Ngira stood thoughtfully, hand on chin. "Most probably this is just bad talk. The people here like to gossip."

"Like people everywhere. But doesn't anyone ever talk about politics, like what they think of the government and so on? Whenever I'm in the teacher's room it's only small talk. I always wonder if they clam up because I'm there."

Ngira smiled and shook his head. "No. For us, to clam up is an old habit. Even as isolated as we are, we can think someone might inform against those who talk too much. Of course, Gordon and I often talk over things he has heard on the BBC, when it reaches this far. The news from the Kampala radio stations is dictated by the government and so is not reliable."

At steeper sections, Ngira would stop and offer his hand to help her down the rubbly slope, which gave her time to study his profile. He had a long, straight nose, rounded lips, a broadly curved forehead, a cushion of black hair cut to the contours of head and neck. Was there a barber in Kisoro? She had never thought to ask. Her own hair did not appear to increase much in length because as the strands got longer they would corkscrew tighter and levitate from her shoulders. When it got too bushy, she would trim it herself.

As they came further downhill something was different in the view of the school. Something new was added, and with a sharp intake of air she registered the reality of a car parked outside her house. No volunteers she knew of had cars. She hoped against hope it might be some off-the-beaten-track tourists, but much more likely, damn it, was that it was a surprise visit from Peace Corps staff.

15

Things Fall Apart

Ngira did not ask about the car. He looked at her quizzically for a moment before he smiled and gave his usual "Cheerio." She wondered if her face had betrayed her upset as she hastily left him on the road in front of her house. It was Peace Corps, all right, most likely on a routine visit. She walked in to see Chip, their Director, a small man with a large mustache and cowboy hat, seated astride a dining chair. Maureen, his sidekick here in Uganda, was the recruiter Laurel had spoken to at the office back in Boston on her wedding day. She sat with legs crossed, foot bouncing. Carolyn, Gregg, and Kevin were in a row on the sofa looking tragic, the smell of bitter smoke still in the air.

Chip said, "Well, these three were caught dead to rights, but they said you didn't smoke, so I guess you're off the hook." Laurel felt a rush of gratitude and the impulse to immediately come clean, but she didn't. She let the lie stand. "Yeah, she's a real goody-two-shoes," Carolyn said between clenched teeth.

Now, alone with Carolyn a few hours later, Laurel was still stunned. She felt miserable about the whole stupid mess. According to Peace Corps regulations, drug use was grounds for immediate dismissal, but why did Chip have to be such a hard-ass about it? Now Carolyn had to leave, the vacation plans were canceled, everything was coming apart. Why not let them off with a warning? The school really was deserted. No one would have known about the weed, but now everyone would know, or suspect something worse.

Laurel was being allowed to stay. They had all lied for her, and now she would be the only one allowed to stay.

"Chip is a fucking fascist!" Carolyn stormed around collecting her things and throwing them into her duffel, and then collapsed on the sofa like a deflated balloon. "And that Maureen. *Nobody forced you to smoke it, Carolyn.* The fake smile and that disgusting orange lipstick she wears." She chipped pink polish from her thumbnail.

Maureen was the one who had given Laurel this most incredible of gifts when she needed it, that day when she had run from the church and down the stairs into the Peace Corps recruiting office. Now, again, Maureen was giving her a break, against all odds. "Maybe they'll change their minds. The punishment doesn't fit the crime."

"They won't, and you know what, I don't care. Fuck this Peace Corps shit. I'm glad I'm going home."

Chip and Maureen had explained everything to Mr. Senwangama and confirmed that it was all right for Laurel to stay on her own. The two staff members were spending the night at Travellers Rest Hotel in Kisoro. Gregg was sent to stay with Gordon, Kevin was dispatched to Ngira's. In the morning they would ride their motorbikes back to Kabale to pack and say their goodbyes. Carolyn was told to be ready to leave in the morning with Chip and Maureen.

Laurel hated the falseness of her situation, the cowardice of hiding behind a lie. If you do something bad, her father had always told her, step up and tell the truth and take your medicine. You'll feel better. Even as a child she recognized the wisdom in this, and had come to believe in the importance of truth. She had wanted to confess to Chip and Maureen, to be relieved of the burden of the lie. But something kept holding her back. She did not want to leave Butawanga, not yet, not this way. What made her keep silent even more, though, was the generosity of the others, lying to save her. Even Carolyn. Somehow, it had not seemed possible to betray such a gesture.

Early Sunday morning they came to get Carolyn. Laurel talked first to Maureen. There were extenuating circumstances to consider – the stress of the term, the knowledge that no one at the school would know about them smoking. "And if you take Carolyn, I'll be here on my own." It was no good. Maureen brushed her off with, "Yes, I know, but we'll send a replacement from the next group. And really, Laurel, you've been a wild card ever since that day you came into my office in your wedding dress. Right now the decision is they're going, but you can stay if you want. So don't push your luck or you'll be going back with them."

Chip listened to her case, but would not change the decision. Rules were rules, and that was that. They had the reputation of the whole organization and the United States itself to consider, to say nothing of all the volunteers who were living by the rules.

After they were gone, Laurel wandered aimlessly through the too-quiet house, still unable to take it all in. So many times she had wished Carolyn would just disappear, taking her irritating ways along with her, but finally they were getting along pretty well and this was too extreme, too sudden. In the bathroom, a few long black hairs were curled around the sink drain, and Carolyn's thick white towel hung mutely from the bar. Not forgotten, surely. That towel was a gift. At the sight of it, she started to cry.

Alone in her concrete box, the window louvers now fully open to the warm air, she was chilled by the solitude. She went into the room that had been Carolyn's, feeling its vacancy, idly opening and closing the dresser drawers, empty now, except there in the bottom one, there was something, a small box. Condoms. Just like Carolyn. Was this an oversight or were the rubbers a gift, too, like the towel? She could leave them there, but then what would the new volunteer think? She took the little box back to her closet and put it in the bottom of her empty backpack, out of sight and mind.

I'll manage, finally I'll get some privacy, not to mention peace and quiet from Carolyn's endless monologues. I'm an adult; I'll be fine. But she couldn't shake a feeling like lead in the pit of her stomach.

By Thursday, the empty house and the deserted school felt too depressing. Except for the headmaster and a few staff, the school had emptied for the vacation. Gordon and Ngira were off climbing a mountain and then going to Ngira's village for the holiday. If only this had happened a little sooner, she might have gone with them. She would love to see Ngira's village.

She grabbed her wallet and big straw shopping bag and headed out to the only possible destination, shopping in Kisoro. It was only 10 a.m., but already the road was a dark river of heat, even with the occasional breeze that wafted out from the shambas, where tin-roofed houses with whitewashed earth walls were surrounded by plots of maize, cassava, sorghum, and clumps of trees that retained some morning coolness. She walked slowly to conserve energy, feeling her exposed skin burn, watching the black dust coat her ankles and her once-white sneakers.

She could still get on the bus and go to Kampala, but there was no way of contacting anyone to make definite plans. She did not want to wander around Kampala on her own. It would have to be a quiet vacation here at Butawanga. She could use the time to prepare for next term. Next up on the fourth form syllabus was James Ngugi's *The River Between,* an African Romeo and Juliet, dark and tragic. She wished it could be something lighter, to make her students laugh. She would pass the time until classes started by reading the curriculum books, listening to music tapes, playing her recorder. Helping Sabinyo in the garden, though he clearly resented her interference. So much for fun with other Americans. But these things could be fun, couldn't they, in their small quiet way?

Some nights she was unable to sleep, noticing every little sound in the profoundly dark night. The nights were going to take some getting used to. She still felt guilty for being allowed to stay, but damn it, why should she be punished for a few hits she didn't even enjoy? If anyone deserved it, it was Gregg and Kevin for bringing the damn stuff in the first place; but Kevin would be draft bait now, and no one deserved that. They might have let Carolyn off, if she hadn't called Chip a fucking asshole, and Maureen a psycho Barbie doll.

Anyway, she was beginning to wonder who was actually being punished here. The others would be back in the States in time for Christmas. It would have been so much easier to confess and be on a plane right now headed for home.

Carolyn had not expressed any concern about leaving her students. Probably Ngira and Walugembe would have to double up on their teaching loads until another volunteer got down here.

She wondered who they would send, and when. Soon,

Laurel thought. Let it be soon.

Children ran out from the shambas as she walked past. They would follow her all the way into town, chanting *zungu, zungu*, and, *you give me shilling, Madam.* They liked to play this game even though by now they knew she would not give them money. Gordon had said that if you gave them something once they would never stop begging. She felt guilty about this, but these children appeared healthy and well-fed, not like the pitiful beggars in Kampala. She had been surprised by the way even the small ones were free to run over the countryside, so unlike her own protected childhood. Today they made her laugh and drew her out of her funk. It was time to stop feeling sorry for herself. It would feel even worse to be sitting on that plane knowing she had left her students teacher-less in the middle of a school year.

She was tired and parched when she reached the main street. Kisoro was quiet, too, since it wasn't a market day. A few men sat talking with the tailor as he worked the treadle machine on the porch outside his shop; she waved, they nodded. Two women carrying head bundles smiled shyly at her; *Mulaho*, Laurel gave the greeting; *Mulahoneza*, came the musical reply as they passed by. She glanced around for Mzee, the resident beggar, expecting him to lurch at her from the shade of a porch, but he was nowhere to be seen.

A child came running down the street and stopped a short distance away. "Wazungu," he shouted to the group of children that had followed her. They all ran after him down the road that led to Travellers Rest and the Rwandan border. There must be white people at the hotel, not all that surprising; here in the so-called Switzerland of Africa, tourists were not uncommon. Kisoro was a gateway to Zaire and Rwanda, the hotel a convenient watering hole for gorilla-seeking safaris and other adventurous travelers. She was tempted to run down there after the children, but the Wazungu might not be English speaking, and the few tourists she had encountered previously passing through Kisoro had been as full of themselves as royalty on holiday. Mostly, she did not want to admit to herself how desperately in need of company she was. Shopping first, then maybe a stroll down to the hotel.

She was comforted by the cool dimness of Gupta's store, the rich scents of material things: fabrics, foods, spices, toiletries, and the paper bags, wood barrels and straw baskets that held them – mixed with the smells of cooking wafting from behind the curtain that separated the living areas from the store. The kitchen would be the province of Mrs. Gupta, who usually came into the store at some point, although Laurel never saw her enter. Suddenly she would be there, announced by her whispering sari and tinkling gold bracelets.

After the usual welcome from the shopkeeper, Laurel placed her shopping list on the counter so that he could fill her order for the few staple foods, paper goods, and cleaning supplies she needed. She selected a bag of English candy called Assorted Fruit Sours, and also a bag of Fruit Gums for the children, if they followed her on the walk home. They were children, after all, and she wanted to give them a treat.

She wanted gifts for Caspar and Sabinyo for Christmas, and was pleased to find an inexpensive watch for Caspar, who was always asking the time. For Sabinyo, a wide-brimmed straw hat trimmed in red fabric would make him the hippest shamba boy in Kisoro.

On impulse she requested some of the red, green, and yellow lentils which Mr. Gupta called dahl, and a random sampling of sweet, earthy-smelling spices. She did not have any curry recipes but why not experiment, try a lentil curry for Christmas, in the absence of turkey with apple chestnut stuffing. Caspar had showed her how to make the local dishes, the ground peanut or bean stew with onions and cabbage. Sweet and white potatoes were always available, and the green plantain bananas called *matoke* were trucked in to the school. It was good food, filling, cheap, and satisfying. Laurel watched Mrs. Gupta weigh out what seemed like huge quantities of the lentils and spices into brown paper bags. It would be a vegetarian Christmas, and she was pleased about that.

The African man who worked at the duka would as usual deliver her purchases to her house. The gumdrops and the two gifts went in her shopping bag. Laurel said goodbye to the shopkeeper and his wife and stepped out of the store into the hot clear air. She walked down the same road where her gang of children had disappeared, taking a brisk pace, anxious now that the Wazungu might have left in the time it took to do her shopping.

There was a Volkswagen van outside the hotel, and a white couple standing on the porch talking to Rajaraman, the owner. Like a thirsty person sighting water, Laurel felt suddenly greedy for conversation that would go beyond the greetings exchanged with local Africans. *Please let them speak English.* The woman was petite, with tightly bunned hair so yellow that at first glance it looked like a hat. She was dressed in khaki pants and a white long-sleeved shirt, standing erect, as if ready to take charge of any situation. The man was only a few inches taller than his wife, but his robust frame looked twice as broad, with a squared-off solidity. They had the air of people who felt at home. Most likely this was the Belgian couple who owned the tea plantation she had seen on her walk with Ngira.

The old beggar Mzee, a now even larger crowd of children, and a few adults had gathered, keeping a respectful distance. The children mimicked the old man and his humpback posture, and he waved them away like flies.

Mzee was first to notice Laurel. He scuttled over with his crablike gait and began his usual routine, hunched next to her in his ancient dusty black jacket and tattered schoolboy shorts, chanting in his private language, leaning close enough to brush her feet with his hands before retreating sideways and starting the same thing over again. The poor old man was half-crippled with some kind of rheumatic condition, and she would have given him money even without the groveling. She was embarrassed by it and tried to get him not to touch her feet, but if Mzee understood any English, he was not letting on. The only way to get him to stop was to give him money, which she quickly did. The old man gripped the shillings in his knobby hand as he withdrew, chanting in rhythm to his hunched, rolling motion. She liked to think Mzee was chanting curses at her, taking his secret revenge on her soft, privileged whiteness.

With a nod to the two strangers, Laurel walked up and greeted Mr. Rajaraman, the innkeeper.

Rajaraman smiled broadly, relishing his role as host to this chance encounter. "Hello, Miss. And do you know Missus and Mister Hauber?"

Laurel turned to the couple and nodded. "Are you the people who live on the other side of Lake Mulehe?"

"Yes, that's right, dear." The woman squinted at Laurel. "And you must be one of the American Peace Corps at Butawanga."

"I'm Laurel Bittelson." She extended her hand. "The only

one now, I'm afraid."

"I am Yvonne Hauber. This is my husband, Karl."

White faces, cool blue eyes. Neat, well-tailored European clothes. Laurel was suddenly conscious of her baggy tee-shirt and bell-bottoms.

"I am pleased to meet you, Laurel." Karl's large hand enfolded hers like a warm blanket. "Yvonne, let us not keep this young lady standing out here. Mademoiselle, please allow us to buy you something to drink."

Laurel smiled. This was another thing she had come to like about Africa: no one here was ever in a hurry.

<u>16</u>

Out of the blue

Inside Travellers Rest, Rajaraman seated them at one of the solid wood tables in the small bar. Laurel asked for a Coke with ice, a real treat. The Haubers ordered Nile Lager.

"So, dear girl," Karl said, "you must tell us about your life at Butawanga. How have you been getting on?" His voice was rather high-pitched for such a stocky man. There was an accent: so was *zo*, have was *haff*. Belgian, Ngira had said.

"But wait, Karl. Laurel must tell us what happened to her companion." Yvonne's English was accented but precise, the "s" razor sharp. Her pale blue eyes bulged slightly. "Surely, you are not at Butawanga on your own?"

"Carolyn went back to the States. Something unexpected came up."

"And when will she return?" Karl asked.

"She won't return."

"Ah. We heard there were difficulties." Yvonne patted Laurel's hand.

Laurel wondered what she could have heard, so quickly, and from whom.

"You do not need to explain, dear. And tell me, is that Englishman Coopersmith still there? We haven't seen him for ages."

"Yes, Gordon's there, teaching Science."

"Does he still behave so indiscreetly?"

Karl frowned. "Now, Yvonne."

"Really, Karl, I am sure Laurel will have noticed his excesses. Between drink and women the man will ruin himself, if he has not already." She sighed.

So it was women, too, Laurel thought, wondering how Yvonne knew more about goings on at the school than she did. Now there was sure to be even more gossip about Carolyn's departure.

"But never mind about him," Yvonne continued. "You must tell us about yourself."

Laurel was out of practice in this kind of conversation, the well-intentioned interrogation that felt all too familiar from home, from her mother. "There's not that much to tell. I grew up in Concord, Massachusetts, near Boston. I studied Music at Boston University, and after I graduated I decided I wanted to see what life was like in another country. Instead of going to graduate school right away, I joined the Peace Corps. So here I am."

The Haubers were both leaning toward her as if expecting a lengthier account. I must sound incredibly boring, Laurel thought, but she was not about to go into the pathetic details about being a failed musician in her mother's eyes, too impetuous in her father's eyes, and in Alan's exact words, a cold bitch –

Karl drained his beer and put the glass down slowly. "Yes, here you are, in the most beautiful corner of the world."

Laurel was surprised and delighted by this simple observation. "Yes, it is beautiful." She had almost forgotten!

"And how do you plan to spend your Christmas?"

"Oh, I'll invite the headmaster to stop by, maybe some of the teachers. I'll cook – something." Better not mention the lentil curry.

Karl looked appalled. "Nonsense. The school is on holiday. You will be on your own, no way to spend Christmas. You must come along with us, don't you agree, Yvonne?"

"Of course that would be lovely, but there is the matter of a visa, no?" She turned to Laurel. "You see, we are just setting out to Rwanda, to visit our friend Ellen Webster. She studies gorillas from her camp in the mountains. She is American. Possibly you have heard of her?"

This must be Ngira's white witch. "Yes, I have, I mean, I'm pretty sure someone told me about her."

Karl frowned. "I am sorry I did not think before I spoke. A visa is necessary at the border. People sometimes bribe their way across, but this is not wise."

"Actually, I do have a visa for Rwanda," Laurel said, trying to sound offhand and not betray a rising flame of excitement. "During training in Kampala, one of the staff members recommended getting them for each border country, in case we wanted to travel."

Yvonne gave a cryptic smile. "What a surprise it will be for Ellen to have a visit from one of her countrymen." *Zur-prize,* sure as a surgeon's knife.

"Yes, a wonderful surprise." Karl smiled benevolently, looking a little like Santa Claus. "You must come along. We will not hear of you being at loose ends on your first Christmas away from home."

Although she suspected Yvonne was not in favor of her going, this was a gift out of the blue, the answer to her doldrums, way too good to pass up. Going to Rwanda to see gorillas was a hell of a lot better than being "at loose ends" at Butawanga for Christmas –

"I'd love to go," she said, while inside her the words *Rwanda* and *white witch* were striking brilliant chords.

"All right then, it's settled," Yvonne said. "First you should have something to eat. Then we will drive you back to Butawanga to pack some warm clothes, and off we will go!" She summoned the innkeeper to their table with a wave. Laurel leaned back in her chair. It was a long time since anyone had taken charge of her like this, the way her mother used to. Strange, one minute to feel like an adult completely on her own, and the next to slip so easily into the childish dependence she thought was left behind.

* * *

The van, which the Haubers called "the Kombi," was heavily loaded, but they made room for Laurel in the back seat. Rumbling down the Kisoro Road toward Butawanga, Laurel was elated by this change in her holiday prospects. She thought about Ngira, spending Christmas with his fiancée in his village. Theresa, Gordon had said her name was. Ngira never spoke of her, and Laurel never asked. It was nice to think of Ngira in love. He was kind and considerate, and she hoped this Theresa appreciated that.

She would have liked to show Ngira how Christmas was celebrated in her home, but here there could be no tree, no glowing hearth, no choral Messiah. No family. Last Christmas, so many things were planned: graduation, then a June wedding. When her senior recital was over, she had rushed around Harvard Square in the biting wind doing last minute Christmas shopping, and then, Christmas Eve with her family, Christmas day with Alan's. Wine, too much food, and everyone knowing who they were and where they belonged.

105

No looking back, Laurel thought as the Kombi bounced along the rocky road, Karl and Yvonne on the seat in front of her.

This Christmas, these strangers would have to be her family.

17

Grease

The border between Uganda and Rwanda was marked by two small concrete guardhouses about fifty yards apart, each standing in a different country. On the Uganda side, the guardhouse looked deserted. Karl got out and tried the door. Locked. Laurel and Yvonne got out, too. Only about 20 minutes outside Kisoro and already a snag.

Across at the Rwandan guardhouse, a man was sitting outside on a wooden crate, and near him a woman and child sat on a cloth, sharing a meal. They waved, and the travelers waved back. Karl pointed at the closed guardhouse, but the Rwandan guard just shrugged and went back to his food.

Karl sighed. "This is typical. If someone does not come, I will have to go searching."

A barefoot boy of eight or nine came running down a path, his long skinny legs and arms pumping, skidding to a stop in front of Karl. "Eh, I know where is this man, Bwana." He grinned and put out his hand, palm up. "I bring for you."

Karl reached in his pocket, produced a shilling and put it in the boy's hand. The boy turned and ran back up the path. Karl smiled indulgently. "That was the first bit of grease needed to oil our passage, eh, Yvonne?"

Yvonne shrugged, shook her head. "I hope at least he is quick. It is already one o'clock. To make it to Ellen before dark we must get to the mountain by three."

"Yes, yes, it will be close. But there is nothing to be done."

Laurel knew she had caused a delay in the time it took to go back to Butawanga for her to pack. They probably regretted asking her along, but it was too late to change that now. "How long do you think it will take to get across?"

"Impossible to say. If it is Samuel on duty today, he is probably at home sleeping, or even miles away at the local bar – ah, but we are in luck. Here comes our man now."

Samuel? There were biblical names among her students at Butawanga, other European names too that were an outgrowth of British colonialism, grafted on to the African heartwood.

An African man of average build, fit-looking, came striding toward them, grinning, tucking the tails of a long-sleeved tan shirt into his beltless black trousers. His black plastic shoes, styled to look like dress oxfords, made a soft flapping sound as he walked. He was young, with luminous brown skin and a handsome face. He extended his hand to Karl, who received it warmly. "Samuel, I am happy to see you."

"Mis-ta How-ba, how are you? And Ma-dam How-ba?" He turned and shook hands with Yvonne, then Laurel. "Oh, and here is a new Ma-dam."

"Yes," Karl said briskly, "this is our friend Miss Bittelson. She is a teacher at Butawanga. We are going to see Miss Webster in Rwanda, as usual, Samuel. But we had a late start today, and must be quickly on our way." Karl handed him all three passports, and Laurel could see there was paper currency tucked into the topmost one.

"Oh, yes, Mis-ta How-ba, I see, I see. I will be only one moment, please."

Samuel took the passports in one hand and with the other unlocked the guardhouse door with a key from his shirt pocket.

He went in, and after about five minutes came out again and peered into the van at the jumble of boxes and bags. "Everything is most in order," he said, smiling and handing the documents back to Karl.

After thanks and more pumping handshakes all around, Samuel lifted the single-hinged gate barring the road and wished them a safe journey. He seemed like a nice man, Laurel thought, and who could blame him for not being at this sleepy outpost every minute of the day? Back in the States, she would have been annoyed at the delay, and outraged by this expectation of grease, as Karl called it. But here, today, she was relieved that things had gone this smoothly.

"It's a casual system, but it seems to work," Laurel said.

"Everything works in its own time in Africa," Yvonne said, "most often at the speed of a snail."

"At least Samuel knows his business, once he gets to it," Karl said. "Lucky for us that his little messenger was on the job."

At the Rwandan crossing, the guard had finished his lunch and was standing at attention waiting for them. The young woman, possibly his wife, and a child of about three lounged on their cloth on the ground, watching. After a similar friendly exchange with Karl, and a bit more grease, they were cordially waved along their way.

"Well, we did not do badly. The road is dry, the petrol is full, now we should make it in good time," Karl said.

"God willing." Yvonne smiled back at Laurel. "Are you comfortable, dear?"

Laurel nodded. There was no point mentioning the hard, cramped back seat and the black road dust blowing at her through the open windows. This was a dirt road through the

African bush, not a highway back home. And she could not ask them to close the windows, in this heat – that would be ten times worse.

Yvonne squinted at Laurel's tee-shirt. "Make a noise in the world – what an extraordinary sentiment."

Laurel looked down at the silk-screened silhouette of Beethoven, bent low over the keyboard of his pianoforte, now faded from Caspar's vigorous washing. What would Yvonne think of Carolyn's purple tie-dyed "Pink Floyd North American Tour," or Gregg's neon yellow "Grateful Dead American Beauty?" But Yvonne would never meet them now.

Laurel had to shout to be heard from the backseat of the van. "I liked the idea that Beethoven would think of his music as making noise – like a rock star or something – when of course his music is nothing short of monumental."

Yvonne raised her blonde eyebrows and smiled uncertainly.

Okay, Laurel thought, now she really thinks I'm weird. "How long has Ellen been living in Rwanda?" she ventured.

"Four years," Karl answered. "Before that, she was a year in Congo. Zaire, it is now called. She had just begun her research when a military rebellion took place in Kivu Province, and for some reason she was escorted down from the mountains and detained by the military. But Ellen was not about to sit in captivity when she could be doing gorilla work, so she persuaded the men who were holding her to take her to Kisoro, and from there she made her escape!" Karl shook his head. "A foolish thing to do, but courageous."

Yvonne rested her hand on Karl's arm. "She was very lucky. There is no rule of law in Congo in these times, Laurel. I know that colonialism is a dirty word now in Africa, but under

Belgium at least there was order, and prosperity."

"That is so, Yvonne. You see, Laurel, after Yvonne and I married in 1952, we came to Congo to manage a coffee plantation near Stanleyville, now called Kisangani. We did very well, employed many Africans, and lived happily there. But when independence came in 1960, it was like pulling the finger from the dike. Right away, there was violence against us Belgians. No matter that we had always treated our African laborers with decency – that is how things go in Africa. We had to flee for our lives."

Yvonne sighed deeply. "Everything we had worked to build there in Congo, we left behind. We started over again in Uganda. Now we are tea growers." She shrugged. "But nothing can replace a good strong cup of our highlands coffee."

"I'm sorry," Laurel said, her voice hoarse from dust in her throat. She did not know what else to say. If she thought about colonialism at all, it was as an evil; but were Karl and Yvonne capable of evil? On the personal level, things sometimes looked different.

Karl squeezed his wife's hand, still on his arm. "And now, of course, their economy is in ruins. But we are well out of it, and thank God we are safe and sound, and so is Ellen."

For the next few minutes there was only the wheezing engine and rattling chassis of the van. Laurel could not imagine making the decision that the Haubers had made, to stay on in Africa after such a scare, and losing everything. She was beginning to see that Africa had a way of getting into your blood, even for white people. The freedoms Africa affords, Yvonne had said. Maybe especially for white people. Owning a big tea plantation like that, with labor cheap and plentiful, would not be possible in Belgium. But was it really another version of what slavery had been in the States?

"Did you bring some warm clothes, dear?" Yvonne's voice was cheerful, chirpy, pointedly closing the subject of Zaire.

"I brought a sweater."

"A good thick wool one, I hope."

"More like Orlon, I think," Laurel rasped, "the only one I have. I never thought I would need warm clothes in Africa. When I got to Butawanga, I wrote to my parents and asked them to send me some warmer things, but they haven't come yet."

Yvonne shook her head. "One sweater will not be enough. You will wear Karl's parka, and we must try to get you into my extra pair of khakis." She eyed Laurel's light cotton bell bottoms. "They will be too short, but they will be better than what you are wearing."

"I can't take your clothes. I'm sure I'll be all right." What she really needed was a drink of water –

"You must not be stubborn about this," Yvonne said. "It gets quite cold on the mountain, and we can't have you catching a chill. This is why Ellen is always coughing and with her nose running. She spends all day outdoors with her gorillas, even in the rain, and comes back chilled to the bone. Then, to top it off, she does not bother to eat properly, but smokes her cigarettes instead."

"It is absolutely amazing what she has done, a woman living alone in the bush. Such dedication," Karl said. "You will see."

Unless I suffocate first, Laurel thought.

"Karl is quite taken with Ellen, my dear." Yvonne gave her husband a teasing look. "That is why I make sure he never goes up there without me."

"Nonsense, Yvonne. You are just as taken with her as I am."

"I have the greatest admiration for Ellen, but not for her dealings with the Africans. She makes too many enemies."

Ngira had said that Ellen once fired a gun at a French camera crew that had come to film her and sent them running back down the mountain.

"She has made enemies, no doubt of that." Karl made a clucking noise. "But she is trying desperately to keep the gorilla from extinction."

Yvonne reached into the satchel at her feet for a pale blue scarf, which she folded into a triangle over her hair and tied at the nape of her neck, tucking the loose end under with her delicate white fingers.

"I would like to see her succeed, but you must admit she is fighting a losing battle. Rwanda is a poor country and an overcrowded one. Ellen must realize that the needs of the people come first."

"The needs of the people will also be served by conservation of the forest, which supplies water for the entire valley. Ellen's objectives are good in the long run for all concerned."

Needs of the people. Extinction. The words becoming faster and higher pitched over the whirr of the engine. Water. She was trying to pay attention, but her rear end was getting sore from the constant bumping, her eyes and nose burning from the dust, now red instead of black –

Yvonne turned abruptly to face her. "The average Rwandan worries about feeding his family today. He is not so interested in the long run. But my dear," Yvonne chortled, "your face is covered with dust. Only around your eyes is still white – like an owl!"

"My throat is very dry from the dust. Is there any water?"

"You should have said something sooner, dear. There is a rucksack behind you, among the boxes, and if you can reach in you will find a canteen of water. Karl, we must stop in Ruhengeri long enough for Laurel to wash up." Yvonne turned back to Laurel. "There is a hotel there with a real bathroom. Quel luxe!"

"But I don't want to delay us any further," Laurel said, feeling around for the rucksack and thinking, a real bathroom, oh yes, please.

"I will pick up a few supplies while you and Yvonne are freshening up," Karl said decisively, adding in a lower voice, "and perhaps we will also make time for one quick beer."

The "pit stop" in Ruhengeri, as Laurel called it, much to the Haubers' amusement, included a Coke for her and a beer that Karl downed with great relish, took only about 20 minutes, and left her refreshed and ready for whatever lay ahead.

18

Virunga Volcanoes

About two hours later their vehicle came to rest in the parking lot used by tourists entering this part of the Parc National des Volcans. Six round metal shacks, roofed with inverted funnels, stood awaiting visitors who might want to spend a night before venturing up the mountain. It would be like sleeping in a tin can, Laurel thought. No wonder they looked unused. More than a dozen local people from nearby shambas were already gathered in the parking lot, talking excitedly as more approached from the surrounding footpaths. Word of the Wazungu had traveled fast.

African men of all ages came forward to get Karl's attention, all talking at once. The women and children hung back and watched expectantly as their husbands, brothers, sons, competed for jobs as porters to carry the tourists' belongings up the mountain. Karl quickly hired a guide, who selected five men of varying ages. Each of the porters hefted a bag or box onto his shoulder or head, laughed and gestured to the others as they turned toward the mountain to begin the long climb to the Virunga Gorilla Research Center. They were all barefoot. Runagaba, the guide, shouted orders to the men as they moved away, then turned and waited for his charges. Laurel watched as the porters vanished into a seemingly endless field of daisy-like flowers. Pyrethrum, Yvonne said, explaining that more and more parkland was being cleared for the farming of this cash crop, exported to Europe for use in the manufacture of natural insecticides.

"And before the car park was put in, here was a stand of bamboo. As you can imagine, Laurel, Ellen hates this chipping away at the park, but what can she do? People's livelihoods must come first." Yvonne glanced in Karl's direction, but her husband was hunched over his equipment making final adjustments.

He turned to them and smiled. "Ready, ladies?"

Karl carried a rifle slung over his rucksack; she and Yvonne carried nothing. Laurel suddenly realized that she was going to be hiking up a mountain on the same giant scale as Muhabura. On walks with Ngira, she had wondered what it would be like to challenge the mountain's steely presence with her marshmallow-soft body. But somehow Ellen's mountain did not look as forbidding as Muhabura. Close up like this, it looked no more threatening than a walk through the open foothills around Butawanga.

Laurel fell into step behind the guide, followed by Yvonne and then Karl. After an easy walk of more than an hour through the cultivated fields, the trail narrowed and entered a cool, dank tunnel of black rock, in some places rough and crumbling, in others smooth and glossy.

"This is a lava tunnel," Karl said quietly. "On the sides it has been rubbed smooth by the passage of elephants that used this trail for centuries, when there was forest here instead of fields of flowers."

Elephants, climbing mountains. Astounding. She had thought they only lived in wide open grasslands. The tunnel now felt like a timeless place, full of secrets that she might be privileged to learn if she kept her eyes and mind open.

116

Emerging, it was like coming out on another planet as a shadowy, dense forest closed in around them. Laurel felt a thrill of adventure such as she had not felt since coming to Butawanga.

As they walked, Karl pointed out the various species of trees, the massive, hunched-over Hagenia dripping moss and vines and long pointed leaves and purple flower clusters, the more slender Hypericum with horizontal limbs hung with ferns. Laurel tilted her head back to watch the sun trickle in through the canopy of branches, the moist foliage shimmering as if hung with diamonds. As the trail got steeper she had to pay attention to her footing, and at places grab onto bushes to help herself along. The guide, Runagaba, or Karl would stop to give her a hand crossing patches of sucking mud. Still, her sneakers and socks were quickly soaked, her bell bottoms wicking the wetness up her legs. Yvonne's spare khakis, tried in the hotel bathroom in Ruhengeri, had been too snug for Laurel to pull up over her hips.

After several hours of steady climbing with only one brief rest stop, Laurel's breath was making clouds in the cold air. Even though she was sweating from the exertion, her legs and feet were chilled. She was very glad for Karl's parka. No one spoke now, whether from fatigue or caution she didn't know. The forest surrounding them was funky with decomposition, seething with moisture and the swishing sounds of vegetative movement, the distant calls of birds and other creatures. Against this background hum, the beat of her own heavy footsteps and breathing, the dull thud of Runagaba's panga as he chopped away the vines that had strayed onto the path, sound displaced thought. She tried to maintain a rhythmic walking pace, her feet and legs like lead weights. Everything began to blur in twilight and mist, the twisted outlines of trees, the dark runnels of shadow snaking through brush and vines. What seemed magical a few hours ago now felt sinister. Could anyone really live here? Maybe the Haubers were crazy, and they were all lost. Or maybe they were bringing her to some hideout where she would be sold to the white slave trade – oh, God, this stitch in her side.

Karl waited for her to recover.

He smiled. "Do not worry, we are just about there. Around the next bend is a clearing, a big meadow, and there we will see the camp." Even in this bracing air, his forehead glistened with sweat.

His voice was comfortable, his words comforting. She put all her energy into each step, to keep her knees from buckling. Soon, Laurel smelled smoke and heard distant voices in the gathering darkness. Ahead were some cabins and an open fire around which their porters sat, talking and laughing.

A man came to greet them, saying *Jambo, Jambo*, smiling with his arms spread wide.

"Binyawakosi, jambo," Karl and Yvonne shook hands with him in turn. "Laurel, this is Binyawakosi, Ellen's houseboy and cook. He has been with her for years. She calls him Ben."

Laurel shook hands. Ben's hand was warm and rough. "Jambo, Madama. Jambo sana." He turned to Karl. "Very sorry, Madama not back yet. She say she back before you come, but not back yet. We go to house. I have ready some hot-a-water."

Karl told Laurel and Yvonne to go ahead, while he stopped to pay off the porters and tell Runagaba when to bring

118

them back for the return trip.

"That is typical of Ellen, to forget the time – and anyone else," Yvonne said. As they walked along the gravel path through a meadow, she looked up at the dark cone of the mountain above them. "I do hope she is all right. But my dear, your trousers are soaked through. Come, let us hurry in, Ben is making tea."

Ellen's cabin was wood with a corrugated metal roof. Curtains showed in the glass-paned windows. Laurel couldn't remember when a place had looked so good to her. "Leave your shoes outside," Yvonne said. "Ben will clean them for us later."

Laurel tried to warm up in front of the stone fireplace. "I can't believe how cold it is up here."

Yvonne laughed. "We are at 3,500 meters, about 10,000 feet. I do hope we have not managed to give you pneumonia for Christmas. I will get something of Ellen's for you to put on. She is taller than I." Yvonne went into another room and came back with a pair of blue jeans. "That little room over there is the guest bedroom. Go and change while I fix your tea. Ben, is there milk and sugar?"

"Ah no, Madama. Milk and sugar gone now, one week maybe."

Yvonne sighed. "Well, never mind, I have brought some, it will be in one of our boxes. You go ahead, dear, get out of those dreadful slacks." The word *zlackz* was like a pointed object. She began rummaging through boxes lined up on one side of the kitchen alcove.

Laurel took the jeans and went into the other room. Pulling on the unknown woman's jeans felt like a delicious invasion. They were inches too long and too snug in the waist, but at least they were dry. She rolled them up, left them unbuttoned and covered the gap with her sweater.

When she came back into the kitchen, Karl was telling Yvonne that the porters had tried to demand more money because it was too late now for them to go back down the mountain, and they would have to stay in the guides' cabin. "As if any of them minded to get away from their families for a night. But these Bahutu are merchants by nature. I said we would give them beans and potatoes for their meal, and they settled for that."

Laurel accepted a mug of steaming tea from Yvonne, cradling it gratefully in her hands. "Can I help with anything?"

"Oh no, thank you, dear. All I need to do is put the stew on the stove to heat. I made it this morning, before we left."

This morning. Walking down the Kisoro Road in the hot sun, killing time. Now, the same day, she was in a place that seemed a world away. She looked around the cabin. It was much cozier than her concrete house at Butawanga. The woven straw mats on the walls added lightness and texture. A sturdy wood table and chairs, a sofa, a stuffed chair near the fire. Glass windows, and so much to look out on. "The only thing missing is a piano," Laurel said, half to herself.

Yvonne looked up from slicing a loaf of delicious-looking bread. "What's that, dear? Oh, I am afraid Ellen has no time for the finer things. Only for her gorillas."

"It's a nice place, even without a piano. Did Ellen build it herself?"

Yvonne laughed. "When Ellen first came here she lived in a tent, and probably would have continued to do so. Bad enough a white woman alone in the bush, but not to have a decent place to live? No, it would not do. So Karl and I arranged for this cabin to be built. Laurel, would you mind stirring the stew now and again, while I change into my dry khakis?"

Laurel took the spoon and potholder from Yvonne, who gathered up her clothes and went into the small bedroom. Stirring the richly fragrant stew, Laurel thought about the way the Haubers cared for Ellen as if she were family. Was that strange? In Africa it seemed white people helped each other more than they might at home in their own countries, but it was also clear that there was affection there.

"Ben," Karl said, stuffing tobacco into his pipe, "Madama is not out alone, I hope?"

"No, surely not alone. She go with Kitumba."

"Good, so at least we know she is not lost." He glanced at his gun, propped in a corner near the door. "Still, I think I will go and meet them with my torch." He laid the unlit pipe on the mantelpiece. "Do you know which trail they took?"

"They go ridge trail." Ben looked nervous now, rubbing his hands together. "I take you."

"Yes, all right, Ben. We will bring Runagaba as well."

Laurel thought of being out there on that darkening mountain, so far from home. Karl was obviously worried and trying to hide it. "Do you think something is wrong, Karl?"

"No, no, I am sure she is just delayed. Kitumba is with her, and he is an excellent tracker." He went to his knapsack and pulled out a flashlight. "Get a lantern, Ben, and we will go." He stood waiting by the door when it burst open, smashing into him.

"Karl! It's so good to see you!" Long arms wrapped around Karl's neck, knocking him further off balance.

"Ellen," he laughed, prying her gently away and looking

into her face. "It is good to see you, too. I was beginning to think some gorilla had you for his dinner."

"Now Karl, you know perfectly well gorillas are vegetarians." She stood facing him with the smile of a delighted young girl.

Yvonne rushed toward her. "Oh, Ellen, thank God." The two women hugged. "You do worry us so."

"I'm sorry for being so late, but wait until I tell you about the contact I made today. Yvonne," she sniffed the air, "dinner smells wonderful. You're just too good to me, I don't deserve– " her eyes locked on Laurel now, for the first time taking in her presence, and the smile vanished. Hollow cheeks, sharp nose, jutting chin; the face that had been softened by joy now turned hard as stone.

19

Gorilla Lady

She stood there dripping in Army style camouflage parka and denim jeans splotched with black mud. Gray-streaked brown hair in a long braid, a corona of wiry strands framing her angular face. Slate gray eyes, staring.

"Ellen, dear, this is Laurel Bittelson, the American Peace Corps from Butawanga. We ran into her this morning and since she was at loose ends for the holiday we thought you would not mind if we brought her along." Yvonne flashed her smile. "She has been so excited to meet you. Oh, and she was soaked through, so I made her put on a pair of your 'jeans,' as you call them."

A calculated silence, then a wary smile. "Laura, is it?"

"It's Laurel, with an -el. I'm sorry to barge in on you uninvited like this." She was aware of sounding too loud and bright, always her reaction to awkward situations. "I hope I'm not intruding."

Ellen was studying her closely. She took off her jacket, shook it, and hung it on a peg behind the door. "Even if you are, there's not a hell of a lot we can do about it, is there."

Yvonne scowled. "Now Ellen, really."

Okay, Laurel thought, this was a mistake. "Well, no, obviously here I am and you didn't have a choice. Karl and Yvonne asked me to come up here with them, but again I am sorry if it's inconvenient."

Ellen shrugged. "Sorry never quite cuts it, in my opinion. But never mind." She turned away from Laurel and hugged Karl and Yvonne again in turn. "Any friend of the Haubers is welcome here."

"There, that's my Ellen," Karl said. "We told Laurel she must come. We knew you would not mind having one of your countrymen to visit."

"You also know, Karl, how glad I was to put America and Americans behind me. But now tell me all your news, and I'll tell you mine, or what passes for news up here."

Laurel kept stirring the food, wishing she could transport herself down the mountain and back to Butawanga. A holiday alone in her house would be better than this woman's rudeness.

"News can wait, Ellen dear. We are all famished, as you must be. You get thinner every time I see you. Laurel has been keeping the stew in good order, but let us eat before it turns to porridge."

"Please," Ellen grimaced, "don't talk about porridge. It's all I've had for days, without milk or sugar."

Laurel stepped back as Ellen barged up to the stove and looked into the pot.

"Chicken tarragon, my favorite. Yvonne, you sweetheart. Let's get this off the stove and dig in!" She grabbed two pot holders and hefted the pot to the table, leaving Laurel to turn off the burner flame. Karl winked and motioned her to the table. She sat down as uncomfortably as if the seat were studded with nails, but the food smelled incredibly good. Ellen's lousy manners or not, she was starving.

Everything in the stew had been grown on the Haubers' farm: the tender chicken, the sweet carrots and potatoes, the herbs in creamy sauce. Yvonne's homemade baguettes were the best bread Laurel had eaten since she'd left the States. The Haubers did most of the talking. Ellen shoveled food into her mouth while nodding or grunting her responses. After they all mopped up the last drops of stew from their plates with bread, Ellen stretched back with a satisfied sigh. "God, that was good." Without looking directly at Laurel she said, "I thought Peas Corpse sent you out in pairs."

Laurel was caught off guard, just when she had started to relax a little. Peas Corpse?

Yvonne spoke first. "Laurel's roommate has in fact departed back to the States. Laurel is on her own at Butawanga now."

Ellen turned toward Laurel with her gray eyes like blank stones. "So, Laura with an -el, two years is a long time to be away from home, alone, here in darkest Africa. Think you'll stick it out?"

"I don't feel like it's a question of sticking it out. I like it at Butawanga." A simple truth, spoken for the first time.

Ellen snorted and brushed crumbs from the table in front of her. "Butawanga is plush compared to other places in Uganda, like the desert up north. Still, it's not the States. All those conveniences, family, friends. Boyfriends, dating, parties. Don't you miss all that?"

"I did get homesick, and I had a bad case of culture shock when I first got to Kampala. But everyone at Butawanga has made me feel almost at home. I came here to teach, and that's what I'm going to do."

"Ah, well said," Karl said, grinning at Yvonne.

For the first time Ellen looked straight at Laurel. "Culture shock, now that's funny. The only shock for me was realizing how much time I wasted before I came here. There I was at twenty-four, trying to survive the brutality of modern America, feeling useless, ready to marry a man who fascinated me because he was from South Africa, from an old Boer family." She sniffed. "It didn't take me long to realize I could have Africa without being saddled with the man."

"I am quite sure you were never useless, Ellen," Yvonne said.

"No, Yvonne, my life before this was just window dressing. I've been here almost nine years now. This is home, here with these amazing animals – this is where I belong." Ellen's voice cracked. Yvonne looked down. Karl reached out and patted Ellen's hand.

"Well, Karl, how about a little schnapps after that fine meal? My version of it, that is."

Karl laughed. "*Ja*, why not? We brought some good brandy, but we will save that for our holiday tomorrow."

Ellen brought a bottle of Scotch from her bedroom. She set down four glasses and poured an inch into each. Laurel picked one up and raised it to Ellen's toast *to old friends*, as if that wasn't an obvious slight. Of course Yvonne added, *and new ones*, but really it was too hasty coming up here to spend the holiday with strangers. Two aging Belgian colonials and their friend who was either magnificent or crazy, probably both. She understood now why Yvonne had hesitated when Karl invited her. Still, if she had not accepted, she would not have hiked up a volcano or seen this incredible place. And, she was here now.

"So, what has Uganda's newest petty dictator been up to these days?" Ellen asked of no one in particular. She snorted. "The bigshot President for Life General Idi Amin Dada?"

Karl retrieved his pipe from the mantel. "The world seems to regard Amin as a harmless buffoon, but I have it from good

126

sources that his first months have been bloody indeed, going far beyond the usual purges of the former president's men. He has made a Gestapo of Southern Sudanese, Kakwas, Nubians. Corpses have been washing up on the shores of Lake Victoria." He turned to Laurel. "As you may know, in July two Americans, a journalist and a lecturer at Makerere, went to the army barracks at Mbarara and have not been seen since."

Laurel was stunned; this was the first she had heard of it.

"Amin's government denies all knowledge of them, but of course they were killed by his thugs, probably for asking too many questions." Karl held a flaming match above the bowl of his pipe, sucking to produce a red glow and stirrings of smoke. "In my opinion, we all need to be aware of such goings on. One of my buyers, a chap named Mahkhani, says that the Ugandan Asians are on high alert. Amin has been blustering against them, calling them the Jews of East Africa among other things."

It took Laurel a moment before the implication of this hit her, and then she was sure she had misunderstood. "I thought most of them were Ugandan citizens."

"Some are, some are not. It may not make a difference, though in any civilized country it would." Blue smoke circled Karl's head like a halo. "There is no way to tell what this uneducated man will do with his new power. We can only wait and see, and of course hope for the best."

"The appetite grows by eating." Laurel realized she was thinking out loud. Ngira's words.

Karl brightened. "Ah, who said it? Francois Rabelais, I believe. Very good, Laurel. Amin has turned loose a hungry beast, namely his army. When simple men have guns and transport and the freedom to eliminate their enemies, whoever they may be, and help themselves to the spoils – this is to be greatly feared."

Yvonne looked at him with her blue eyes wide. "When these tribal hatreds flame up, like Hutu against Tutsi in Congo and now Rwanda – the Africans are capable of great cruelty. At such times, no one is safe."

Karl took a deep drag on his pipe and slowly exhaled the smoke. "I am sorry to upset you, Yvonne. But do not worry. As Brecht writes, it is exhausting to be evil. Soon even Amin will tire of such lawlessness, as it will not benefit the country or his own interests. And the foreign press and their governments will condemn his actions, forcing him to call back his men."

"Yes, well," Ellen said, "I wouldn't bet on it."

This new information was unsettling, but somehow unreal. The atmosphere in Kampala had been friendly and welcoming, and certainly at Butawanga there was never any feeling of danger. Gregg and Kevin had talked about something going on around Kampala, and if the report about the two deaths was true that would be cause for worry. Yet she was living far away from Kampala, and Peace Corps would not leave them in these remote schools if there was any danger. It was understandable for Karl and Yvonne to be overly concerned, given their bad experience in the Congo.

Laurel was exhausted and began to drowse as Ellen spoke of her dealings with the Rwandan government, her African employees, the foreign benefactors who were continually disappointing her.

Then Ellen sat up and rubbed out her cigarette. "I must tell you about my encounter with Bruno today." Laurel perked up. "He's the silverback leader of my most habituated group."

Yvonne stood up. "Ellen, dear, I am sure Laurel is

interested to know all about your gorillas, as we are, but may I suggest that we all might benefit from a good night's sleep first?"

Ellen stretched her arms back and yawned, as if just remembering how tired she was. "You're right, Yvonne, it's very late. I'll ask Ben to move a cot to the living room of the guest cabin for Laurel."

Yvonne and Karl exchanged a glance. Great, Laurel thought, now they're all wishing I hadn't come.

Ellen huffed. "Or, if you think you can stand being here with me, you can take my spare bedroom."

Laurel did not have to think about the choice. She liked the Haubers, but was glad not to have to invade their privacy at the guest house. "I'll stay here, thanks. And if you're not too tired, I'd like to hear more about the gorillas."

"Maybe."

Laurel thought there was a shaft of light through a chink in the armor.

* * *

They talked for almost an hour after the Haubers had retired to the guest cabin. Mostly, Laurel listened while Ellen talked about her work among the mountain gorillas, about how they are not a predatory species like humans, that they have a social structure based on the family group and are capable of emotion in the same sense that we use the word. Laurel wasn't sure how much of it she believed, but as Ellen spoke, her face and eyes animated, she began to revise her earlier negative impression. This was a woman living her passion with incredible strength and fortitude – so what if she lacked some of the social graces? The work she was doing was scientific, important, very demanding and incredibly brave. These animals were at risk of being hunted to extinction. Whatever Yvonne thought, it was wrong for people to take everything, kill everything. And here was Ellen, on her own, fighting against overwhelming odds. No wonder Karl admired her.

Before going to bed they visited the pit latrine, about a hundred yards behind the house. Ellen carried a flashlight but did not switch it on, since the rain clouds were gone and the clearing was bathed in moonlight. At the small wooden enclosure Ellen went first, saying she would get rid of any "nasties." Laurel wasn't sure whether this made her feel better, or worse. When Ellen emerged she handed over the flashlight, and by its light Laurel saw a narrow wooden seat straddling a dark hole, but nothing more sinister, nothing on the wall but a roll of toilet paper suspended on a hook. There was the characteristic sour outhouse smell, but she had known worse in parks and fairgrounds at home. She got done quickly and joined Ellen for the walk back to the cabin.

In the tranquil cold of this clear night, the mountain's cone was illuminated against the blue-black sky. Laurel now felt glad to be there, and something else, a sudden expansion of her whole state of being, the knowledge of being connected to something infinitely large. It was like being in music, playing, listening, surrounded by sound, being filled by it. She raised her arm and sighted along her pale fingers, finding three stars spaced like piano keys for a minor Triad, pushing each point of light to produce a note, and she could hear it, the minor third resolving to a perfect fifth. Then, there were arpeggios swirling into chords around her, faint, distant – where was it coming from? The air, the forest? "There's music here," she said.

If Ellen heard, she made no sign. "The sky up here at night

is like a tonic. Good for what ails you." Ellen's face now was pale and deeply lined. "Sometimes when I'm feeling low, I come out into the meadow and drink it in."

"It's beautiful here, Ellen, so beautiful it's surreal. I've never been any place like this before." She looked at the gangly figure of Ellen loping along next to her, smoking, outlined against the black wall of tropical forest. "But you must get lonely sometimes."

"I have, at times, but not so much anymore. No time to get lonely. Plus, you'd be surprised at the number of people who come traipsing up here, uninvited."

"Oh."

Ellen snorted. "Sorry if I gave you a hard time before. I'm like a gorilla, suspicious of strangers. It takes me a while to adjust to new faces. Especially white ones."

As they came around to the front porch there were the huge dark shapes of elephants walking almost noiselessly through the grass. She stopped, holding her breath, and Ellen stood silently beside her. Laurel was not afraid as the massive forms floated quietly past her, trunk to tail. "My God," she whispered after they had passed, leaving only a lingering odor like freshly cut green grass.

"They come through here almost every night. Sometimes they hang around to graze with those little antelope we call duiker," Ellen whispered. "Elephants are extremely intelligent animals. They know poachers don't usually come this close to camp."

"How do they ever make it up the mountain?"

Ellen snorted. "They were coming up here long before people ever did. You were following their trails when you came up today. There used to be large herds of them. Now, just a few scattered groups are left."

Laurel remembered the lava cave, the steep trail, the parking lot.

The cabin was like entering a different universe, with the sounds of the mountain's moonlit world shut outside. Inside in the soft light of fire and lamp, the world of people and things felt undeniably good. Ellen lit a lantern in the small second bedroom, and Laurel unrolled her sleeping bag on the cot. She was suddenly, totally exhausted. Her legs ached, and the blisters on her heels throbbed painfully.

"So," Ellen said as she adjusted the wick flame, "what do you think you'll do after you finish your little stint in the Peace Corps?"

Little stint? Laurel was determined not to be offended by things Ellen said. She sat down on the cot, hoping Ellen did not want a long conversation. She was too tired. "I'm planning on graduate school, a Master's in Music Education, so I can teach music in a school back home."

"Ugh," Ellen grunted. "The idea of babysitting other people's brats never appealed to me."

Laurel sighed. "I actually like children, at least I think I do, although as an only child I never had any around except at school. But I know I like the idea of turning people on to music. Children seem like the logical place to start."

Ellen turned away, clearly finished with the topic. "I've got a little typing to do in the other room. Field notes from today. Will that disturb you?"

"No, not at all. I'm tired enough to sleep through Armageddon." It was a favorite expression of her father's, from the war.

Ellen grimaced. "You may have to, with Amin on the

warpath."

"I don't see why Amin would bother with Butawanga. There's nothing there except the school and the mission."

"Well, probably not. It is pretty isolated, and former president Obote was Langi, so the tribal purging should stay up north. Like Karl said, things will calm down once Amin's eliminated the competition." Ellen coughed and pushed stray hair away from her face with a limp hand. "But did you see poor Yvonne's face while he was talking? She's tough as nails, but after what they went through in the Congo, she must be wondering if it's all going to happen again." Ellen stopped in the doorway. "It never fails. Just when one of these countries looks like it's making some progress, some maniac comes along and sets them back a hundred years."

After Laurel got into bed she tried to analyze the possible dangers. Right now she felt comfortable and secure and finally almost welcome, in any case too tired to worry, falling quickly and deeply asleep to the rhythmic pick-pock of Ellen's typewriter keys.

<u>20</u>

DON'T RUN

Laurel woke to cold sun boring through the small grimy window, smells of frying food and sounds of activity. She pulled on her clothes and smoothed down her hair. Everyone was already in the kitchen, with breakfast being prepared by Yvonne and Ben. There were avocados, Yvonne's homemade sausages, biscuits with marmalade, and fried bread that Ben had made, and most tantalizing of all, the prospect of a whole day at Ellen's camp.

"What a feast," Ellen declared. "This is more food than I've seen in a week. A month, maybe."

Yvonne smiled thinly. "Well, the first time we came up here, if you will remember, Ellen, the cupboard was very bare indeed, and Karl had to go all the way back to Ruhengeri to get supplies. So now we have learned our lesson. If we expect to eat when we are here, we bring plenty of food."

"I'm terrible, I know. I put off shopping until the last possible moment, usually when I run out of cigarettes. But listen, you two, little Ellen has a few tricks up her sleeve." She walked over to a cupboard and opened it to reveal a large box. "See this? This is Christmas dinner with all the trimmings, compliments of me. Lots of canned goodies: a ham, mushrooms, baby onions, applesauce, green beans and squash for a pie. Cornmeal, flour, Crisco. I've been stockpiling it for months, and tomorrow, after my little party for the men and their families, I'm going to treat you all to a real American Christmas." She looked smugly self-satisfied, even more when Karl erupted into a cheer.

"Ellen," Yvonne said, "do you mean to say that you have had all that food in your cupboard while you have been living on porridge?"

"That's right. The box was strictly off-limits."

Yvonne sat back from her plate, her small white hands resting in her lap. "Really, Ellen, what are we to do with you?"

Ellen shuffled her feet and smirked. "Take me out and shoot me, I expect. But not today, please, because it's going to be a beautiful day, and I think we can all take a short stroll to meet some gorillas."

Karl agreed enthusiastically, and even Yvonne said what a fine idea. Laurel had blisters from yesterday's climb and her thigh muscles were incredibly sore, but she was not about to pass up the opportunity to actually see gorillas close up in the wild, instead of caged up in some sad, smelly zoo.

They all stood outside the cabin, dressed and ready, while Ellen gave them their marching orders.

"This isn't at all likely, but if for some reason we're charged, the main thing to remember is – DON'T RUN." Ellen took a long drag on her morning cigarette. She rationed them, she said, four a day, so as not to run out in between shopping trips. No bumming smokes from her, Laurel thought, even if I wanted to, which I don't, except like right now –

"The gorilla's charge sounds like a freight train bearing down on you, but it's usually just a scare tactic, nothing more than a big bluff. If it happens, though, all your instincts will make you want to get the hell out of there. But if you run they will probably chase you, and they can do some damage."

135

Karl, Yvonne, Laurel, each glanced at each other, registering what Laurel thought might be simultaneous second thoughts. Damage? But surely Karl and Yvonne had done this before, hadn't they?

Close to camp the trail was wide and clear. They walked in silence yet disturbed a group of small duiker antelope that sprinted into the trees, white tails flagging their retreat. Then Ellen and the guide Kitumba led the way onto a narrower trail that got steeper by the minute. The air smelled cold and clean as snow. Laurel walked in a kind of breathless euphoria, the ache of blisters and legs reduced to background noise. Then Ellen began to wheeze and slow her pace. She whispered to Kitumba at intervals, examining things on the trail, and showed the others the dung deposits they had been following. They were from yesterday, dried out and hard to see. It was important, Ellen said, to keep following gorilla sign so as not to stray onto a buffalo path and surprise one of those dangerous animals.

The vegetation was changing. There were fewer majestic Hagenia trees, and more shrubbery; low-growing trees and bushes embroidered with vines. "See that plant?" A red-flowering vine clambering up one of the trunks. "That's Loranthus. Gorillas love it." Ellen winked at Laurel. "Belongs to the mistletoe family." After about an hour, Ellen explained they were climbing up a ridge that would lead them to a place just above the hollow where she had seen the gorilla group yesterday. "In about another hour or so" – Ellen stumbled in mid-sentence, went down on her hands and knees, face contorted with pain. She stood up, winced, insisted she was all right. "As I was saying before I tangled with that damn vine, as we get to the top of the ridge, we'll need to be very quiet. The hollow is about 500 yards down the other side. They won't catch our scent from that distance, and we should be able to get a good view while staying hidden. They're habituated to me, but they'll be frightened by strangers, especially since the group has a new infant. Better if they don't know we're in the neighborhood."

They walked on, Ellen limping slightly. The trail was almost not a trail, more a narrow passage through a dense dark green lattice of bushes, trees, and vines. It was strictly single file, with Kitumba in the lead, followed by Ellen, then Laurel, Yvonne, and Karl. There was a rich, earthy smell, like from one of the huge piles of oak and maple leaves she would play in as a child back home. The air dripped with moisture like soft rain, yet the sky above the forest canopy was blue and cloudless. Their pace now was slow enough that Laurel did not feel tired as much as a strange contradictory mixture of being giddy with anticipation and worried by Ellen's warnings. She tried to step as silently as she could with the squelching of her sneakers, soaked again.

"Okay," Ellen said, "We're about 15 minutes from the crest of the ridge. Let's take a break before the final push. I have to go answer the call. All this good food is playing havoc with my bowels." She rummaged in her knapsack and pulled out a small shovel. "It's important to bury your waste. Gorillas love to investigate feces, and they are susceptible to human diseases."

Yvonne frowned. "Really, Ellen."

Ellen took Kitumba's panga, a straight-bladed machete with a wooden handle. In case of snakes, she drawled, and waded into the forest to one side of the trail. They all turned their backs, although Ellen was invisible in the dense brush.

"She's favoring that ankle," Yvonne said quietly.

"Yes, I noticed," Karl replied.

Snakes, Laurel thought, turning the word over in her mind while glancing around at the surrounding vegetation, the hanging vines, the myriad wet nooks and crannies where reptiles might hide, but then an overpowering odor and ear-splitting screams broke in a crashing wave. Her heart stopped then started, beating too hard and fast, the unbearable noise splitting her head. Something was coming at her, something big mowing down branches and leaves, *oh, God,* she turned to run but Karl grabbed her shoulders and with Yvonne and Kitumba, arms tight around her and each other, pulled her to the ground. Those deafening screams, crashing noise, the horrible odor – shaking, breathing in gulps, she buried her face in someone's shoulder as they huddled on the ground, the world ending, sure they would be torn to pieces.

Suddenly, the roaring stopped.

In the uneasy quiet, no one spoke. Laurel was beyond speaking. Her heart felt ready to break out of her chest. Thoughts started to form again, racing, disconnected words, Ellen's words: gorillas, freight train, don't run, damage. The noise started again for a moment, then stopped, followed by a hollow thumping. Something like hooting or barking, but not the explosive screams.

She began to breathe again and cautiously raised her head to see Ellen crouched on the ground, casually reaching for vegetation and putting it near her mouth, pretending to chew. As she did this, she made soft grunting noises. And there, about 20 yards away from Ellen, a glimpse of a dark shadow in the thick foliage, a huge dark hand parting the mesh of vines, a face of black leather! Laurel could make out the eyes, wide and fiery red, a snarling mouth with long canines exposed exploding in a loud bark, a violent shaking of trees and brush. Terrified again, she curled back into a tight ball, shut her eyes and thought *please God, please God –*

It felt like an eternity of waiting, with arms and legs numb. Then, the sounds of movement in the vegetation, the occasional hoot, a gathering silence.

Finally Ellen's voice said, "Okay, he's probably just watching us now. Let Kitumba get up first, the rest of you follow him. Kitumba, *tutakwenda Wazungu.*"

Kitumba stood up in slow motion, then Karl. All was quiet. Laurel unrolled from her crouch and moved lead-footed down the path, followed closely by Yvonne, her face pale, Karl with his arm around her waist.

A short way down the trail Karl said, "is everyone all right?" He looked tenderly at Yvonne. She nodded, then rested her head in the hollow of her husband's shoulder as they walked.

Laurel was still trembling, fighting back tears. "What happened?"

"We came too close."

"What about Ellen?"

Kitumba turned and said, "We go. Madama come soon."

"She is keeping their attention on her. They know her, you see. That is why they broke off. I was charged like that once before, and I was not any less terrified this time," Karl said. "Except that other time, I shot the brute. Lucky I did not have my gun today."

"Yes, lucky," Yvonne said. She sighed. "Ellen would not forgive you. She would rather sacrifice us than one of her animals."

"Now, Yvonne," Karl said, "you know that is not true. You are just upset."

As they walked down the trail with Kitumba in the lead, no one spoke. After about ten minutes, Karl told Kitumba they should wait for Ellen, that he was concerned about her ankle. Kitumba agreed.

Yvonne offered food, but no one was hungry. Laurel still felt shaky, but she was strangely exhilarated. That was the most frightened she had ever been in her life, but when she thought about it, she almost wanted to laugh. What noise, what terror! And that god-awful smell! But she had seen only a glimpse of the animals causing it. Of course, that was enough. Bluff, Ellen had said, but it sure as hell was convincing. It had felt dangerous, and very real. Don't run – she was mortified that she had not had the presence of mind to follow that simple rule. "I feel so stupid that I tried to run. Thank you for holding on to me."

"Never mind, Laurel," Yvonne said. "It is a natural instinct. We are all very lucky. Ellen should not have put us in such danger."

After about 20 minutes, Ellen came limping along the trail. Karl and Kitumba helped ease her down to sit on her knapsack. "Damn trick ankle," she said, grinning at them sheepishly. "Well, boys and girls, what did you think of that little show?"

Karl said, "I hope there will not be an encore."

"Really, I do apologize." Ellen looked at Yvonne. "I never dreamed they were so close. We startled them, that was all. But what timing! There I am in a tangle of brush with my pants around my ankles and all hell breaks loose."

"It is not a joke, Ellen." Yvonne's voice was level and tight. "You put us all in danger."

140

"I know it was terrifying for you, but you remembered not to run. There wasn't any real danger." Ellen fiddled absently with her boot laces, avoiding eye contact with anyone. "I'm pretty sure it was Bruno. The old fraud puts up quite a display."

Yvonne let out a deep sigh. "The important thing is, we are all of us all right. But I am not so sure about that ankle of yours."

Ellen looked up at Yvonne with a pained smile.

"You must keep your weight off it. Lean on Karl and Kitumba while we walk."

Back at the cabin, Karl and Yvonne hovered over Ellen, helping her remove her boots, remonstrating over the swollen ankle. Ellen kept saying that it was nothing, but they wrapped it in wet towels and insisted that she remain immobile with the ankle elevated, to which she agreed only if she could sit and type up her notes.

Laurel and Yvonne began putting out things for dinner. Laurel went over the afternoon's excitement in her head, the awful charge, Ellen's presence of mind saving the day – really, she had been magnificent. Yvonne's reproach, Ellen's explanation. The affection between the two women had won out, and everything was all right now. Laurel started to sing, softly, in her fuzzy mezzo-soprano that was fine for a chorus but not for solos – *Amazing Grace, how sweet the sound, that saved a wretch like me –*

Ellen stopped typing. Laurel stopped singing.

"Don't stop," Ellen said.

Laurel resumed and Ellen joined in, her contralto reedy and off key. Next, Karl's nasal tenor, then Yvonne in a rich soprano.

I once was lost, but now am found, was blind, but now, I see.

141

They kept on singing the same verses in their found harmony, and for the first time that day, Laurel remembered it was Christmas Eve.

21

Ngira

Why haven't I told Laurel about Theresa? I know that Gordon has already gossiped to her, but to say it myself would have been the proper thing. Just to say, when I see my fiancée Theresa this holiday – that would not have been so difficult.

There is a terrible conflict within me, a confusion of feeling for Laurel. When I saw her that first day at Senwangama's, I was not impressed. Untidy hair, skin that looked like it was rubbed with sand, and sometimes an expression of tasting something bitter. I judged her dry as a bleached out bone, but in this I was mistaken.

Laurel is doing very well here. She always goes on time for her classes, marks her lesson books, talks with the students, and this has put more than a few of the other teachers to shame. She has a smile for everyone. She has charmed us.

I understand her face now and the beauty which is there. Her hair floats in the air like the puff from a seed pod – when she walks it moves like the wings of an angel. She pushes it behind her ears, but it will not be tamed. And her eyes – they are lakes of blue and green, both hot and cool, a fire of spirit with a goodness of mind. Yes, now I see her properly. She compresses her mouth when she is deeply thoughtful, or disturbed, not from peevishness as I first thought.

Between man and woman there is always an attraction, and I can only infrequently relieve myself with Theresa. But for

Laurel I feel something beyond simple desire. She is like an emptiness in the stomach. There is a need to see her, to hear her speak, to look into those eyes. When I am near her, I want to hold her. Just that, to hold her; to breathe her in, to meet her thoughts, to keep her safe. But alone, in my undisciplined moments, my thoughts wander into more intimate scenes.

What can I be thinking, to imagine such a communion? We can have no future together. To her I am just an amusing African who is educated enough to converse in English. Carolyn told Gordon that Laurel is engaged to someone at home in the United States. She is not free, and neither am I. She is trusting me not to push our friendship beyond the bounds that keep it intact, and I must never betray that trust.

I am grateful that she was posted to Kisoro. Here at least we have enough to eat, the climate is mild, the water excellent thanks to British-dug wells, as Gordon never tires of reminding me – and please God we are isolated enough to escape the dangerous whims of new governments. At Christmas, Theresa spoke of fear in Kampala, as if a sharp knife hung over the city.

Laurel is young and trusting, her head filled with music. The thought of her blundering into danger in Kampala, or anywhere, fills me with fear. Like all Bazungu from powerful countries, she carries with her an assumption of safety. She cannot see that, here, such assumptions are only illusions.

I want to care for her, protect her, help her, while staying within moral and ethical bounds. But such constraints can fall away when the heart runs wild. Now that Carolyn is gone, I must be careful not to be alone with her. It is a problem, being friends with a woman. There must be boundaries.

Perhaps I will ask Gordon for advice, but his understanding of such things is clearly limited. He called

Carolyn a cocktease, but then when I said he was well rid of her, there came such a look on his face, rolling his eyes wide as a cow that has received the first blow of slaughter. He was dejected after she left. How could he have cared for her, knowing she only used him for her convenience?

Certainly, that young woman in my village would do anything for Gordon. She would marry him, live with him, be his servant if he asked it of her. He has been with her on three occasions that I know of, evenings when I was occupied with Theresa, but he is unable to appreciate the girl's simplicity. Well, and am I any different? Theresa was never a village girl at heart.

Gordon would have Theresa in a moment if he could. I have seen the way he looks at her. He must know she could never be for him, that he would be consumed like dead acacia in a grass fire. Gordon must like to be abused by women. This would explain the degrading behavior with Carolyn.

This also explains why he takes only a paternal interest in Laurel. She is serious, and disapproves of Gordon when drink makes him act the pig. I can see it in her face. But she remains polite. It is not in her nature to abuse. With me she is always ready to listen, to discuss, unlike Theresa, who has little patience for what she calls my philosophies.

Little Theresa, you were always so much stronger than I. When we were children, you wanted to join the boys in our war and hunting games. Refused, you became a tiny demon, shaking your fists at us. On Sundays when my family went to the mission for Mass, there you would be, scrubbed and in your best dress, and when I tried to speak, you cast me away with all the pride of an angry goddess.

Then, there was the time at school you took my hand at

recess and pulled me through the courtyard to the teacher's room, where we were not permitted to enter. You took one bold look around before you opened the door, and I, spellbound, followed.

The room was empty. On the wall was a full-length mirror, the first I had ever seen. We stood in front of it, side by side; there I was, all of a piece. I was two years bigger than you, but my eyes were fixed on that small girl, turning round in slow circles, smiling.

I knew then that we would share our lives, and this has been borne out by time. We have had our secrets, our adventures, our quarrels. Our ambition to be modern, to live where we do not have to see cattle, thatched roofs, open cookfires, to get the best education and good cash-paying jobs. To leave the village behind and never return. What I saw in that mirror was your determination to rise up, like the cream from the milk, and be someone special.

We both wanted to be teachers, but now all you talk about is Business Law. It will mean more schooling, this Business Law, but you say it will make you more in demand for jobs when we go to America. It is a "hot career," you say, lying naked in our night place among the sorghum rows, your eyes awakening points of flame in my flesh.

When I said we would be together always, I knew it was a lie. I now want to stay in Uganda as a teacher among our own people. You will always be a part of me, like the blood flowing in my veins, but my heart is no longer with you.

Education is the key to Uganda's future. We need more good teachers for schools like Butawanga. The former government supported the schools at least, but God knows what will happen under this new one. Surely, African teachers will be the ones to ride out the storms, whatever they may be.

These white teachers are like ghosts that come and go as quickly as the souls of stillborn infants. It is hard to tell about whites, and perhaps better not to depend on any of them. Why should we be obliged to import teachers like televisions or automobiles? Who better to teach in his own country than someone who loves it?

In this country if you want success, you must go to school and study hard. My own brother refused to go to secondary school and ran off to Kampala, full of schemes to get rich quick. All he cared about was acquiring new things: shoes, a western style suit, an expensive watch, to be "Wabenzi" by owning a Mercedes car. Did he imagine that such things just fall from the sky? Now, he is living on the streets, poor except for the money I give him, too ashamed or too proud to come home. God knows how he lives. He is a disgrace to our father, who is an important man in our village; a healthy tree does not bear rotten fruit, he says, shaking his head.

I tell my brother he should enroll in one of the new technical training schools. I will gladly help him to pay his fees, if only he can be persuaded.

If only Theresa can be persuaded. But she is just as dazzled by the western Tower of Babel. Perhaps she will yet change her mind. Still, it is a deception to let her go on thinking that I am just as determined to go to the U.S. I must find the courage to tell her to follow her dream without me. And I must also find the courage to keep my feelings for Laurel well hidden.

What a muddle. No, I will not confide in Gordon, sober or drunk, since he will surely let something slip to Laurel. Gordon might have his suspicions, but I must do nothing to confirm them.

Perhaps I will ask Father Matthew. I have heard that he visits some of the village women, and this is not a good thing for a priest. But he studies philosophy, and may have some knowledge of the heart.

For now, at least, I will try to put Laurel out of my mind. Three days with Gordon climbing in the Mountains of the Moon will make all earthly concerns seem diminished. We may even reach Elena glacier, high on Mt. Stanley. How Theresa and I marveled over pictures of this white miracle when we were children. Ice and hail I have seen, but to feel my feet sink into a field of snow stretching ahead like the desert plains of Karamoja – surely, this will be worth the climb.

22

Surrealistic Pillow

Laurel's first Christmas morning away from home dawned thick with a mist that soon burned off in the clear high altitude air moving its hand over the camp like a blessing. After a light breakfast of toast and tea prepared by Ben, Ellen shooed everyone outside, to clear the decks while she baked and prepared for the Christmas party. Laurel strolled around the clearing with the Haubers, then sat on the front porch enjoying the sun, with nothing more strenuous to do than to wait for the invited guests. Karl explained that Rwanda, like Uganda, was a largely Christian country, and even if some of the guests might hold more traditional African beliefs, everyone loved a party. A party, on top of a mountain in Africa! Ellen had accepted her, so she now felt it was a real stroke of luck to have run into the Haubers in Kisoro, how grim the alternative of Christmas alone in her concrete house. Right now, she had to admit with a twinge of guilt, she did not even miss her family.

"Madama mtumzuri, mzuri sana sana." Chanting praises as they walked, hips and shoulders swaying in time, Ellen's guides and trackers and their families arrived at camp. There were eighteen men, women, and children, some carrying cloth-wrapped bundles on their heads. The wives and grandmothers were all in traditional *basuti* style plain cotton dresses, with long shawls for warmth. The men and older boys wore sweaters or jackets with their trousers, while the young boys shivered in

149

shorts and shirts. The little girls had shawls over their school dresses. Each man, woman, or child had hair trimmed close to the head in a neatly rounded cap, same as most people in Uganda; clearly the bushy, free flowing "Afro" of young American blacks did not reflect hairstyles from this part of the continent.

Laurel followed Ben into the cabin and there was Ellen in a pall of flour, hastily wiping her face and smoothing her hair. "I hear them, Ben. I need to fix myself up a bit or I'll scare them all back down the mountain."

He stared into the kitchen.

"I know, I've made a big mess, but I'll clean it all up later."

Ben still looked stricken, but he managed to croak out, "No matter, Madama."

She grinned. "Come on, Ben, cleaning up can wait. Let's break out that good beer for our guests, and I've got Coke for the kids."

When Ellen came out, people smiled and greeted her: Nyirangagi. She beamed as each family presented a gift: a plucked chicken, a basket of potatoes, a hollow gourd, a straw mat.

Everyone was invited inside, and they moved the furniture and lifted the straw rug to make space for dancing. Ben shouted for the men to help themselves to the beer, and Laurel brought out the bottles of Coca-Cola that Ellen had stockpiled for the occasion. The children were excited when they saw the beverages, but each waited politely until Laurel or Yvonne handed over an uncapped bottle.

Ellen distributed gifts for the adults and their families: toiletries, lengths of cloth, small toys, boots, shirts. More beverages were passed out, along with three large pans of cornbread Ellen had made, and the food that the guests themselves had brought: cold roasted sweet potatoes and dried meat jerky. Then the music started.

First it was rounds of Christmas carols, in English, French, or Kinyarwanda. A white-haired man came front and center, dressed in a tweed jacket with suede elbow patches over a faded black turtleneck, carrying a long scoop of wood fitted with strings. Everyone moved back and quieted down. The old man bowed to Ellen, fixed his cloudy eyes on some point in space, and began to chant and pluck the strings of his instrument. His thin, high voice was in constant modulation, leaping and leveling against the regular, repetitive line of notes as bright and shiny as those from a harpsichord – the combination was mesmerizing. In fact, in its monody, it was almost Baroque, Laurel thought. This was it, the connectedness, the humanity of music and its power to bring people together and plug them in to the greater universe, whether Beethoven, Bach, or this old man with a zither, the basic human need to communicate and express, and here it was now in this room, in music so simple, so beautifully simple – she should be recording it, writing it down, or something, and there was probably a story in the song that she couldn't understand, but it didn't matter – she let it flow over her, the hypnotic sounds, the voice carried along by the zither like a leaf on a bubbling stream.

When the old man finished, the head guide Kitumba beat out a rhythm on a pair of small cylindrical drums. One of the men joined in on a bamboo flute, others clapped and hummed, and everyone danced, including Ellen and the Haubers. Laurel danced, with or without partner, enjoying herself among the friendly, festive crowd, as she had at the clubs in Kampala, transported by the repetitive rhythm. Even at home, dancing to the Stones or Jefferson Airplane, it had been different, more self-conscious, with some snobbish internal classical music major voice telling her she should not be enjoying the popular stuff quite so much. But here, no brain games, just the pure, elemental joy of music and movement.

After several hours when people finally began to tire and all the food and drink was gone, they took their leave and started back down the mountain, chanting as they had on the way up.

Ellen slumped on the sofa, perspired and grinning. "I think everyone had a good time."

"It was a very nice party," Yvonne said. "You outdid yourself this year, dear."

"It was wonderful," Laurel said, still on some kind of high. "I loved the instruments, especially that zither the grandfather played."

"That's called *inanga*," Ellen rasped.

"The sound is enchanting. I wish I had brought my tape recorder."

"Why didn't you say something? You could have used mine."

Laurel had thought of this, but had not wanted to take one of Ellen's blank cassettes, which she used to record gorilla vocalizations. "That's okay, maybe next time." Realizing how presumptuous that sounded, she quickly asked, "What was it they were calling you, sounded like Nee-ran-goggy?"

"Nyirangagi, 'woman who lives with the gorillas'." Ellen snuffed. "I'm not sure it's a compliment. Well, dears, let's not stand around jawboning. It's already six o'clock and there's still Christmas dinner to see about."

They all helped in the final preparations for their holiday meal. Ellen had hung a sprig of African mistletoe in the doorway to the kitchen and demanded that Karl do the honors. When Karl quickly touched his lips to Laurel's, they were warm and moist, a pleasant sensation. They all shared yet another bottle of wine brought by Karl and Yvonne, and more brandy after the meal. It was 9 p.m. and fully dark outside the cabin when they finally left the table.

Laurel sat on the straw mat before the fireplace. Karl took the easy chair and lit his pipe. On the sofa, Yvonne was stroking Ellen's hair with a pearl-handled brush, their gift to her. The hissing of the fire, Karl's rhythmic sucking on his pipestem, the sound of bristles raking through Ellen's hair, the tonic of drink and good food, the warmth of the fire: it all felt so comfortable, so familiar, as if she had been coming here with the Haubers every Christmas for years. Or, it was almost as if she lived here and tomorrow would say goodbye to the Haubers and stay on to help Ellen with her incredible work in this timeless place. But no, it would be the long trek down the mountain back to Butawanga, life there calling her like some inscrutable, unfinished symphony looking for an ending.

Tomorrow, she would be back, and what a story she would have to tell Ngira.

<u>23</u>

The Sun and I

On this sunny, quiet afternoon at Butawanga, four days after her return from Rwanda, Laurel thought she would die of boredom, sitting on her back step overlooking the vegetable garden where radishes, cabbages, peppers, Brussels sprouts had taken off from seed like rockets exploding toward the sun. The soil here was not just fertile, it was Jack in the Beanstalk magical, she thought, watching Sabinyo's new hat dip and rise as he gathered today's glut of ripe tomatoes.

The green globes had been only touched with orange when Carolyn left; now, as if at some secret signal, they were all turning red at the same time. While Sabinyo and Caspar, Ngira and the other teachers gladly shared her bounty of other vegetables, no one besides Gordon cared for the tomatoes. They were not commonly grown here, so people were not used to eating them. At Laurel's urging Caspar had taken a few home to his family, to add to the groundnut sauce, but he had politely declined to take any more. Maybe there was some kind of food taboo against tomatoes, like the local one about eating eggs. She had tried her hand at tomato salad, sauce, soup, but still could not use them all.

Sabinyo laid the basket of tomatoes on the step next to Laurel. They were so beautiful, so firm and glossy, she picked one up and bit into it. Juice and seeds splurged down her chin. Sabinyo looked away. It would not be proper to laugh at his employer, at least not to her face. Laurel had little doubt that he and Caspar laughed at her freely between themselves. She wiped her chin with the back of her hand, took another bite, then held one of the perfect fruits out to Sabinyo.

Sabinyo shook his head decisively. "No, thank you, Madam." Under Caspar's coaching, he was learning to be more conversant in English. The first complete sentence he had spoken to her in his impatient monotone was "Thank you for hat Ma-dam," for the Christmas gift she had given him. "You are welcome, Sabinyo." She had pronounced it carefully, to model the correct English response, not the American *yur welcum*.

She had managed to learn so little Kinyarwanda. Sabinyo and Caspar would give her basic vocabulary if she asked, but only if she asked. Possibly they thought it was strange for a white woman to try to speak it, or maybe she just mangled the pronunciation so badly that they wanted to spare her the embarrassment. Most likely they regarded it as proper to the social hierarchy that they learn to speak her language, not the other way around. And English was officially the national language of Uganda. Gordon spoke Kinyarwanda fairly fluently, but then he frequented the local bars, and as she had heard, he often kept company with African women, though he did not seem to bring them around the school.

Ngira's native language was not Kinyarwanda, it was Runyankole, but she had never heard him speak it. As a teacher he was mandated to speak English in class, as were the students. That policy was meant to discourage tribal prejudices. We don't say 'tribal,' he had once corrected her, because it was a term imposed on them by the colonial government and tended to reinforce divisions among the Ugandan people that were no longer really relevant. She could only imagine how many mistakes she was making every day in her interactions and was glad that Ngira cared enough to explain things to her.

She watched Sabinyo fill a steel basin and carry it from plant to plant, scooping draughts of water to each. Caspar was inside mopping the kitchen floor with liberal amounts of water, like a sailor swabbing the deck of a ship. In most tasks, he seemed to think more was better, that the more water and soap he used, the cleaner things would be.

You should teach him how to do it properly, to prepare him for his next job. You won't be here forever. Gordon, too, was proving to be an invaluable source of insights into things white people needed to understand about Africa. But she was still uncomfortable with her role as employer. She was only a visitor in this timeless place. She and Caspar and Sabinyo were like a family in their daily routines, maintaining this simple household together, yet it seemed there were boundaries that were better if not crossed. If she asked to visit their homes and meet their families, they would be embarrassed and bewildered at the request. And would she be any less embarrassed, the white Madam descending on the hired help?

Gordon and Ngira were committed to this place, in their own ways, and what did they really think of her, anyway? Ngira probably thought her spoiled and useless compared to African women. Like Theresa. 'The firebrand' Gordon called her, though he didn't exactly say why. Next to someone like that, Laurel thought, she must seem all the more bland and inconsequential.

After completing her two years she would leave, and the school would drone along just fine. *These people are lucky to have us,* Carolyn had said, but to Laurel, by the time she learned to do the job well, she would be leaving.

The miracle was that no one here seemed to expect her to be more than what she was. No one seemed to care if she was bland and inconsequential. The headmaster, the other teachers, the students, had all given her the gift of acceptance, and because of that her self-doubts had emptied a handful at a time, like the water in Sabinyo's basin. I'm the lucky one, she thought.

The sun at one o'clock sliced the mountain giant Muhabura's bulk into sharp pyramids of light and shadow. Sabinyo's dark skin glistened with sweat. He was thin and lanky with oversized hands and feet. Laurel watched from the shade, envying him his tasks. But he didn't like anyone to meddle in his work. And where were Ngira and Gordon? When she had got back from Rwanda brimming with news about her trip, they were gone. It was too golden an afternoon to spend inside reading her texts, and anyway there was still plenty of time before the holiday was over. A walk into Kisoro, then, and the off-chance of lucking out again and meeting someone exciting, as she had with the Haubers.

* * *

Her eyes were still adjusting to the dim light of the duka when Mr. Gupta sang out, "Hello, Miss. I am sure you know Father Matthew, from the mission?"

"Yes, of course." He looked very different in a short-sleeved shirt and khaki trousers, hair tousled, dark circles of sweat under his arms. "How are you, Father Matthew?"

"I'm fine, thanks. Yourself?"

"Just fine. Did you have a nice Christmas?"

"It was quiet, but very nice, Miss –"

So, he had forgotten her name. "Bittelson. But it's Laurel, please. Father Matthew, I wanted to thank you all for the invitation to Christmas tea at the mission. Mr. Senwangama told me about it. I was away in Rwanda, but if I had been at Butawanga I would have been very glad to come." She hoped he would renew the invitation, but instead he just nodded in reply and reached out for the small package Mr. Gupta handed him. "And of course I would have come up for services on Christmas."

"The chapel doors are always open." He smiled and headed for the door.

He didn't look gay, but could you tell just by looking?

"And how are Father Phillip and Father Lawrence?"

He turned to stare at her with his brilliant blue eyes. "They're fine. In fact I came here to find this gift for Lawrence's birthday tomorrow. He hates a fuss, but I think he enjoys our little gesture." He addressed this to Mr. Gupta, who looked confused.

"That's nice. And when is your birthday?" How dumb, but she wanted to keep him talking, to reveal something about himself. Instead he just looked trapped, like a mouse being toyed with by a cat.

"My birthday? September. I'll leave you to your shopping now, Miss Bittelson."

He fled out the door with the small brown parcel under his arm.

"Wish Father Lawrence a happy birthday from me, and please, call me Laurel," she sang out after him, but he did not stop or turn.

She smiled at Mr. Gupta and handed him her grocery list. "I'm sure he found a nice gift for Father Lawrence?"

She hoped Mr. Gupta would divulge something, but no, he just smiled oddly and started to fill her small order.

Laurel selected the few personal things she needed, taking her time browsing. Mrs. Gupta came out quietly from the back; Laurel said hello, and the woman nodded. She had luminous light brown skin and looked younger than her husband, maybe in her early thirties, to Mr. Gupta's mid-forties.

Laurel found a box of floral note paper from England on which to write her "bread and butter" notes, as her mother called them, thanking the Haubers and Ellen for their hospitality. She loved finding these luxury items from rarefied other worlds: the stationery, a box of French-milled soaps, a quilted tea cozy. It was a kind of guilty indulgence, not exactly in line with the Peace Corps ethic of living like the local people, but on the other hand purchases would support the small business economy in this out-of-the-way place. She wondered if these were things that Mrs. Gupta had selected for the sheer pleasure of having them in the store. She wasn't exactly clear about how to mail anything to Ellen or the Haubers, but bought the paper anyway.

As usual, her food purchases were packed into a box to be delivered. She put her few toilet articles: toothpaste, soap, and sanitary napkins, which Mrs. Gupta had wrapped discreetly in brown paper, into her straw bag. The shopping had not taken long, and she would be back at Butawanga in half an hour. Without Gordon and Ngira around, what to do with the rest of the day? She might stop into Travellers Rest for a cold drink, but it would feel awkward sitting there alone.

Tonight, another solitary dinner, the remaining groundnut sauce from last night and the two matoke plantain bananas Caspar would peel for her with the sharpest kitchen knife before he left for the night. The tough, bright green skin of the matoke banana had to be peeled like a potato. The groundnut sauce was made from finely ground, raw peanuts, boiled up with water and whatever other vegetables were on hand, and served over the cooked, mashed matoke. It had taken some getting used to, but now she preferred it over other things she knew how to cook, except for spaghetti.

Tonight she would write to her parents, a prospect she dreaded, since she would need to tell them about Carolyn's departure. They would worry. Her mother would picture her daughter on her own in some godforsaken place. She would write them that a replacement would be arriving any day now, even though she was beginning to have her doubts.

Walking home, the air was warm and dry, not a dark cloud in sight. A strong wind from the mountains blew the dust around with an eerie blend of whine and whisper. Sound traveled differently here than at home; there was no background noise level, no pollution to muffle and dissipate. It was like the clear frigid air high over a ski slope when the chairlift stopped unexpectedly, with only the occasional clack of skis or clownish yodel to shatter the icy silence. Here, her footsteps made a sound as intensely bright as the snap of lightning balls.

Even the usual children had deserted her. They had followed her all the way to Kisoro – lucky she had thought to bring the Assorted Fruit Gums, which they had eaten with loud lip- smacking and giggling. Now they were nowhere to be seen. Hoping she was not being watched, she explored the rhythm of her own movement, allowing hips and shoulders to sway freely while balancing the straw bag on her head. Africans did this so easily and gracefully from long practice, but Laurel knew how awkward she must look, trying and failing to keep the bag balanced. No wonder the children always laughed and shouted when the Mzungu in bell bottoms and blowzy red hair came marching stiffly down the road.

It wasn't that she was trying to be African, it was just that Africa had seeped in through all her cracks, and she had never known she had any cracks. Back home everything had operated within proscribed boundaries, each day plotted into its proper place on the grid of past, present, future. Time was not to be squandered in a well-ordered life: school, homework, family dinner, piano time, reading time, bed time. Concerts, museums, theater on the weekends; music camp and family vacation during the summer. College was a similar kind of daily structure, yielding security and comfort. Even down-time had to be filled, with studying, music-making, planning the future in detail with Alan.

Here, she was learning to live more slowly. Released from the clamor of life back home, the busyness, the need to account for each minute, she was coming to appreciate simple pleasures like conversation and the company of other people. Here, no one told her what to do. The way she taught, how she acted, how she used her time, was all up to her. This had been frightening at first. Now, it felt liberating, like noodling at the piano instead of worrying over each note. She had the strange feeling of composing herself, note by note, measure by measure, improvising new variations and harmonies, recalibrating her tonality from a minor to a major key. Life as an impromptu, or a symphony. Why not? The thought was exhilarating. So much for bald university professor Krantz and his belief that women don't have an aptitude for composition. He should just see her now, walking down this road in Africa. She was positively effulgent with aptitude. Yes, that was the word, effulgent, a

161

Gilbert and Sullivan word, *in something gold he glories all effulgent* – she was singing now – *I mean to rule the earth as he the sky,* a song from *The Mikado*, a few pitches lower than written, because damn, she was no soprano, but one of the great things about music was its flexibility –*we really know our worth, the sun and I.*

She thought about Mrs. Gupta back at the store, how pleasant it was to have a woman there, even though they could not really communicate. Laurel had not seen any other Asian women in Kisoro; did she have women friends here, or was Mrs. Gupta lonely, too? She had not appeared during the time Father Matthew was there –

Gay or not, there was something daunting about him, something unattractive, despite his good looks. A September birthday meant he was Virgo, like Alan. Fussy perfectionist, needs to be in charge, demands loyalty. Intelligence, and courage. The profile according to Tessa seemed eerily close in Alan's case, but Father Matthew was too much a mystery to be so predictable. Maybe he wasn't born under any planetary sign at all, and at his birth the sky was momentarily empty, like a concert hall during intermission.

Her throat dry from slogging along the ashy school road, her house in sight, and there was someone sitting on the front step. It was Ngira, looking like someone waiting for a bus. She wiped her forehead, gritty with sweat and dust. "What are you doing here? I thought you and Gordon were away."

Ngira's smile faded. Why had she taken such an aggressive tone? She didn't want to chase him away. She wanted him to stay and talk to her.

"We were to go climbing to the Ruwenzori, but Gordon was troubled with his gouty toe. He went to Kampala to visit friends, and I came back here."

Laurel laughed. "That's too bad, but anyway I'm glad to see you. I've been dying to tell you about my trip to Rwanda. Do you have time?"

He moved over to make room for her on the step. "How could I not have time for such an important story?"

"Wouldn't you like to come inside?"

He gestured at the sky. "It is a very nice afternoon."

"Yes, but it's more comfortable inside, and I'm thirsty from my walk." Suddenly, she understood that after Carolyn's departure he did not think it proper for them to be alone together in the house. She laughed out loud. "As far as I know Caspar is still here –" his expression stopped her. He was right, of course. Being alone in the house, even with Caspar present, could be a source for gossip. He was looking out for her reputation as well as his own. "I'll just ask him to find us something to drink, and I'll be right back."

He looked at her and smiled. "All right, Laurel." Such a rich voice, and she liked the musical way he said her name, *Lah-rel.* He was a good person, a good friend, and she hoped he didn't think she was trying to get him to come inside to seduce him. God, that would be embarrassing, and absolutely the furthest thing from her mind.

<u>24</u>

Father Matthew's Journal

Kisoro, 5th January, 1972

"Nunc scio, quid sit Amor." Now I know what love is, Virgil wrote, but I wonder, in his promiscuous and permissive pagan time, what could he know of forbidden love that is both joy and torment?

It is my soul's torment, my love for this African man. I call him Rabelais and he indulges me, thinking it only another peculiarity of an already peculiar priest. He cannot know how I relish the nickname, hoard it as a part of him that is all my own. When he tells me of his travels with Gordon, who takes his generous friendship with no thought of gratitude, I feel envy burn inside me like a tumor. It should be me as his confidant and close companion instead of that debauched Englishman. I would climb mountains, travel anywhere with him. Right now the very idea of love with another man would repel him. Friendship first, and then – the hope that in time I might win him, body and soul –

Last Sunday when he stayed after Mass to discuss the writings of St. Augustine – he is interested in philosophy, and this is how I tempt him to visit me – I thought I would go mad, not being able to touch him, his beautiful skin, strong thighs. I became a serpent in the guise of priest, speaking of the soul's journey toward God! I fully expected God to crush me on the spot, but no, my punishment will be revealed to me in God's way and time. I behaved impeccably, and he left satisfied with our discourse and, in his trusting innocence, suspecting nothing.

Later, needing a receptacle for my passion, I once again brought Mtembo's sister to the mission orchard. There on the ground beneath a tree I made her kneel, the vinous smell of rotting fallen apples nauseating as I fumbled with the condom. Then I lifted her skirt and took her from behind like an animal, her brown haunches quivering. But animals are innocent and only following their natures, while I was a man possessed by the demon of lust and its inevitable result: self-loathing. Afterward, I told her to leave and turned my face away. She touched me gently on the back, and her touch brought forth my flood of tears. The poor, sweet child – not a day over 16, I'd guess – shows me a compassion I don't deserve. I defile her, breaking my promise to God and my duty to Christian principles. There can be no hope of my salvation. No hope, no hope! As long as I allow myself to be ruled by concupiscence I will never receive the blessings of divine grace. Only the thought of Rabelais's bright presence keeps me from despair.

Lately, he always turns the conversation to that girl at Butawanga, and this upsets me more than it does even when he speaks of Theresa. Theresa lives far away, and I never believed that she had captured his spirit along with his body. This American girl is an unwelcome complication. Laurel. An ironic name. Some might call her pretty in a soft-boiled, Rubenesque way, but not striking like her departed companion. Still, he finds her appealing. She acts the proper Bostonian, but I'm convinced she has a wanton nature. In the States these days, immorality is commonplace among the young. It didn't take long for those girls to be involved in an orgy of sex and drugs with two young men, as we heard. But then I should be the last to judge.

I do believe she's predatory, judging from the way she tried to interrogate me today in Gupta's store when I was buying the condoms. Gupta believes I buy them for the village boys, so he didn't betray my bald lie about Lawrence's birthday. It was a joke I couldn't resist, while she stood there like Pandora consumed with curiosity over my little box – but shame on me for embarrassing poor Gupta.

No, the girl is not as guileless as she pretends. When Peace Corps took the dark one away, why didn't they take Laurel as well? Thankfully she was not at home when we sent to invite her to Christmas tea. I do not think I could have borne her scheming presence with equanimity.

Of course my dear Rabelais is taken in completely, having no experience with spoiled, self-centered American girls. The prospect that he will be wounded at her hands is intolerable to me. *Varium et mutabile semper Femina.* This time Virgil is right, women are fickle and not to be trusted.

I pray that God will protect poor Rabelais from the damage she might do, even in her limited time here. Yet I have no right to ask God to hear me in my unclean state. When I bestow the sacraments on His flock, I feel God judging me, looking into my soul and seeing only the weakness of the truly fallen. My love seals my fate. I accept it, even embrace it. I no longer ask for, nor hope to receive, forgiveness. This is nothing I am strong enough to change. I am damned.

25

Letter to Tess

Monday, 12/27

Belated Merry Christmas, Tess. By the time you get this it will be 1972 and I'll have started second term. Lots to report, not much space on these damn little airmail fold up things, so here goes:

Spent Christmas in Rwanda with a Belgian couple and Ellen Webster, who studies gorillas from her camp on a mountain – check out National Geographic, article about her a couple of years ago. We hiked out to see some gorillas but got too close and they charged which was holy shit terrifying but just a bluff. No one was hurt.

Carolyn is gone, "terminated" along with Greg and Kevin. Worst luck, P.C. brass walked in when they were smoking weed. I actually tried it (o.k. stop laughing) and got a little stoned but I didn't get caught and the others didn't tell on me. Got to say you nailed it, Tess. Carolyn the Bull was headstrong and prone to excess, but she was loyal. Now I'm feeling guilty and alone in this empty concrete house. At least I still have Gordon and Ngira. By the way, Tess, if you bump into my mother somewhere don't tell her about all this. No sense worrying my parents.

Ngira and Gordon are a comedy routine, with Gordon the whiner (with a weakness for gin) and Ngira the sensible one. Assuming I get through this term, I plan to persuade them to take me back up to Ellen's camp (Gordon has a car). I really want to go back, and as you know, once I set my mind on something –

If it wasn't for Gordon and Ngira, I don't think I'd be able to stick it out here on my own. Everyone is friendly but mostly it doesn't go beyond small talk over coffee in the teacher's room. I forget Ngira's African a lot of the time, which when you think about it is a racist thing to say. There was a Peace Corps psychologist screening volunteers back in DC, big Afro, African style clothes. She said all whites are racist, whether we know it or not. What if she was right? Let me tell you, I was really glad to see Gordon's white face when we first arrived. Remember how the handful of black students on campus stuck together and didn't mix? Here, I'm the minority. People stare because they're curious. I don't think anyone hates me just because I'm white.

Our headmaster agreed to let me start a student chorus. I'm excited about it. My ghostly brain sonatas have been breaking apart like shipwrecks and coming back with new things worked in – voices, rain on a tin roof, an instrument called inanga. Prof. Krantz wouldn't approve but to me it is some extreme high, and the more I do it, the more I have to do it. If only I had my piano to work it out on!

Oh, I don't think I told you there's a mission nearby with three white priests – weird, weirder, and weirdest. One of them creeps me out, and would you believe I actually tried flirting with him because he's American and good looking. Carolyn thought he was "gay," maybe she's right, but I'm embarrassed at myself for even trying to find out, I mean he's a priest for God's sake.

Sorry your paintings didn't sell this time, but you know

just getting a show like that was a real coup. You are a great artist, and sooner or later everyone will realize it. I absolutely will not tolerate any negative thinking from you of all people, Tessa. I do enough of that for the both of us.

Comera, L.

<u>26</u>

Adam and Eve

The hard-packed dirt path that Laurel and Ngira followed up to the mission passed through the compact shambas on the hillside, then climbed straight up to where a high stone wall enclosed an apple orchard. In the heart of Africa, a crop reminiscent of New England's fall bounty winked from the sequestered trees like forbidden fruit. The path skirted the wall and veered through an archway covered with grapevines that had spilled over from a trellis on the other side of the wall. A white pebble walkway led from the arch to the heavy wooden doors of the church, always wide open when they arrived. Laurel liked flowing in along with the chatting, laughing people. A hush descended inside, where the fresh morning air did not penetrate the damp, musty smelling interior.

Father Matthew conducted the Sunday morning Mass, striking in white alb and embroidered chasuble cloak that followed each gesture in a sweeping arc. With his tanned face, he looked more like some exotic sultan than a priest.

The Protestant services she remembered from childhood had been simpler, and in English. The Mass was in Latin first, followed by the Kinyarwanda translation. Laurel admired Fr. Matthew for this effort of outreach to the people. Hymns were in English, and the congregation did a credible enough job of singing the words. Ngira sang out naturally and effortlessly in a round baritone with an ebullient tone that made her look at him sideways and smile. It was the first time she had heard him sing. She wanted that voice for the school chorus, started more than a month ago.

She had written to one of the faculty in the Music department at B.U. to ask if the university could purchase some songbooks to send over, but as yet had not heard back from them. For now, the students were having a good time with simple songs and rounds, and singing the Ugandan national anthem at school functions. Kizuma had joined, which pleased her. In fact, the whole thing had turned out so much better than she thought it would at the first meeting, with four students who were as nervous as she was. Now she had a group of ten, enough to really begin working on voice parts. Some of the other teachers ran extracurricular activities, like sports, so as the only female teacher Laurel was glad to open this avenue for herself to contribute more than the required teaching duties.

Ngira said he was too busy coaching soccer and advising the Maths Club to join the chorus, but he sometimes stopped in at rehearsals and could always be persuaded to join in. All the students liked Ngira, but the chorus loved him for his voice. Laurel judged it to be almost operatic in its dynamics. It seemed to embarrass him, this gift for which he could find no practical use.

When Mass was over, people lingered in small groups. Students who worshiped there liked presenting her to their families. *Mulaho, Mulahoneza*; hands were clasped, the women averted their eyes. Laurel wondered if African women felt oppressed, and if they should demand equal rights with men as American women were doing. Young African women, like the ones she had met during Peace Corps training who were studying at Makerere, clearly had ambitions for good jobs, travel, higher education, but it was harder for women in rural places like Kisoro. There were no jobs to speak of, and life centered around family and shamba. An idea like women's lib would be very foreign here, even threatening. But then, she thought, it was threatening to any established male-dominated society, including the U.S.

Eventually everyone filed out through the door, nodding to their priest. Father Matthew gripped Ngira's hand and chatted with him in English, *sotto voce*. How rude, excluding her like that. He did not even smile when he mumbled, *Miss Bittelson, how nice to see you again*, then turned to the next person in line. Now she was even more curious about him, about the secrets behind his ravishing blue gaze.

Today he could not escape as easily as he had at Gupta's store. "You know, Father Matthew, I think I would sell my soul for one of the apples in your orchard."

The priest narrowed his eyes, and Laurel caught a look that made her inhale sharply. But then he smiled.

"Then of course you must have one. You and Ngira can help yourselves from the kitchen, or straight from the trees if you like. When everyone is gone I'll show you the way. But Miss Bittelson, do try to put a higher value on your soul. It's always dangerous to tempt the devil, even in jest."

Tempt the devil? "Oh, don't worry, Father. I don't believe in the devil."

Ngira laughed. Fr. Matthew turned away to greet the few remaining parishioners.

Walking down the hill to the school, the priest became more and more irrelevant with each bite of the small yet unblemished Red Delicious. This was Ngira's first apple. At first he judged it a bland, unfulfilling fruit; but Laurel noticed

172

once he got going, he ate it all the way down to the hard, seed-filled core, licking the sweetness from his fingers.

* * *

Toward the end of January, two *TIME* magazines and some other mail arrived for Carolyn. Laurel forwarded the mail but kept the magazines. Even belated news was proof of another world still out there. If the other continents destroyed each other in a nuclear holocaust, she sometimes wondered how long it would take the news to filter down to Kisoro.

The issues were from December, 1971. *Last year*, she thought with amazement, as if somehow left out of this passage of time. Little was reported about Vietnam: an article about the final court-martial resulting from the My-Lai massacre, an acquittal; fighting in Cambodia. Were American troops still being sent over there? Were there casualties? This information was not given; the American press and public were tired of this war. The creation of the new nation of Bangladesh was covered at length. There were articles on "The Good Samaritan;" Gloria Steinem's plans to publish a feminist magazine titled *Ms.*; "pop" singer Isaac Hayes; high unemployment among Vietnam vets. Laurel felt removed from it all after being in Africa only eight months. How would she feel after two years?

There was a letter from Tessa, the third. Tessa's letters were like personal works of art. Laurel knew she wrote them with a calligraphy pen on rice paper stationery from a store in Boston's Chinatown. It was so like Tessa to splurge on lovely expensive paper while barely supporting herself, trying to get established as an artist.

Surprisingly, Alan had been in touch with Tessa. It was surprising because she had never liked him much, and he had been critical of Tessa's free-love lifestyle. *He's been so needy since you left. He started calling me, so finally we went for a walk one afternoon down by the Charles.*

Walking by the Charles! She used to walk with him there, too, his arm around her shoulder, wrapped in the scent of his English Leather.

He needed a shoulder to cry on. I know you had your reasons, but still you were kind of hard on him, you know?

"Give me a fucking break," Laurel had said out loud before crumpling the delicate translucent paper into a ball and throwing it onto the floor. After some pouting, she picked it up from the straw mat and smoothed it out on the table. A letter from Tessa was too precious to waste on residual jealousy over a man who, by her own choice, was no longer hers. Tessa had a weak spot for men who played on her sympathy. But really, Laurel thought, now all of a sudden she says I was hard on him? Before, she said the only thing hurt by the breakup was Alan's pride.

This was just Tessa's Libra showing, Laurel decided, the feeling sorry for anyone with a sob story. She and Alan were too different for it to be anything else.

* * *

Over a weekend in February, Gordon took Laurel to Kampala for her medical checkup at Peace Corps headquarters. She was grateful to avoid the bus, although Gordon's rickety Saab didn't inspire much more confidence. At least he stayed sober for the drive.

Kampala was more subdued than it had been during the months of Peace Corps training. There were still smiles and greetings from people on the street, but now they seemed anxious to get on to where they were going, and only soldiers lingered on the street corners. Though flowering plants still blossomed purple, white, pink, spilling out from alleyways and tiny city gardens, their scent was now mixed with more urgent smells of hot asphalt and vehicle exhaust on the sultry air.

Peace Corps and the Embassy were monitoring the political situation, she was told. Although Karl's words at Christmas were always in the back of her mind, she trusted Peace Corps to keep tabs on what President Amin was up to and let the volunteers know of any real danger.

She was glad to get back to sleepy, quiet Butawanga. Although the pace of life was slow, her days seemed full. It was three months since Carolyn had left, but Laurel no longer worried over the delay in sending another volunteer. Even though James Ngugi's *A Grain of Wheat*, Shakespeare's *Hamlet*, and Plato's *Republic* were tough going, she was determined to get her students through it. Beyond that, the tantalizing vision of summer break. Most tantalizing of all, if only she could arrange it, was her secret plan to travel back to the cool primeval forests of Ellen's mountain.

III

Elephant Mountain

"There are times when one cannot accept facts
for fear of shattering one's being."

Dian Fossey, *Gorillas in the Mist*

27

Captain Aiwa

Chip made another routine Peace Corps visit to Butawanga in late June, the one-year anniversary for her volunteer group being in-country. He was sorry to have to tell her that there would be no new volunteer coming in the foreseeable future. Rumors of violence by Amin's regime had discouraged some trainees from coming, so the latest group was smaller than anticipated. Laurel didn't mind, not really. Once she had got used to the idea of living alone, she had hardly thought about a new roommate. He asked her if she might like to transfer closer to Kampala, now that the school year was over. Think about it, he told her, but there was nothing to think about. She wanted to stay at Butawanga.

Chip smiled under his moustache and said, "That's what we like to hear, Laurie." He advised her against traveling to Kampala because there were some Army roadblocks along the way. "The Army's a little riled up right now because there are rumors of a so-called invasion coming from Tanzania. Just sit tight until all of this blows over," he said. For her next medical checkup at the end of August, Peace Corps would send a car.

She told Chip that she was fine and promised not to travel to Kampala on her own. What she did not say was that Gordon and Ngira had agreed to take her to Rwanda next month. Laurel had written to Ellen, care of a post office box in Ruhengeri, asking if they could come, and a letter came back saying July would be a good time. She was thrilled at the idea of seeing Ellen again, and since Chip might advise her not to go, she had thought it best not to mention it. Anyway, she reasoned, they would be traveling away from danger, not toward it.

This time she felt better prepared for the hike up Ellen's mountain. Shortly after Christmas, a package had arrived from her parents containing her hiking boots, jeans, socks, ski sweater, flannel shirt and rain parka. There was a short note from her mother saying that she had never thought there would be a Christmas when their *Laurelchka* would not be there with them. The Polish-ized endearment made Laurel wonder if that meant she was forgiven for going away. A note from her father said, *we miss you, glad all is going well, hope the duds will keep you warm and dry.*

The package from home gave her a sharp jolt of homesickness, wishing she could be with her parents long enough to hear her mother say *Laurelchka* in that voice she used when, for once, Laurel had not done anything wrong; to look into her father's eyes as he faced her, holding her shoulders, and know the simple pleasure he took seeing her whenever she came home. These were things she had taken for granted in that left-behind life, that now felt like precious gifts.

Now, though it was warm enough at Butawanga, she was very glad to have warm clothing to take along for this trip. Excited almost to the point of giddiness, early on this cloudy Wednesday morning in late July she put on the jeans, flannel shirt, hiking boots and ski socks, shoved the parka and sweater into her backpack and zipped her passport into the top. Then she went out the front door and locked it behind her.

The "boot" of Gordon's Saab would only hold his gear and the provisions they were to pick up in town. Ngira stuffed both his and Laurel's packs into the back seat and crawled in after them. Seeing how cramped he was, his knees coming up even with his shoulders, she offered to sit in the back. Ngira shook his head and smiled at her.

They stopped at Gupta's store for food to bring to Ellen. Laurel agreed to do the shopping while Gordon and Ngira walked down to Travellers Rest for a coffee. Beer, more like, she thought when they were gone, and why did I stick myself with doing this while they're down there relaxing? But since Gordon had to drive and Ngira had saved her from the cramped backseat, she had decided not to protest. They would split the grocery bill afterward.

Instead of Mr. Gupta and his usual burst of cordiality, she was startled by a stranger's face behind the counter. He was a big man, very black, not the delivery man but someone she didn't recognize.

"Hello, Madam." A slow display of white teeth, purple gums.

"Hello." She glanced around, still expecting the store's owner to emerge from the back. "Where is Mr. Gupta?"

"Guptas are gone, out of Uganda, if they are wise." He waved his arm in a sweeping gesture, taking in the breadth of his property. "This my store now."

She was dumbstruck. "Oh, I see." But she didn't see at all. "I thought they were happy here."

"No matter. All of them must go, very soon. Africa for Africans, you know." He continued to grin at her. "Our great president General Idi Amin Dada said this will be so." He motioned toward the familiar picture that hung over the curtained doorway to what had been the Gupta's home.

Laurel couldn't force herself to smile. She wondered where

the shopkeeper and his wife could have gone. Back to India, so suddenly, when their life was in Uganda? "It's a terrible thing."

"Do not worry, Madam. I am getting everything that you are needing. You will find everything in order."

Laurel was completely shocked. This was all so sudden, and so unfair. She hardly knew what to say. "Are you from Kisoro?"

"No, from Arua, in the North. I go for short time to Makerere, but I am not liking it. Then I am in Uganda Army, in Jinja. I am liking it fine, but General Amin he says I am too educated to be soldier. There is very fine store in Kisoro, he says, and you can have it." He cleared his throat. "I am not liking to refuse."

"No, I suppose not." She couldn't help the sarcastic tone in her voice and didn't care if he noticed.

"But the people here," he cocked his head to indicate the village outside his door, "they are very backward. Not many whites here also, I think." He grinned at her again. "I am Munde." He extended his hand. The palm was broad and spatulate, like a shovel.

She tolerated a quick, finger-brushing handshake. "I'm Laurel Bittelson. I teach at Butawanga."

"Yes, Madam. I know who you are."

Of course, he would have heard about her. The only white woman in the nearby area would be an important customer.

She selected the things she needed, except there was no jam, canned milk, coffee, or sugar. Munde told her Gupta had let those things run out, but that he was making arrangements to get them in again soon. After some discussion about the high price of Weetabix cereal, which Gordon liked, she conceded and paid the bill. They would have to make a stop in Ruhengeri to pick up the missing items.

Munde called the delivery man, who had been sitting on a chair in the corner, to pack her purchases, addressing him in Swahili, whereas Mr. Gupta had used Kinyarwanda. When the box was packed, he motioned to the man to take it outside.

While the delivery man wedged the box into the boot, she tried to make some sense out of what she had just seen. Just last week, the Guptas acted as if nothing unusual was happening. Now they were gone, forced to give their livelihood and their home into the hands of this stranger. Mr. Munde. She felt a flame of anger. Although she shouldn't blame him for what was the government's doing, that smug grin behind the counter would take some getting used to.

The delivery man had worked for the Guptas for years, and she wished she knew enough Kinyarwanda to question him about all of this. She pressed a shilling into his hand and thanked him with *Wakosi*. He nodded and turned back to the store. A bitterness came up in her throat. On top of all this, there was no sign of Gordon and Ngira. She would have to walk down to the hotel to get them.

The small, dark dining room of Travellers Rest was hazy with smoke and filled with the noise of a group of soldiers in Army uniform, drinking beer among a legion of empty bottles. It was 10 a.m. Ngira and Gordon were seated at a table, two beer bottles in front of them, and no coffee in sight. So, Laurel thought, that's why they've been so long, partying with these men while I was stuck dealing with Mr. Munde.

As she walked across the room, the soldiers looked her up and down, making comments and clacking their tongues. It made her feel like merchandise. She remembered that there were rumors about the Ugandan Army being on the rampage, and the roadblocks Chip had warned about, but somehow she had never imagined they would bother about Kisoro.

Gordon and Ngira stood up, the soldiers remained seated. "My friends," Gordon said loudly, "this is Miss Bittelson, who is also a teacher at our school."

A tall soldier seated at their table grinned at her. He had pockmarked skin and a thin line of moustache. "Then she is very brave, to be teaching so many bad boys." He cackled, extended his hand. "I am Captain Ali Aiwa."

The fuzzy hair on the back of her neck bristled. She didn't like this man, this whole setup. He did not release her hand for several long seconds.

Gordon offered her his seat, an uneasy smile plastered on his face. "Would you like a beer?"

Ngira caught her eye and frowned.

"No thanks, Gordon." Thankfully, the Captain did not insist on her joining them. Ngira looked stiff, nervous. The men were loud and clearly drunk. Mr. Rajaraman was not in sight. She was beginning to feel frightened.

Ngira stood up again. "Yes, thank you very much for your hospitality, Captain, but in fact we must be going now."

Laurel took his cue and walked with him to the door.

"Oh, well then, I guess we'll be off," Gordon said briskly. He shook hands with the Captain and waved a broad, awkward salute to the other men.

They walked quickly, not talking, back to the car.

Inside the car, Ngira said, "They might make trouble for us. It would be better to call off the trip and go back to Butawanga."

Laurel had never heard him sound so tense. "Maybe Ngira's right, Gordon."

"Nonsense." He started the engine. "They seem harmless enough, just stewed to the gills. They'll sleep it off and be on their way before we get back from Rwanda."

Ngira made a sound deep in his throat. "Heh, I am not so sure. That Captain Aiwa has the eye of a vulture."

"For Heaven's sake stop worrying, Ngira. You sound like an old woman."

Gordon wrenched the car into gear and sped down the black dirt road toward the border.

The New York Times, April 14, 1972

[Excerpted from an article by Charles Mohr]

KAMPALA, Uganda, April 13 —The burned-out automobile of an American journalist who disappeared last July with a companion was found yesterday, just where a deserter from the Uganda Army said it had been hidden.

The missing, and presumably dead, Americans are Nicholas Stroh, 33, and Robert Siedle, 46. Mr. Stroh was a freelance journalist who covered Africa for The Washington Star, the American Broadcasting Company and several other United States and Canadian news organizations. Mr. Siedle was a lecturer at Makerere University in Kampala.

Mr. Stroh, accompanied by Mr. Siedle, drove his pale blue station wagon the 180 miles from Kampala to Mbarara, Uganda, on July 7 of last year to investigate reports that 150 soldiers of the Acholi and Langi tribes had been massacred by fellow troops at the barracks there. The two never returned, but an anonymous telephone caller with a British accent told the United States Embassy on July 8 that he had seen them under arrest at the barracks.

Last week Lieutenant Tibihike, who was stationed at Mbarara barracks last July but later went into exile in Tanzania, told a British journalist in Dar es Salaam that fellow officers had boasted of stabbing Mr. Stroh and Mr. Siedle to death because Mr. Stroh was "proud." Lieutenant Tibihika said that several days later he was ordered to dig up and burn the bodies and to dispose of Mr. Stroh's car.

The car was identified from the chassis number and other details, informed sources said.

28

Papa

To: Senator Edward Kennedy

Re: Concern for the safety of Peace Corps volunteers serving in Uganda

25 May, 1972

Dear Senator Kennedy:

I am writing to follow up on my telephone call to your office earlier today, when I spoke with your aide, who gave his name as Martin.

In April, there was a report in the New York Times that two Americans missing in Uganda since July of last year are now known to have been murdered. In recent months, there have also been reports of widespread killing in Uganda under President Idi Amin, and of course his proclaimed prejudicial expulsion of East Asians from that country. News of atrocities by the regime are causing my wife and I great anxiety about the safety of our daughter, Laurel Bittelson, who is stationed near the remote town of Kisoro. I have contacted the Peace Corps office in Washington and the Department of State on this matter, and received only non-specific assurances that the situation is being monitored. Under the circumstances I feel that such assurances are both insufficient and unsatisfactory.

I appeal to you as our elected representative to find out what is going on over there.

I request that you use your position in our government to urge the immediate withdrawal of Peace Corps volunteers from Uganda. Secondly, the U.S. should intervene to prevent what is beginning to appear as a wholesale genocide in that country. Both my wife and I have all too vivid memories of what was suffered in Europe when the U.S. government delayed taking action in the second World War. My wife's parents were lost in a death camp in Poland. I was in one of the English divisions that liberated a camp in Germany and I can assure you, Senator, I will never forget the scale of the human tragedy I witnessed there.

And now, our young daughter is living in a country ruled by a military government under direction of a madman who openly boasts that he admires Hitler. He compares the Indian population of his country to Hitler's Jews. Many thousands of Indians even with Ugandan citizenship are now stateless, forced to leave their homes and possessions behind and flee for their lives. Amin respects neither human rights nor international law. We must recognize that there is no way to ensure the safety of any person of any nationality living now in that country.

Laurel is young and American and therefore accustomed to the rule of law. We do not know if she is aware of any threat. There is no telephone service where she is, letters are infrequent, and her last letter was largely blacked out by censors – in itself a cause for great concern. Senator, as a parent, I know you will understand how excessively worrying it is to feel that your child is in serious danger and be unable to help her. We do not want to find out too late that the unspeakable has happened because of our government's inaction.

I hold our government directly responsible for the welfare of my daughter and other volunteers who are serving there in the name of our country.

Martin has our address and both my work and home telephone numbers, which I have also provided at the end of this letter. I will expect an urgent and personal reply.

Respectfully,

Arthur J. and Margaret Bittelson

<u>29</u>

Sitting on fire

Laurel raised her voice over the Saab's whine. "What are so many soldiers doing in Kisoro, anyway?" The smells of sweat and beer at the hotel, and a vibe that was aggressive, hostile, especially from that freaky captain. She needed to know what to make of it, whether her discomfort at the whole situation was justified.

Gordon chortled. "Throwing their weight around, frightening Rajaraman into dispensing free beer, that's all." He wrestled with the gearshift as the car grappled for traction up a slight incline on the dirt road. "That Aiwa bloke said they were on exercises."

"I think Captain Aiwa is Nubian, or a Sudanese mercenary," Ngira said. "They are foreigners who care only for money. Amin's army is full of them. Why did you tell him we were traveling to Rwanda?"

"Why in bloody hell not, Ngira? Laurel and I have our passports, and you don't need one. We can go if we like. Really, my friend, you should not let these bullies worry you."

Ngira frowned. "Really, my friend, you should learn that bullies with guns can shoot you if they want, and there is no one to stop them."

"Bollocks. Pardon me, Laurel. I am a British subject, and Uganda is still a Commonwealth country. Even Amin knows better than to take on the Queen."

"The Queen?" Ngira waved dismissively. "May I remind you that this is the Republic of Uganda. We are no longer under the English high heels. Your Mzungu queen is very far away in her castle, drinking tea."

"Bloody hell, Ngira – you know what I mean!"

Gordon flushed red and yanked on the steering wheel to keep the car on the road. Ngira waved his fist. "Can't you see that soldiers like those will not be impressed by shaking your English sword? If they answer to anyone at all, it is only to that captain there, and Amin."

Gordon began muttering to himself, and Ngira sat with his arms folded, staring out the window. Green shrubs and low spreading trees tilted and bumped with the motion; the sun was already high, broiling the car, and the dust was suffocating, even worse than when she had gone with the Haubers in their van. Everyone was edgy, and there were still those damn soldiers to worry about. Bullies, Ngira had said. *Shoot you if they want.*

Laurel felt queasy. She really wanted to go, but not if it was going to be dangerous. Or cause trouble between the two men. "Gordon, I think we should call it off."

The car skidded to a halt. Gordon let out a hiss of air and shook his head. "Fine, Laurel, whatever you say. This was your bloody idea to begin with."

"I know it was, Gordon, and believe me I was thrilled when you agreed to go. But Ngira's right. Who knows what that Captain is up to?" This was the right thing, the safe thing, wasn't it? She trusted Ngira's judgment, but on the other hand –

She avoided Ngira's eyes. "On the other hand, we are going away from where the soldiers are."

Ngira let out a long exhalation. "We all of us agreed to go, and now that we have come this far, let us go." He smiled then at Laurel. "Most probably I am worrying too much. And perhaps after all it is better not to pass through Kisoro again right away."

A surge of hope. "Really?"

"Yes. Anyway, I want to meet your American gorilla lady."

Gordon said, "there we are then, that's the old Ngira."

Was he implying that Ngira was different because she was there? Gordon could be so juvenile sometimes. But she didn't care. She pushed aside any lingering reservations and settled back, satisfied with their noisy progress down the road toward Rwanda.

Then she remembered. "What on earth happened to the Guptas? I walked in and there was this man behind the counter named Munde. He gave me the creeps."

Ngira shrugged. "It is a cruel solution to a problem that has been building for some time now. In Uganda there has always been resentment of successful Asian merchants, but President Amin has pushed it to the extreme. All Asians must leave Uganda by the eighth of November."

"Why didn't you tell me before this?"

"I am sorry. I thought you knew. Some say that 50,000 Asians now live in Uganda. Many are Ugandan citizens, but this does not matter to Amin. He has told them they are sitting on fire."

"I didn't even have a chance to say goodbye. Where did they go?"

"I know they have family in England," Gordon said. "Their son is in school there, but it's possible the quota might make it hard for them to get in. God knows where they'll end up. Still, it's just as well Gupta got out early. Rajaraman better close up Travellers Rest and get going, too, or he'll end up in detention, or worse. Amin's put a stop on Asian bank accounts. The fool thinks they'll all get rich on Asian money and property, but who will run the businesses? Christ, this bloody transmission –"

Gordon applied himself to his reluctant machine as Ngira sat silently looking out the window. Mr. Gupta had never mentioned a son. They must have always felt on guard, unable to trust anyone. She hated to think of them suddenly homeless. It was so unfair. Amin had no right to persecute people. He should be stopped. Surely the U.S. and the U.N. would do something.

Gordon announced, "Ladies and gents, it's the border." Concern for the Guptas did not stop a flash of pleasure. They were really, truly on their way to Ellen.

The customs officer at the Ugandan border post was not Samuel, as at Christmas when she had crossed with the Haubers, but this new man was also polite and friendly. He talked with Gordon and Ngira in Kinyarwanda. Gordon tipped him. The official looked at their passports, then waved them through without searching the car.

At the Rwandan border they were detained a bit longer, while an officious guard questioned Ngira. Gordon folded a ten shilling note into his hand, and they were cheerfully allowed to pass.

"You see?" Gordon said. "The proverbial piece of cake."

30

Someone else's dream

The long, dusty drive into Rwanda finally ended at the car park at the edge of the Parc des Volcans, where they hired two porters and a guide for the hike to Ellen's camp. The guide was Runagaba, as before. He remembered Laurel and greeted her loudly, *Mzungu Madam*, explaining to the others that she was a friend of Nyirangagi. She shook hands all around, enjoying this new-found importance.

Along the trail, through the Hagenia trees and the dark lava tunnel used by generations of elephants, everything was just as beautiful and other-worldly as she remembered. She had packed two music cassette tapes for Ellen. Music would be just the thing to help get her through the solitary nights. Brahms' *Hungarian Dances*, for their upbeat folksiness, and although she hated to part with it, excerpts from Mozart's opera *The Marriage of Figaro*, for the comforting sound of the human voice.

She also packed a blank cassette, intending to use Ellen's machine to record the forest sounds that had made such an impression on the first trip.

The climb was easier this time. She was warmly dressed, the trail was drier, and she was able to keep up with the men. It was just dusk as they walked into the clearing of the Virunga Gorilla Research Center. Laurel felt on top of the world. She couldn't wait for Gordon and Ngira to meet Ellen. Any minute now would come the warm welcome, assuming Ellen wasn't going to fall into her suspicious-of-strangers mode. But something was different this time. The open pit fire was down to a thin line of smoke, the compound deserted. Strange. It was always possible that Ellen had forgotten they were coming. She was a busy woman, engrossed in her work. It was stupidly self-important to think Ellen would plan her day around their arrival.

But there was no sign of Ben, either, and as houseboy he would have been left in charge of the camp.

They piled their belongings on the front porch. Gordon paid the porters and dismissed them. Since there were none of Ellen's men with whom to share a beer and a fire, they took their pay and went back down the trail.

"If Ellen made contact with gorillas, there's no telling when she'll be back." She looked around the empty camp, trying not to worry.

"All I need right now is a fag and I'll be happy." Gordon sat on the step and lit a cigarette. Like most Africans she had met, Ngira did not smoke. Laurel almost asked Gordon for a drag, but stopped herself, knowing that even a taste might be enough to re-start the habit. It might calm her nerves for a moment, but it would not help her figure out what was going on.

She called out Ellen's name, then Ben's, her voice swallowed by the deep silence. She tried the latch. "Oh, good, she left it open for us. I guess she expected to be late. Might as well go inside."

Laurel went in first. In the dim light there was a sharp smell of Omo laundry soap and the startling sight of Ellen bent over the sink, up to her elbows in mounds of suds. A washboard, an article of clothing. She was struck silent at the sight of Ellen's mechanical scrubbing, wondering what the hell was going on, and recovering enough to say in a fairly steady, forcibly cheerful voice, "Hello there, Mrs. Clean. Did you forget we were coming?"

Ellen did not reply or change the rhythm of her scrubbing.

Now Laurel was alarmed. "Ellen, what's wrong?"

After a long, agonizing moment, Ellen lifted a dripping hand and wiped her brow. "They killed Bruno." The voice was a growl, barely recognizable.

"Oh, no." Not Bruno, the gorilla that had eaten wild berries out of Ellen's palm. At Laurel's touch, Ellen pulled away. In the basin a white shirt floated in brownish suds; next to the basin, a crumpled pair of blue jeans, saturated with what was certainly blood.

"We found him about an hour ago. They took his head and hands, to sell for their damn jujus."

Gordon and Ngira came in then. Ellen didn't acknowledge them. She went back to scrubbing and made a sound, somewhere between groan and deep sigh. "No matter how hard I try I can't protect them. I just can't win. It's only a matter of time."

Laurel looked helplessly at Gordon and Ngira. "One of her gorillas was killed." She glanced back at Ellen. Whatever she was washing must be shredded by now. "I think you should sit down for a while, Ellen."

"I'm all right."

"Miss Webster, you may be in shock." Ngira walked to her and gently took hold of her forearms. With her mechanical motion halted, Ellen's knees buckled. She allowed them to guide her to the easy chair. Laurel got a blanket from the bedroom and tucked it around her. Gordon found an open bottle of whiskey on the table and poured a glassful. She gulped it down.

"Thank you," she said. "Hell of a welcome for you and your friends, Laurel. I was so looking forward to your visit." Something like a whimper, then a cough. "Really, I'm all right now, no need to fuss. I just took some time to – but now I'm fine. I do need to go down to Park Headquarters, make a report and get some rangers to help in the search. My men are out tracking the poachers now, even Ben." She threw off the blanket and lurched to the door. "Please, make yourselves at home, there's food here for a change. I should be back tomorrow, and then we can make up for lost time."

"Ellen, it's almost dark. You can't go down now."

"Sure I can, Laurel. I've done it lots of times. You know where everything is, so just help yourself. The men can bunk in the guest house." Ellen's brow contracted in concentration. She pulled on her parka, grabbed a flashlight and the shotgun that hung over the door.

Laurel looked desperately at the two men. "But Ellen, you're still probably in shock, like Ngira said. Can't you wait until morning at least?"

"Yes, that's the better plan," Gordon said. "I'm certain the Park office will be closed by now."

"That's true, Gordon," Ellen said as if she had known him all her life, "but I know where the head ranger lives. I'll roust him, don't you worry."

"I'll go with you." Gordon put on his hat, despite Ellen's protestations.

"I will go too," Ngira said.

Laurel reached for her parka. "Yes, we'll all go."

Ellen was already out the door. Gordon paused long

enough to say, "Ngira, you stay here with Laurel. No sense in all of us crashing around in the dark," then tromped out after her.

Laurel ran to the door. "Hey, you might need some back-up!" she shouted, but Gordon had already vanished. All right, more than likely she would slow them down, but still, she wanted to help, damn it. Turning back inside, she saw Ngira's crestfallen look.

"Really, Ngira, I don't need a babysitter. Go catch up to them. I know you want to go, and they need you more than I do." Even as she said this, she knew she didn't want to be left alone.

He hesitated only a moment. "No. You should not stay here alone. Anyway, Gordon will be the best one to deal with the authorities."

"Maybe," she said. Yes, a white male would definitely carry more weight with whomever they were going to see. She would be excess baggage. But Ngira certainly could have gone. "Anyway, thank you for staying with me."

"You are welcome. But what a dreadful thing. That poor woman."

"Yes, she works so hard, tries so hard to protect those animals, and then something like this has to happen. Shit," she said. "Shit shit shit." She was aware of pacing around, Ngira watching her. The bottle of whiskey was still there on the table. Laurel reached for it, as if to study the label. "Want some?"

"I don't like it much. But if you're having some I will join you."

Laurel found two clean glasses and poured an inch or so into each.

Ngira took a sip. "I have never understood what Gordon

sees in this stuff." They laughed.

"I don't know how I can be laughing at a time like this," Laurel said.

"Laughing is better medicine than whiskey."

"I'm glad Gordon went with her. Otherwise she would have gone on her own."

He shrugged. "She is very determined, but I doubt they will catch the men who did it."

Laurel went to the washbasin. "It must have been horrible for her, finding Bruno like that. She was so fond of him. She told me his trust was the best gift she had ever received." In the basin was Ellen's shirt, in water made brown from blood. "God, why did it have to be Bruno?"

She squeezed out the shirt and put the jeans in the basin, wondering for a moment if these were the same pair she had borrowed when she was last here. The scrubbing motion felt good, and she understood why Ellen had needed to lose herself in it. As she drained the basin and pumped in clean water for the rinse, she released a heavy sob.

Ngira came up and gently touched her shoulder, then moved away. "I will go to the other cabin now, so you can rest."

"Actually, I need to eat something. How about you?"

Ngira glanced doubtfully at their small box of food. "What is there?"

"Well, I picked up some Trufru peanut butter, one of the staples of my diet." She quickly squeezed out the shirt and jeans, dried her hands. "Did you ever have a peanut butter and jelly sandwich?"

He smiled. "I have always thought the sandwich a useful invention. A neat package, and you can eat it all up. As for peanut butter and jelly –" he rolled his eyes – "tonight, even that will be most welcome."

"Okay, two PB and J, coming up."

"I will make some tea."

They moved awkwardly in the small space, avoiding contact with each other. For some minutes they ate in silence, the weight of Ellen's grief still heavy in the cabin's little kitchen. Laurel had wanted to share the magical beauty of this place, but all that was shattered. She hoped they would be able to salvage something of their visit when Ellen got back.

"Poor Ellen. Her work here is everything to her. I admire her courage."

"She has chosen a difficult life."

"My mother wanted me to be a concert pianist, but I always knew I would never be good enough. I've always wondered if it was just a lack of courage."

Ngira smiled. "But how can a person live in someone else's dream?"

"It felt like failure. Still does."

"But now you have decided to be a teacher, and already you are not a failure at that."

"I don't know. I hope not. The students here are very motivated, and that really helps. When I go back home I plan to teach music to young children. I want to teach them to listen, to think about how they feel when they hear, and to make their own music. But I don't know if I know how to think like a child. I never had many playmates my own age, and I don't have any brothers or sisters."

Ngira rested his chin on his hand. "But a good teacher must have a mature wisdom. And while it is true that brothers and sisters are blessings, they can also be troublesome. My older brother John was put in charge of me, and both of us were expected to tend my father's cattle. When we took them to the hillsides to graze, John always told me he would take care of the cows on the upper slope, so I would not have to climb so far." He chuckled. "Of course we both knew that cows prefer the lower part of the hillside because it is wetter and has better grass, so I always had twice as many cows to worry about."

Laurel laughed.

"But I did not really mind, allowing him to think he was tricking me. I always made better grades in school, which caused our father to berate him. This was a source of resentment. At times I think he hated me."

Laurel had not had to compete with a sibling; but she knew how John must have felt, not living up to a parent's expectations.

"I've actually been trying to do some composing. I know it's not something to stake my future on, but the more I do, the more I want to do." She had never spoken this to anyone besides Tessa. Not even Alan, who would have regarded it as a hobby. She felt her chest constrict the way it did whenever she allowed this dream to take shape in her mind. "And I don't see why I shouldn't. Just because there haven't been many female composers, doesn't mean I can't succeed." Now that it was out, she felt good. Saying the words gave them the force of possibility.

Ngira smiled. "You will shine in whatever you do, Laurel." His eyes held hers for a moment before breaking away. "Now you should get some sleep. I will go down to the guest house."

"Wouldn't you like to stay a little longer? I don't feel very tired. I guess I'm still upset."

He picked up his rucksack. "I do not think I should, Laurel."

She did not want him to leave. "The truth is, I'd rather not be alone tonight, with the poachers still out there. Do you think you could sleep here instead of going down to the cabin? You could take the spare bedroom, and I'll stay out here on the sofa."

"Since you ask it, I will stay." He glanced at the small sofa. "But you must have the bedroom. I will be fine out here."

All right, so it was not exactly proper, but she really was frightened at the prospect of being alone in Ellen's strange, dark, violent world. Though it occurred to her that she was being childish and probably selfish to make him sleep where he would not be comfortable, she was really, really glad he had agreed.

31

Moonlit Sonata

She woke up in the middle of the night with the moon streaming through the small window of Ellen's spare bedroom. There were the unfamiliar shapes and musty smells, then the pressing need of a walk to the outhouse in the dark. She pulled on her damp jeans and socks and went into the living room, expecting to find Ngira asleep on the sofa.

His sleeping bag was on the floor, empty.

She went to the window. The clearing was awash in moonlight, and there as before were the elephants moving like great ships on a calm sea. Ngira was sitting on the front step, looking from the back like a Buddha seated at the entrance to a temple.

She picked up her boots and went out to sit next to him in the cold air. He smiled at her but did not speak. The only sounds were the gentle crack and snap of vegetation as the massive elephants and small, slender duiker browsed together in the moonlight. A large rat scurried out of the forest, sniffed around the cold ashes of the pit fire, ran back to the dark wall of trees and disappeared.

She hated to break the spell. "I have to go to the outhouse."

"I will walk with you."

They moved slowly and calmly, drawing only a few huffs from the animals. At the latrine Ngira waited some yards away while Laurel went in. The moon was so bright they hadn't needed a flashlight, but inside it was dark except for a ghostly slit of light on the toilet paper. She tried not to think about rats and spiders and got out of there as quickly as she could.

"It was very dark in there." She shuddered. "By the way, why are you up?"

He smiled. "Same as you, only I was not brave enough to use the latrine. Then," he nodded to indicate the moonlit clearing, "I did not want to go back inside."

"I know what you mean. This place is incredible at night."

"Yes, incredible."

Laurel looked into the blackness of the forest. "I wonder where they are, how they're doing."

"They are no doubt searching for the poachers, though it is difficult at night. Don't worry, Gordon is more sensible than he seems. He will take good care of her."

They walked back to the house, lingering on the porch.

"Ellen's pretty good at taking care of herself," she said. "Coming in?"

"Yes, in a minute. You go ahead."

Laurel washed her hands at the kitchen sink, shivering. In the bedroom she quickly took off her jeans and socks and huddled into her bag. She heard Ngira in the main room, getting into his bag.

As warmth pulled her toward sleep, uneasy thoughts and images kept her awake. If only she could rewind the last two days and save Bruno, she would wake up to find Ben and Ellen in the kitchen fixing a hearty breakfast and making plans for their day. It was generous of Gordon to go with Ellen. She knew Ngira would have gone, too, if it wasn't for her.

He was so near, just in the next room, she might be able to

hear him breathing – but no, nothing. Outside, walking side by side, if only he had put his arm around her. At the recollection, her breath came fast and shallow. Oh God, she thought, I'm attracted to him. Really attracted; the force of it made her sit up. She was not a virgin. She and Alan had made love whenever they could arrange it. But Ngira? They were just friends. And what about his engagement to Theresa?

Impressive, Gordon had said. Was she tall and thin, or short and voluptuous? Did she have light brown skin, like Ngira, or shiny black like Mr. Senwangama? Ngira had spent whole nights with this Theresa; Carolyn had heard that piece of gossip from Gordon. She tried to imagine what kind of lover he would be, but what did she really know about him? Carolyn's rule number one: *No Africans. There's VD and crabs to think about, for starters.* But that was Carolyn. Carolyn had not bothered to know Ngira in her months at the school, his intelligence, sense of humor, the way he laughed. The way he said her name, his voice wrapping around like an embrace. "Live for Today," it was a rock song sung with smooth vocals and taut electric guitar; she could hear it drumming in her head like a mantra.

Laurel was hit by a wave of panic as she knew what she was going to do. She held the bag around her waist to cover her bare legs and let them carry her into the living room. She saw Ngira's form inside his bag, motionless. She could hardly breathe, her heart was beating so hard.

"What is the matter, Laurel?"

"I'm sorry, um, the cot in the spare room is too lumpy. I'll try Ellen's bed."

"Good idea." He turned on his side, away from her.

Leave now, she thought, before it's too late. But she felt frozen in place, every cell in her body going taut even as she tried to sound casual. "So, now you can sleep in the spare bedroom, if you want."

He sat up. "I am fine here." He sounded fully awake. "The floor is not lumpy, at least." There was teasing in his voice. She could just make him out in the dim light. He was wearing his khaki shirt. His shorts and socks were draped over the hulking back of the easy chair, the way laundry was dried over the crowns of bushes. A wave of nausea welled up. They were friends, friends, it would be stupid to spoil it, he would think all American girls were oversexed like Carolyn, and she didn't want him of all people to think that.

"All right then." She forced herself to turn toward Ellen's room, the bag swishing behind like a bride's train. *Regulate*, for heaven's sake. *Regulate*.

"Laurel." *Lah-rel*.

"Yes?"

He lay back and let out a long sigh. "Nothing. Sleep well."

She stood there a moment with the blood pumping loudly in her ears before she spoke his name.

He sat up again, and something, some vibration of thought or desire, overcame the distance between them. She dropped the blanket from around her waist and, bare legs catching the moonlight, walked toward him.

"I – I just want to –"

"Shh. Come to me." His voice entered her like a caressing hand. She sank down next to him. Now she could see the outlines of his face, his lips slightly apart, dark eyes intense with wanting. He touched her hair, brushing down over her neck, then took her head in his hands and held her eyes with his. *Laurel*. His lips met hers in a quick shock, like static. Their eyes reconnected, and she felt another spark of heat. She pulled back.

He said, "Do you want to stop?"

"I don't know."

He let out a long breath. "You are so lovely."

"I'm afraid."

"Yes." He sat back, smiling. "I am too."

She giggled nervously. What to do, how to act? He was looking at her, tense, waiting. She felt a tremor, a bloom of sweat. She unbuttoned his shirt and awkwardly pushed it from his shoulders, not quite daring to touch his skin. When he fumbled with her buttons, she undid them, exposing her breasts and watching his eyes take her in. She was suddenly calm.

"Are you still afraid?"

She smiled. "No."

"We must be careful. I don't have anything."

It took her a moment to register the sudden memory of Carolyn's gift, still in the bottom of her rucksack.

Clutching her shirt closed again she went back into the bedroom, and when she came back to him with the little package folded in her hand, she felt absurdly happy. There was this golden moonlight bathing everything like a warm rain, and there was nothing to stop them now –

He unzipped his sleeping bag and she saw that he wore jockey shorts, a knowledge that seemed touchingly intimate. He took them off, then helped her slip out of her panties. It pleased her, this sudden nakedness; it was right that they should be naked together. He took her hand and pulled her to him, held her so close there was all of him against her, each muscle and bone, every movement of breath. "I will be happy just to hold you like this," he whispered.

As she clung to him, there in the moonlight, the truth of

what she wanted most at that moment came to her, and there was nothing to prevent it, and it was all that mattered.

A tremor, and then, no words, no thoughts, no memories. His moist sweet smell the pearwood of her recorder; skin against skin, warmth, wetness, stillness.

When they lay resting, she watched her white fingers trace over his dark skin and the sprigs of hair on his chest and belly, down the thick strong muscle of his thigh.

* * *

She reluctantly left his warmth and went back to her bed, so they would not be found together if someone returned early in the morning. Away from him, regret flowed in and kept her awake. Why had she gone and spoiled things? Until tonight he had never indicated any desire for her; maybe he had only pretended, to avoid embarrassing her. She must be crazy. They could not become lovers, it would be impossible at school. And he would not want rumors to get back to Theresa. They would have to act like it never happened. Blame it on the night, the tragic circumstances, and put it behind them. Just as it was starting to get light, she finally fell asleep.

She awakened with a start to broad daylight, the smell of food cooking and the sound of voices. Ben was busy in the kitchen, Ngira sitting in the easy chair with a leg draped over one of its arms. His smile reached into her, but she walled it off with embarrassment and regret.

"We should forget about last night, Ngira, and go on as before. It's better that way, don't you think?"

He looked at her intently, but did not answer.

"Madama." Ben nodded at her. "There is coffee."

"Thank you." She didn't like coffee, but a cup in her hand

and Ben's presence provided a distraction from the unanswered challenge still hanging between her and Ngira. "Ben, have you seen Ellen and Gordon?"

"Oh yes, Madama say, all is okay. She come back soon."

"Thank goodness." Laurel looked at Ngira. Their eyes met, but she broke the contact. There had been no pretending in the way he held her. Now she felt like a traitor, a saboteur.

"Break-fast?" asked Ben. Laurel was very hungry. As she and Ngira sat down to the rare treat of corned beef, eggs, and toast, Ngira questioned Ben in Kinyarwanda. Apparently Ellen, Gordon and some Park guards had taken custody of the one poacher whom they had succeeded in capturing, and were taking him to the Park Conservator in Ruhengeri.

"I wish there was some way to help, but there is no use asking Ben to bring us down," Ngira said, "since we would have no way of getting to Ruhengeri. All we can do is wait."

"Yes, I suppose. Ben must be exhausted anyway, being out all night like that."

They decided to fill the time by taking a walk around the camp. As they were getting ready to go, Ngira said, "I know you are already engaged. I am sorry if last night caused you some regrets."

Laurel stopped lacing her boots. "Engaged?" Of course, Carolyn had planted that idea with Gordon. "No, I'm not engaged. I was, but not anymore. There's nothing for you to be sorry about, Ngira. It was my fault." She drew in a deep breath. In the light of day it was time to be adult, face reality. They could not be lovers at school. "I wasn't thinking straight. I was upset, I guess. Let's forget it ever happened."

"Yes, perhaps that would be best after all." He turned away and walked out the door.

Her heart sank. So I was right, she thought, he really doesn't care, only went along with me because I gave him no choice. Give the white woman what she wants, ugh, how embarrassing. She didn't know whether to be relieved, or angry, or what, but all she wanted was to cry. She didn't. She quickly finished putting on her boots and ran to catch up with him. "Speaking of being engaged, why don't you ever talk about Theresa?" It came out sounding accusatory, as if he were suddenly the enemy.

He turned toward the forest and sighed. "Because I will disappoint her, and that makes me ashamed."

Laurel felt her face get hot, her pulse quicken. "I'm sorry to be nosy, but how will you disappoint her?"

He avoided her eyes. "Nosy. What a comical sort of word." That was all he said.

They wandered past the guest cabin, stopping to look into the windows at the clean rooms and bare cots. She could picture Ngira as he should have been last night, asleep on one of those beds, safe from this lascivious white girl who he thought was a friend. How much easier things would be now if she had just let him go.

"Ngira, just so you know, I don't expect anything from you because of what happened last night."

He made a motion as if to reach out to her, but then the arm changed course to lean against the rough surface of the cabin wall. She knew that arm, the strength of it, how smooth and warm his skin would be under the parka sleeve.

His eyes looked past her to the forest. "I understand."

Her mouth was tacky with some bitter taste, probably from the coffee. "It just seems to me that we shouldn't rock the boat right now, you know, with school and everything."

212

He sighed. "I would never want to cause your boat to rock, but I don't believe that is the true reason –"

Suddenly there was a sound of voices from the trailhead. They froze for a moment like startled antelope. Good, Laurel thought, there would be time for this conversation back at Butawanga, after she had time to think things through. She had to be careful about rushing into things. That was her usual way, her *karma* as Tess would say, like last night; the flip side, too often, was regret.

Laurel felt the relief at this diversion was mutual as they walked quickly to meet the sound. It was Ellen and Gordon, Kitumba, Ellen's two trackers, and two men in uniform who must be Park guards. Gordon was flushed from exertion and talking animatedly.

Ellen looked haggard, her eyes staring blankly out of dark sockets. She coughed deeply. "Laurel, sorry we've been so long. Are you all right?"

"I'm fine, Ellen. How about you?"

"I'm okay. I just need a cigarette." She rallied her mouth into a brief smile. "We managed to get one of them, you know."

"Yes, Ben told us. I'm glad. How are you, Gordon?"

"I'm all right." He grinned. "Ellen knows her way around this bloody mountain. I could barely keep up." He winked gallantly at Ellen. Laurel suddenly remembered that they had not moved Ngira's things to the guesthouse, but it was too late to worry about that now.

When they trooped into the cabin, Ben was again standing at the propane stove cooking. He must have seen them coming. "Madama," he said, eyes glistening.

"Oh, Ben." She let her hand rest like an injured bird on his shoulder.

He patted her hand. "Sit-a down, Madama. You must eat."

Ellen slumped into a chair and invited Gordon to join her. She asked Laurel if they had eaten. Ngira began rolling up his sleeping bag.

"Did you two have a peaceful night, then?" Gordon said.

"I slept very well, thank you. Laurel took the guest room, and I slept here as guard."

Gordon raised his eyebrows, but turned his attention to the plate of steaming food before him. Both Ellen and Gordon ate in silence for a few minutes.

"Food is good, Ben. But you must be about dead on your feet. You go down to the bunkhouse and have a rest, we'll clear this up later."

"Yes, Madama."

Ben wiped the cooking area and poured the grease out of the frying pan, folded the dishcloth and walked out the door.

Ellen got a pack of cigarettes from her desk. Gordon accepted one, produced a silver lighter from his shirt pocket and lit Ellen's, then his own. Ellen settled back in her chair, took a long deep drag, exhaled slowly, coughed. "Laurel, thanks for bringing Gordon up here just when I needed him. He was a big help. His French is a lot better than mine."

Gordon gave a smug grin. "Glad to be of service."

"And thank you, Ngira, for guarding my camp and keeping Laurel company."

"It was my pleasure, Miss Webster." Ngira answered in such a formal voice that Laurel giggled foolishly.

"I'll bet it was," Gordon said, then gave out with a loud yawn. "Good Lord, I'm knackered. Ngira, let's move our gear down and I'll get a bit of a rest, if that's all right with you, Ellen."

"Of course. Make yourselves at home. I might grab a nap too."

After the men left, Laurel sat down, feeling the unbridgeable gulf of Ellen's pain between them. Ellen's hand propped on the table was trembling enough to knock ash from the cigarette hung between her fingers. Her face looked as lifeless as a mask, except for a line of tears that flowed from one eye leaving a trail down her dusty cheek.

32

Pandora's Box

"From now on I will never love another living thing." Ellen sounded offhand, as if remarking on the weather.

"Ellen, why don't you go in and get some sleep? You must be worn out."

"You're right, Laurel, I do need to sleep. But not yet." She grabbed the quarter-full bottle of scotch and two dirty glasses, poured some into each, and drank hers down as if it were water and she was dying of thirst. It was one o'clock in the afternoon.

"They took his head and his hands, but I've decided they did that as an afterthought. Most likely they were after the infant. They bring top dollar from foreign zoos." After another sucking swallow, she refilled her glass. "Bruno died defending his family. They were able to escape, while he stayed behind to fight the dogs and spears."

"Oh, Ellen. I'm so sorry."

"No, don't be sorry, sorry is useless. Talk to me, talk to me about anything. Tell me about you and Ngira."

"Me and Ngira?" Laurel gave a tense laugh. "What do you mean?"

"Gordon told me there might be a budding romance between you two – but forget it, none of my business." Ellen sipped at her whisky with unfocused eyes.

Laurel reached for the whiskey Ellen had poured for her, for the cool steady weight of it in her hand, and looked down into the amber liquid.

"Ngira and I are friends, Ellen. Whatever Gordon might think is going on, he's wrong."

"Oh, well then, I suppose he was trying to take my mind off things with a little idle gossip. He's kind of sweet, in his way."

Laurel did not relax her grip on the glass. "I'm glad you and Gordon got along so well."

"And his French was a big help with the Park Director, who is Belgian. Usually I rely on Karl and Yvonne to help me deal with Monsieur le Directeur. The smug little bastard, I know he authorizes a lot of these zoo deals, but he always plays innocent."

Laurel was relieved at the change of subject.

"He's a criminal, that one. A big, fat, lying colonial son of a bitch." Ellen snorted into her glass and swallowed another jolt of whiskey. "But never mind him now. Where were we – oh, yes. Ngira seems intelligent, and Gordon says he's a brick. That's Brit for a good, reliable sort. But how would you tell your parents you were coming home with a black African?"

The words hit Laurel like a blow to the spine; her mouth fell open, and for a moment she couldn't speak.

"What's wrong? Is it the whiskey?"

"He's not a black African, Ellen. I mean he is, but he's not some nameless person, he's Ngira."

"Well, okay, but is that the way your parents would see it?"

Laurel let go of her still untouched glass of whiskey. She could feel herself bristle. "It doesn't matter how my parents would see it, or anyone." This had to be true, because it was right. "It only matters how I see it, and Ngira. And I lied

217

before. There is something between us. Last night we made love, right here in your living room."

Ellen sank back into her chair. "Oh, my."

"And I thought we could just put it behind us, but how can we really? He has a fiancée, but he told me – I'm not even sure what he told me. It sounded like he might not marry her. To tell you the truth, I was glad."

Ellen looked overwhelmed. "So you love him?"

"Yes. No. I don't know." She laughed miserably, recalling that day that she and Carolyn first arrived at Butwagana, the tea at Mr. Senwangama's, Ngira like the bull in a china shop. "When I first met him, I wasn't impressed. I think it was Shakespeare who said that it can't be love if it isn't love at first sight. That makes sense, doesn't it?"

"Not necessarily."

"But I've never trusted first impressions. People and places have to grow on me. Now there's no one I'd rather be with. He's my Brahms." If that sounded silly, so be it.

"What?"

Laurel took a deep breath. *Regulate.* "Clara Schumann, the pianist and composer, married to Robert, who was way more famous as a composer. But Brahms was such a good friend that he became an indispensable part of her life, even though she was married." Everything was beginning to come clear, like the sudden connection of musical phrases into a coherent, brilliant line. "Most historians think their relationship was strictly platonic. If they were lovers they were very good at not getting caught. But who wants to live that way, never showing your real feelings, sneaking around like criminals –"

Ellen's raised eyebrows scored her forehead with hard lines. "What will you do now?"

"God, I don't know." Now, the smack of reality. Theresa. Butawanga. Ngira, walking out the door that morning with his dismissive *Yes, perhaps that would be best.* "We won't pursue it, that's all. We've already agreed."

"That's probably wise. It's just as well not to set yourself up for a fall."

"What do you mean?"

"What will you do when you go back to the States, take him along?"

"Well, why not?" She tried to imagine Ngira with her in Boston, the two of them in some cheap apartment, his ebullient voice boxed within its walls. "Or I could stay here, sign on for another tour with Peace Corps, for a start, and then be some kind of contract teacher. There's not that much I would miss in the States." As she said this, she knew it wasn't true. Home was still back there. "I could have a piano brought in –"

Ellen reached out and squeezed Laurel's hand. "Laurel. You're from two different worlds. My advice is, leave it that way." She poured herself another glass of scotch.

Laurel flared at this. "If you can be happy living here, why can't I? If we were determined enough, I think we could make it work, Ngira and I." Ngira and I; saying it was like riding the perilous Kabale to Kisoro Road, with nothing to keep the bus from falling off the cliff. "Crap, I don't know. I used to think I knew what I wanted – a musical career, a husband, children, not necessarily in that order. I was all set to marry Alan, but I broke up with him and came over here."

As Laurel talked, Ellen listed slowly from side to side, like a boat caught up in the wake of a larger one.

"Alan saw everything through his eyes, never through mine. At least when people come from different worlds, like

219

Ngira and I, they have to try to understand each other. Right?"

Ellen looked up, bloodshot and bleary. "There was a moon last night. It's nice the way it comes into the cabin. The only thing missing was the roses." She emptied the last drops from the bottle into her glass and swallowed it down. "Last month when Paul came up here, he told me he was going back to his wife, this time for good."

Paul? Laurel scrambled to catch up with what Ellen was telling her. She had never considered that Ellen might have a lover. "I'm sorry."

"So was I. You see, that's what I mean about setting yourself up for a fall." She exhaled a sickly smell of liquor. "I knew it was coming, he made that clear right from the start. Little wife back home and so on, damn her. A real brick of a little wife." Her shoulders slumped as if the normal pull of gravity was suddenly too much for them. "I never told him about the abortion. What difference could it have made?" She got up and stumbled into her bedroom, fell heavily onto the bed and slept.

Laurel was stunned. Abortion was not something people usually talked about. But of course, there would be no other choice for Ellen. She went in and laid a blanket over her, walked out and closed the door.

* * *

They stayed two more days. Laurel was heartened by the strength of Ellen's embrace at parting. Ellen accepted the two cassette tapes and promised to listen to them when she was feeling less fragile. In return, she gave Laurel a tape of recorded forest sounds. Laurel had completely forgotten about asking, so this unexpected gift was even more precious.

Laurel hoped they could come back again soon, perhaps at the end of August before the new term started. Gordon was obviously captivated by Ellen and would no doubt be easy to persuade.

As for Ngira, he was captivated by the place. "Most of the ancient forests are gone now, but this," he said, "this is almost untouched. We are seeing what God put here with the first wave of His hand."

No wonder Father Matthew called him Rabelais. It had puzzled her before. Ngira, the philosopher. He had not spoken again about what had happened between them. If he could forget it, so could she.

It would be friendship, then, even more polite and proper than before. Like Clara and Brahms. Avoid the complications. Forget the sense of guilt and betrayal. Ignore the terrible attraction. Put desire in a box and lock it away. It would be much, much better that way.

Two different worlds. This mountain was another world, separate and somehow sacred. Ngira was right about that. She could hear it all around, the susurrations of respiration and growth, the creaking, groaning, shuddering of a life force so strong it seemed capable of transforming her own guilt, even Ellen's grief, into the most forgiving of melodies.

As they picked their way down the steep trail, Runagaba and Ngira in front of her, Gordon behind, Laurel felt oddly buoyant. Everything would be all right. The music of this magical creation, Ellen's parting gift, was tucked away in her backpack, yet to be savored. Ngira was just ahead, moving easily, gracefully, and more slowly than he would be if she were not there. He had always been considerate of her, deferential even, and she had taken advantage of it. She had decided that

221

what came next was up to him. She wanted him, but she wasn't sure if this was love, and of what his feelings were toward her. Let things rest for a while. However it went, at least she would always have this one silver chord of their night on the mountain to hold to herself, shining in memory like a perfectly played sonata.

33

The Border

The Saab clamored over bumpy, dusty roads through green countryside, taking them away from the mountain and back toward Butawanga. Laurel tried to unravel the implications of everything that had happened. She felt guilty about leaving Ellen alone with her grief. And then there was Ngira, folded into the seat behind her. She did not need to look at him to feel his presence like a pedal point, the constant tone around which other musical parts move. The way they had come together, the incredible harmony of it, was the memory that reproached her for that morning when she had denied him the truth of how he had made her feel – his mouth brushing her skin, the soft probing of his fingers and that particular way he had entered her, slow, certain, the intensity building with each new layer of feeling until she lost herself in it, in him. Sex with Alan had been like climbing a ladder, always the same steps, and afterward he would ask how it was, scale of one to ten–

"She's quite a woman, isn't she?" Gordon's voice was a jolt.

"Yes." Ngira said. "I would agree, quite a woman."

Ngira's intimate tone, as if he had read her thoughts, made her blush. She kept facing forward. "Poor Ellen. I hope she'll be all right."

Gordon snorted. "She's tough, but she's fighting a losing battle."

"Now you sound like Yvonne Hauber," Laurel said. The terrible thing was, they both might be right.

Ngira sighed. "It is very difficult, but she is a person who follows her heart. In the long run, I think she will succeed."

Now she glanced back. Ngira was studying the scene outside the tiny side window, the monotonous low shrubs and dry red earth, the occasional small shamba set back from the road. She looked at him sitting with his face turned away, his bent knees almost level with his shoulders. She knew the smooth tight skin of those hands and forearms, glossy and cool like the skin of a mango, and she craved his touch the way her struggling carnations craved the sun. She knew his uncircumcised penis, how she had been unsure about how to touch him and he had guided her, then put on the condom when no pleasure of foreplay could delay them any longer.

She had not come to Africa to fall in love. Ellen was right: where could a relationship like this go? Pursuing it at Butawanga would mean complications for them both. Assuming he even wanted to. She would need to keep temptation out of the equation: no more intimate conversations on her steps with the darkness gathering outside, no walks into the hills, no being alone together anywhere.

Maybe loving her was the furthest thing from Ngira's mind. That would make things a whole lot easier. After all, he had Theresa. Still, that heat between them, it made her pulse race even now as she looked at him, wanting to read him, to know what he was thinking. As if feeling her look he turned, unsmiling, and her heart sank. Of course, he had lost all respect for her. It was that simple, a one-night stand. Love was an order of magnitude different. And what did she know about it, anyway, given the way she had thought she was in love with

224

Alan – she blinked back tears.

Ngira looked at her. "What is the matter, Laurel?"

"Nothing," she said miserably. "Some dust in my eyes."

"Keep them closed the rest of the way, then. We are almost home."

The concern in his voice touched her. She smiled. "It's okay, they're better now." She wanted more than anything to reach out and touch his hand, but settled for keeping him talking, the first thing that came into her head – "Do you have another name besides Ngira? Father Matthew calls you Rabelais. That can't really be your first name, can it?"

"When I first came to Butawanga, I borrowed a book by Francois Rabelais from the mission library. So the name is Father Matthew's little joke. He is a strange man. In fact I am Ngira, David."

This unexpected revelation was like a bolt of electricity. Laurel tried it out on her tongue. "David." Just a moment ago she had not known this about him, and now she did. David Ngira. A good name, a remarkable name.

Gordon turned full around to stare at Ngira. "Well, old son, aren't you the close one. In all these years, you never told me you were named David."

"In all these years, you never asked," Ngira said, winking at Laurel. "Anyway, I prefer my African name."

"Right, well, and I'm the bloody king of England, and I decree a beer at Travellers Rest as soon as we clear the borders."

* * *

This time, the Rwandan border guard insisted on searching their belongings. The guard in charge made a cursory inspection of each bag, which by now contained mostly soiled and odoriferous clothing. After a small tip from Gordon and a brief exchange out of Laurel's hearing, he sent them on their way.

Back in the car, Ngira said, "I don't like the sound of that."

"It's probably just some misunderstanding."

"What are you two talking about?"

"That guard said the Uganda border is closed. Some rot about keeping spies out of the country." Gordon waved his hand in the air, as if shooing a pesky insect. "Things do tend to get exaggerated. At any rate, nothing to worry about. The Ugandan guards know us, they'll let us pass."

But there was no sign of any guard at this border station, only four Ugandan soldiers in dusty tan uniforms. Each man grabbed one of the guns lined up along the side of the small guardhouse, ran out into the road and pointed it at the car.

"AK-47s," Gordon rasped as he braked hard. "Bloody hell."

"There is our Captain Aiwa from Travellers Rest," Ngira said quietly.

Laurel looked around hopefully for the guard who had passed them through just a few days earlier, or for Samuel to come striding down the path, smiling, plastic shoes flapping. But there were only soldiers. They circled, guns level, bobbing up and down from the waist to peer into the car. Laurel sat frozen, her hand over her mouth.

"That bastard Aiwa must have known they would close the border, but he let us go anyway," Gordon said. "I can still jam it into reverse –"

"Bad idea –" Ngira did not have a chance to finish,

because Captain Ali Aiwa jerked open the driver's door and motioned Gordon out of the car.

A soldier yanked open the door on Laurel's side. She got out on wobbly legs. Ngira squeezed out of the back seat to stand next to her.

At a barked command from their Captain, the men pushed Gordon and Ngira against opposite sides of the car's gritty roof, forcing them to stretch forward over it, and pinned them with rifles against the backs of their necks. Another soldier searched each one, slapping his hands along pants pockets and legs, while Laurel stood by, wide-eyed, heart racing.

Gordon tried to protest, his words choked off by renewed pressure on his neck. When the search was over and the two men allowed to stand, Gordon's eyes were shot with red. "Now see here, you can't do this. This will mean big trouble for you. I am a foreign national, and I will report this to the Ugandan government and the British High Commission."

Aiwa smirked. "I am begging your pardon, *Bwana*. We have orders to stop the crossing of spies and mercenaries over our borders."

"But Captain," Ngira said, almost jovially, "you know that we are teachers living at Butawanga. We are not spies."

"But, Mis-ta Teach-a," the man drawled, "who can say that a teacher is not a spy? Or, a woman?" He came so close that Laurel could feel the heat of his breath, smell the sour beer. She took a step back. He looked her up and down. "You must also be searched." A leering chuckle was echoed by his men. "For weapons."

She stood looking back at him, mind racing, face stinging hot. "I don't have any weapons."

"Why, you bloody bastard—" Gordon said between

227

clenched teeth.

"You must not do that," Ngira said. "It would be most improper –"

Aiwa pivoted to stare at Gordon and Ngira. He broke into a loud guffaw, again chorused by the other soldiers. "You must all be held for questioning." Although no one had touched her, Laurel was shaking.

Captain Aiwa told them to get back into their car and follow the Army Land Rover to Travellers Rest. Two soldiers rode in the back with guns pointed at the Saab.

No one spoke for a moment as Gordon wrestled with the gears. Laurel fought back tears. "This is all my fault. It was my idea to go in the first place."

"Don't be silly, Laurel. This is just a bloody game they're playing at. They're full of the local *pombe* and throwing their weight around a bit, that's all."

Ngira leaned forward from the back seat and put his hand on her shoulder. "Yes, that's right." She felt the firm pressure of his fingers and palm. "Try not to worry."

Laurel pressed her cheek against his hand. She didn't care if Gordon saw. She turned to look at Ngira, and knew that he would be waiting for her to decide, as he had that night at Ellen's. Knowing this calmed her. She wanted these soldiers to stop this stupid game and let them get back to Butawanga, where she could not wait to put her arms around Ngira and let him know she had already decided.

In front of Travellers Rest, Gordon parked the Saab behind the Army Land Rover. As they sat waiting, more soldiers came out of the hotel, and Captain Aiwa strolled back to the Saab and shouted at them to get out of the car.

He bowed like a doorman, indicating the door to the hotel.

228

"Step inside, if you please."

Gordon went first, followed by Laurel and behind her, Ngira, passing through the men now grouped on the porch on either side of the entrance. Suddenly there was a hand low on Laurel's back, a clucking sound, a man grabbing her buttocks so hard she cried out, *Hey*, tried to turn and push his hand away but he grabbed her wrist, twisted her arm behind her back and leaned in to bend her forward at the waist, leaned his hips hard against her. *Uh.* The others laughing, goading. A sharp pain in her shoulder, no breath, no words. Gordon was already inside and had not seen. Ngira, walking right behind her, wheeled around and shouted, "I see, Captain, that you have lost control of your men."

The tall man glared, and for a hair's breadth everything stopped. Laurel was still doubled over, a raw, gasping sound coming from her throat. Then Aiwa shouted: "*Kwisha*." The soldier took his hand away and she stood up, turned, but her attacker was already back standing with the others, all of them grinning, and she didn't even know who it had been. Her arm flopped loose, her other hand went to her shoulder. Breathing hard, unable to think, she stared in their faces and saw nothing there but cold indifference. As if she were not human but something else, something not worthy of respect. Ngira's hand on her arm nudged her into motion, and together they walked into the hotel, followed by titters from the men.

Gordon stared at her. "Wha — did something happen out there?"

She looked at the floor. Her face was still flushed, and wet, she realized, from what must have been tears.

"Bloody hell, Ngira, what happened? Laurel—are you all right?"

"One of the men was very rough with her. Aiwa called him off." Ngira said.

Gordon raised his voice, waved his arm. "What? The bastards—if they think they can get away with that sort of thing—"

"I'm all right, Gordon. Please, don't make a thing of it." She was weak now with dread of what might happen, what could have happened to her just a few minutes ago if Ngira hadn't—the soldier's hips, the hard line pressed into her buttocks. His brute power. The guns. They needed to go along with whatever it was this captain wanted, and get out of there.

It was a scene very much as before they had left, men seated at the bar and tables, smoking and drinking, with Mr. Rajaraman in nervous attendance. He glanced at them helplessly. There was no one to help them, no one who could help them. What happened now was up to this captain.

She stood between Gordon and Ngira in the middle of the dining room. She was sweating, heart pumping hard, as before a recital, as when the gorillas had attacked. Back by the door, Captain Aiwa was talking with Munde, the new storekeeper, Munde thick and stocky, the Captain long boned, lean.

Gordon whispered, "I can't hear much, but this Munde bloke seems to be trying to get us out of this."

"Yes, I think he was in the Army once. He has said Amin's name a few times." The soldier nearest Ngira poked him in the shoulder.

The conversation was short. Munde slapped Aiwa on the back in a friendly way and walked out the door. The Captain entered with the unhurried gait of a man in power. Maybe now he would say it was all a mistake, a bad joke, and let them go.

"Sit." He motioned impatiently for the soldiers at the

nearest table to get up. Laurel and Ngira sat down. Gordon remained standing.

"Let's get this cleared up right now, Captain," Gordon said. "As you know, we went to Rwanda on holiday. We had no idea there would be border restrictions when we came back, so I am sure you can see it was just a case of unfortunate timing." He cleared his throat and added in a confidential tone, "we will pay any fines you might think necessary –"

The hard-angled face looked bemused. "You are making bribe to me, Sir? *Unataka fanya chichiri?*" He boomed this out for all his men to hear. There were cackles from around the room.

"No, no, of course not. Only to compensate you for your time and trouble."

The Captain shook his head. "This very bad. First you try to cross border illegally, then you try to make bribe to me. Sit down."

Gordon's face was stiff with anger, but he took a seat with Laurel and Ngira. The Captain remained standing opposite them, flipping slowly through their passports and Ngira's identification. The silence pressed down. Laurel could hardly make herself look around, couldn't make herself look at the scarred twisted face of this man who, right now, unbelievably, held her life in his hands.

"I think you are spies. You go to Rwanda to bring information to enemies of government of Uganda. Admit to this!"

They all said "No" at the same time. They looked at each other, then Ngira said, "You are wrong. I am Ugandan, and my companions have come far from their own countries to teach our children. We are only what we seem. We have no other purpose."

231

Laurel and Gordon concurred and looked hopefully toward the Captain. His face was impassive. "This country has too many like you, little *msukumizi*."

Ngira looked stunned, then angry. "But surely, Captain, I am not the one making trouble."

Oh no, Laurel thought, don't antagonize him.

The man stared back, unblinking, the whites of his eyes yellowed and mucous. One of the soldiers who had remained outside walked officiously to Aiwa, diverting him from Ngira. The soldier held her cassette tape, the gift from Ellen, in the palm of his outstretched hand.

The Captain took it, asked the man some questions, then dismissed him. "So, what is this? A tape, but no machine for playing it? I think it is information from your traitor friends hiding in Rwanda!" He let the translation of his words ripple through his men before raising a hand to silence them.

"But it's only the rainforest." Laurel's voice sounded thin over the wild beating of her heart.

"We will see. Rajaraman! *Nataka machine-ay*."

He waved the cassette in the air without taking his eyes from them. Rajaraman disappeared into the hotel kitchen and returned a minute later with a small cassette player. He handed it to Captain Aiwa, who turned it over in his large hands and then thrust it back at the innkeeper. "Play it!" Rajaraman looked apologetically at Laurel, snapped the cassette into the machine and pressed the play button.

The first minutes were barely audible swishing sounds, the movement of air and vegetation. Rajaraman fiddled with the volume, turning it up to maximum. Suddenly a roar blared out with deafening clarity, and everyone in the room jumped. On the second roar the men started to laugh.

Then began what Ellen had called hootseries, a type of gorilla vocalization. As the hoo-hoos built in intensity, the laughter in the room got louder and less restrained. By the time the tape moved on to pig-grunts, the Captain was outraged. He signaled Rajaraman to turn it off.

He took the cassette, pulled long curls of silky brown tape out of its plastic housing and threw it all on the floor.

"The woman can go," he pronounced through clenched teeth. "The men must stay."

Laurel had not expected this. She looked at Gordon and Ngira. They looked back at her, wide-eyed.

She found her voice. "But – they must come with me."

"Go now, woman, or you be very sorry!"

She stood up and headed for the door, knees weak, then stopped and turned around. Gordon was pale, incapacitated with rage. Ngira's face glistened with a fine layer of sweat, but he smiled at her and nodded. She turned and went directly out.

She walked quickly away from the hotel, quickly past the faceless forms of the men searching Gordon's car and a litter of garments from their knapsacks, down the road into town, certain at any moment that she would feel arms, hands grab hold of her. Keep walking, don't panic, she told herself, folding her arms tightly across her chest as if it were the cold making her shudder. The late afternoon sun was lowering red.

At Gupta's store, Munde was leaning in his doorway, smoking a cigarette. She didn't trust him, but there was no one else to turn to. She took a deep breath.

"Mr. Munde, they are still holding Gordon and Ngira at Travellers Rest. Can you help?"

Munde took a long drag on his cigarette, then exhaled. "Ah, this a bad business, Miss. I cannot help your friends. They are in the hands of God – and that Captain there."

Laurel stiffened. "I can't just leave them there. You know the Captain, I saw you there talking to him. Please, come with me now, tell him he must let them go."

He answered with a slow grin, then a decisive head shake. He was not going to help.

"Then at least tell me, what can I do?"

"Go away, before he change his mind. I get you out once, but I am not succeeding again."

"You got me out?"

"I say to that Captain, I tell him General Amin he likes Americans." He chortled, scrubbed out his cigarette with the ball of his huge sandaled foot. "Aiwa, he is stupid man."

"But why would you do that for me?"

Munde shrugged. "I see you some time at Makerere, only passing by, but you are giving me nice smile." He turned away into his store.

Laurel stood for a moment trying to get control of her breathing, then stumbled off the porch and ran down the dusty road toward Butawanga.

34

Vortex

No one was on the road. No children, just the familiar clusters of banana trees, stands of sorghum and maize, cabbage patches, thatched rooftops. The dark rich earth, studded with stones. Everything and nothing was the same. Laurel ran as fast as she could, her only thought to get help, but how, where? The only short-wave radio was back at Travellers Rest. The mission was far, and would priests be able to deal with soldiers? Mr. Senwangama was her best hope, best hope, best hope, the words propelling her until she rounded the school road and staggered to the headmaster's door.

He was just finishing his supper. Her head was pounding and her mouth so dry for a moment her tongue felt paralyzed. "The Army is holding Ngira and Gordon at Travellers Rest," she rasped. "We have to get them out, right away."

Mr. Senwangama frowned and got up from the table.

"Please, may I have some water?"

He motioned to his servant and led her to a chair. "What is all this? Tell me again, and please be calm."

Laurel took a deep breath and drained a glassful of water. This was not a time for calm. "There are a lot of soldiers at Travellers Rest and the Captain in charge detained us. He kept insisting we were spies. He let me go, but not Gordon and Ngira. We have to go now, in your car. And let's stop at the mission. It might help to have them along."

His frown deepened. "Please, Miss Bittelson, try not to

upset yourself. I think there is very little danger. At most they will question them and let them go."

Laurel stood up. "No, Mr. Senwangama, I don't think so. This captain wouldn't listen to anything we said. He was very threatening, and he's got something against Ngira."

The Headmaster gave her the stern look usually reserved for troublesome students. Chest heaving, she returned his stare. "And one of the men hurt me."

"But this is terrible. Are you—"

"I'm fine. But please, let's go."

"Yes, yes, all right." He instructed his houseboy to get the driver, then went to put on his jacket and shoes. She waited as if trapped in the slow motion of a nightmare, an electric urgency firing her every cell.

They drove up to the mission. Father Matthew was not there, but she explained the situation to Phillip and Lawrence, all the while distressed by the pressure of time passing. Father Lawrence said that Laurel was most likely suffering from an overactive imagination brought on by having watched American television, but at Mr. Senwangama's urging both priests agreed to go along.

When they were finally on their way, she almost began to doubt her own assessment of the danger. The man was rough with her but he had not hurt her, really, not the way he could have – and they had all let her walk out of there. If they were intending to harm anyone they would not have let her go to sound the alarm, would they? Maybe the Captain was just having his little power game, as Gordon had said, and would let them go when he got bored. But why not let them all go at the same time? *Your friends are in the hands of God – and that Captain there.* Munde's words still echoed. She sat on the edge of the back seat in Mr. Senwangama's car, searching the road for any sign of Gordon's Saab. The two priests followed in the mission Mercedes.

About halfway to Kisoro, the driver pointed to a cloud of dust ahead. Mr. Senwangama said, "There they are now, you see?"

"Oh, thank God." She anticipated their voices: Gordon angry as a wet chicken and railing about reporting them to the authorities, Ngira deeply angry but covering it with humor. He liked American movie westerns; she could joke with him about bringing the "posse" to the rescue.

The Saab was not slowing down. Mr. Senwangama's driver had to swerve to avoid it as it barreled past and skidded to a stop off the road behind them. They all got out and ran to the car. It was Gordon, but his motionless form was slumped over the steering wheel.

The two priests opened the door and eased Gordon to the ground. He was unconscious. A bright red ribbon of blood ran down the side of his face, and one shoulder of his shirt was dark with blood and dust. Laurel choked back a scream.

"Concussion, shock at the least," Father Lawrence said. "We must get him to hospital."

"Oh my God," Laurel said when the full implications of what was happening hit her. "But where's Ngira?"

Mr. Senwangama's eyes widened. "We must find him." The men quickly decided that Father Phillip and Mr. Senwangama would go on to Kisoro, while Father Lawrence and Laurel took Gordon back to the mission hospital.

She clutched at the headmaster's arm. "Let me go to Kisoro with you."

Father Lawrence gave her a severe look. "I need someone

237

to keep pressure on the wound while we drive."

"Yes, that is best, Laurel," Mr. Senwangama said, gently removing her hand from his arm. "Father Phillip and I have more experience in these matters."

They had no idea what they were up against, but let them go, she thought, don't delay them.

"Well, let's not stand about any longer," Father Phillip barked. "We had best go see about the other chap, quick as we can. You'll manage, Lawrence?"

Father Lawrence nodded. "Yes, yes. Godspeed."

Father Phillip and Mr. Senwangama drove off with the driver in the Peugeot. Laurel watched the car recede with its pall of dust, wanting to be there to take Ngira's hand and see him smile at her. Msukumizi, troublemaker, the Captain had said. Godspeed, yes. There was Gordon, motionless on the ground. Father Lawrence touched her shoulder.

"All right, Miss Bittelson, we must get him into the back seat. You support his head and neck as I lift him."

The priest lifted Gordon's gangly frame with surprising ease. "Now, you get in the back seat and help pull him in."

They struggled to get Gordon lying as flat as possible on the backseat, his head on Laurel's lap. Blood oozed steadily from a blue-black gash on his temple and trickled down onto her jeans.

"Head wounds bleed a lot." Father Lawrence removed his white shirt and folded it into a compact square, covered the wound, then took Laurel's quaking hands and placed them one over the other on top. "Now, just a little pressure with the top hand." He gave her a thin smile. "You are all right?"

The question took a moment to register. "I'm all right, yes."

"Good. Let us go, then." The priest, white arms bare in his undershirt, got behind the wheel.

The Mercedes smoothed out the road, mercifully. She felt somehow emptied of emotion, as if her real self had gone to Kisoro to find Ngira, and what was left here in the car was a mannequin. She studied Gordon's face, his pale skin streaked with dried blood, his finely veined eyelids fluttering as he struggled toward consciousness. He groaned and coughed, his lips flecked with foamy spittle. Suddenly his head jerked in spasms. She snapped back into her body. "Father!"

"Good, he is coming around."

Gordon opened his eyes and stared blankly.

"Gordon? It's me, Laurel."

He blinked slowly, as if just raising and lowering his eyelids took the greatest effort. He groaned, then mumbled something.

"Gordon, we're taking you to the hospital." She steadied her voice. "Father Lawrence is here. You're going to be fine."

"No, no." He said this several times.

"It's all right. Just rest now."

He turned his head to look into her face.

"Gordon, you need to keep your head turned that way –"

"No, no, no," he wailed, suddenly loud. "There were shots, get help, go back." His face contorted with pain as he struggled to get up.

"Gordon, don't get up. Father Lawrence!"

The priest stopped the car and reached into the back to grab Gordon's shoulder. "Mr. Coopersmith, you really must lie down."

"No, no. Can't you understand?" He slumped back into the seat. "They shot Ngira." He closed his eyes and moaned.

239

Laurel sat paralyzed, holding the blood-soaked shirt, taking her breath in short sharp bites.

"He is quiet again. See if you can apply the compress please?"

She reached out and tried to hold the cloth against Gordon's wound as his head bobbled with the jostling of the car.

Then Father Lawrence's voice, sounding far away. "Ah, mon Dieu, mon Dieu." There was coldness, as if her heart had stopped, then a hot sickness so sudden that she barely had time to open the window before vomiting into the whirling black vortex of dust outside the car.

35

It was Marlowe

"Where both deliberate, the love is slight; Who
ever loved that loved not at first sight?"
Christopher Marlowe, *Hero and Leander*

Her mind a waterfall, a constant shush. She was cloistered
like a nun at the mission, and the fathers treated her like a
delicate, damaged instrument that no one knew how to put
back in tune.

Going over and over that night at Ellen's, what was said,
remembering that need to pull back from the exposure of
feeling. Those words she had not really remembered enough to
quote properly but had offered up to Ellen like some kind of
profound truth, when it was really an excuse not to trust what
every part of her besides her brain already knew. Father Phillip
had given her the original source: yes, Shakespeare, but
Shakespeare was quoting Christopher Marlowe. The priest's
mind contained a collection of such knowledge as rich as the
leather-bound books in the mission library. He didn't ask why
she wanted to know, or whether or not she agreed with the
sentiment. It had been love at first sight with Alan; but that love
had dwindled away. With Ngira love had grown, almost
unnoticed. Now it was too late.

The soldiers still billeted at Travellers Rest had not
intruded into the school or mission. The general opinion was

that if one stayed clear of them, there would be no trouble. Still, at Father Phillip's urging, Laurel had agreed to spend a few days at the mission before going back to her house at Butawanga. By then it was hoped the soldiers would be gone. He told her that the teachers at the school were reluctant to talk about things they heard. In Kampala, President Amin's secret police were picking up people from their homes or businesses, never to be seen again. From all over the country came reports of the Army stopping and robbing busloads of people, raping women and girls, stealing private vehicles and killing the owners. Stories of torture, blood rituals, executions, corpses floating in the Nile.

Laurel felt as if she had dropped off the end of the earth into some forgotten place, among people who were powerless to protect themselves from evil. The fathers at the mission, the teachers and students, the villagers, were all pretending nothing had changed. Everyone went about the business of daily life as usual; she lived each day as usual, while inside her a voice was screaming. Everything was at odds now, silent or clamoring, the fabric of everyday sounds unmeshed. Father Matthew seemed to have taken it upon himself to try to cheer her up, but his words were meaningless to her, the drone of a robot man.

<u>36</u>

The Account

After leaving Gordon in the hands of Laurel and Fr. Lawrence, Mr. Senwangama and Fr. Phillip drive straight to Travellers Rest. The soldiers there deny that anyone has been detained. They find out that Captain Aiwa is at the border station and drive out to confront him.

The Captain is cleaning his rifle in the last rays of sun. He says that three persons who had illegally crossed the border were questioned and released. Although Father Phillip speaks of God's all-knowing justice and Mr. Senwangama of his intention to alert the Ministry of Education and the Ugandan police, the Captain assures them there is no more to be said. Not knowing what else to do, they return to Kisoro.

It is almost fully dark by then and there is no one on the streets. The two men stop at Munde's store. Munde says he has not seen or heard anything and advises them to go home and forget the whole affair, saying that Ngira most probably fled into the countryside and would turn up sooner or later. With this in mind they drive slowly out of town, hoping to find Ngira making his way along the road back to school.

When they arrive back at the mission, still hoping that Ngira has preceded them, they are met instead with the implications of Gordon's disjointed account. Later, as he regains consciousness for longer periods, he fills in details that make plain the full horror of his story:

After Laurel was released, Gordon says, the verbal abuse worsened, and they were accused of being everything from spies and mercenaries to homosexuals. With their hands tied behind their backs, they were pushed out of the hotel and ordered to get into the Army Land Rover. When Ngira refused, the Captain pulled a *panga* from under the seat and in one downward stroke cut off Ngira's ear.

"Get in, msukumizi," the Captain said, "or you will lose the other one." They both got into the vehicle. The Captain put the severed ear in a cup and held it under the wound to catch the blood, which he pretended to drink – or perhaps did drink – for the amusement of his men.

Words were exchanged between the Captain and one of the soldiers. Ngira was nearly unconscious, and as Gordon tried to support him a soldier raised his rifle and brought the butt crashing down onto his head.

When he came to, he realized he was lying on a road on the other side of town. Half-conscious, he made his way back to his car, still in front of Travellers Rest. Inexplicably, they had taken his money but not his car keys. He heard the soldiers gathered inside the hotel, then the unmistakable sound of gunshots – three gunshots, in the distance. Struggling to remain conscious, he drove away. No one tried to stop him.

Father Phillip and Mr. Senwangama return to Kisoro the next day to again confront the Captain, who again denies everything. The search expands, people are questioned about anything they have seen or heard. Rumors begin pouring in; many heard the shots, someone saw something buried, or dumped in a lake; another saw the Land Rover speeding out of the bush. No one has actually seen a murder, and no body has been found. Everyone agrees on one thing: this is the way things happen now in Uganda.

37

Poison

"I loved him," she said, because it was there inside her, burning to come out, and this priest would be the one to condemn her, and she was ready.

Father Matthew hesitated, eyeing her. "And did he love you?"

"I don't know." The lie was poison on her tongue. "Yes. Yes, I think he did."

"You didn't tell him how you felt?"

"No. I never told him."

"But why?"

She stared at her hands, lifeless, unconnected things laid on her lap, and sighed. "I suppose I was afraid."

"Because he is African." It was not a question.

She wanted to scream, *No, not because he's African*, but her throat stuck on the word. She couldn't be sure, maybe now would never be sure, if that was part of the reason, a deep-rooted prejudice against the color of his skin.

"Never mind," the priest said, his face blurred in the dim light of the mission parlor. "Friend or lover, what can it matter now?"

She hadn't cried, only sat as still as stone in the failing light as silence closed around her like water. Father Matthew said something about God's love, then got up to light the gas lamp that would drive the darkness into shadows inhabiting the empty recesses of the room.

38

Negative Space

Sabinyo was in the back garden, straight-legged but bending at the waist as he moved down the rows pulling weeds. Caspar was in the kitchen making a bean and cabbage stew for their lunch. Even though Laurel finally persuaded him to put a few tomatoes in, the stew smelled blandly unappetizing. After three days sheltering at the mission, she had had enough of Father Lawrence's clinical sympathy, Father Phillip's blustering condescension, and Father Matthew's – attitude, was the only way she could think of it, outwardly solicitous but always the undertone of disapproval, dislike.

She was not ungrateful. Faced with the prospect of returning to Butawanga and the unbearable reality of Ngira's absence, she had gladly accepted the invitation to spend some time in the quiet security of the mission. The fathers meant well, and they could just as easily have left her to her own devices. Looking back on her stay she could smile now, imagining how relieved the priests must have been to say goodbye to this basket-case of a girl who had sat, silently staring or uncontrollably crying, whenever she was not closeted in her small mission room. No, the priests, including Father Matthew, had been nothing but kind; it was her own responses that were blunted, as dead as the low D on her piano had been with a broken connection between key lever and hammer. The key goes down, but there is no sound. She did not consciously understand that she would need to learn how to trust the world again, the world as a place with evil in it, just as her mother had said.

Regulate; the word would come to her occasionally but felt as stupidly empty as everything else. Fucking childish, and no wonder Carolyn was irritated by it. What a nerve she had to tell anyone how to conduct herself, Laurel thought. She wished Carolyn could be there, so she could say, you're right, I'm smug and self-important and naive about the world. Even if Carolyn could be offensive, at least she was honest. And I call myself a truth-teller—

Caspar was learning to cook, proud of his new command of the stove. She ate the lunches he prepared, praising the result, which was as good as his rudimentary skills and the simple ingredients would allow. Sabinyo generally ate without comment. With Laurel eating alone at the table and the two boys on the back step, the three of them filled their bellies. That was the African way, the Butawanga way, and maintaining this basic interaction with her employees as she prepared for the year of teaching was enough to lend a comfortable predictability to her days. The nights in her concrete house were another matter, because then she was alone with her thoughts and the reliving of that terrible day, the grief, the guilt. They should have stayed longer at Ellen's. She should not have left the two men at Travellers Rest. She should have run faster, spoken louder. Everyone told her she was right to summon help; but she knew the truth. The right thing was to have stayed and saved him, joining Gordon in using whatever power their white skin might have had.

She hated to remember how she had sat in that car on the way back from Rwanda, those last hours with him, without one word to let him know how she felt. "Friend or lover, what can it matter now?" Father Matthew must have been trying to console her, not understanding how the words would hurt.

How to resume life here? Nothing would be the same. She could no longer sit in the sunshine on her front step with the expectation of Ngira's solid presence and booming voice, or go with him to Mass on Sundays, or walk with him into the hills overlooking the school.

With each night's fear and uncertainty she would resolve to ask Peace Corps to send her home. Each morning, as the sun kindled a golden glow in the sky behind Mt. Sabinyo and the emboldened air billowed the curtains, she would resolve to stay.

Both states of mind waxed and waned like the moon, and she came to accept each of them as part of some inescapable process. She felt incapable of action or reaction, submerged in her temporary niche of madam teacher in this foreign country and wondering if she persevered long enough in this negative space, surrounded by all the constant reminders of Ngira's absence, the pain would finally go away. Like the Sleeping Beauty character, suspended in time waiting to be awakened by someone who, in this case, would never come.

There was almost no mail, and what did get through was heavily censored for any content critical of the Ugandan government. She had one letter from her parents that had mostly escaped the censor's marker, expressing only general concerns for her health and welfare. There was a *P.S.* from her father that told her that her parents knew of the censorship and violence and were frantic with worry: *Don't be caught sleeping through Armageddon.*

Tessa sounded blissfully unaware of the situation in Uganda, her most recent letter relating little of substance except what "Alan and I" were thinking and doing.

A year ago, the idea of Tessa and Alan would have struck Laurel as bizarre, the most unlikely pairing imaginable. Even though Alan was no longer hers to possess, she might have felt angry, betrayed by the speed and eagerness with which Tessa had taken him up. Now she could not bring herself to be angry with anyone she had loved. If they were coming together as a couple, she wished them well with all her heart.

There was no correspondence from Peace Corps. She had given up on the arrival of another volunteer and didn't much care. In some strange convoluted way, looking for solace in the presence of another American seemed a betrayal to everything she and Ngira had shared. She would always be American, but now she felt separated by more than physical distance from her life as a college student. Even with a roommate, she would still be alone.

* * *

A memorial service for David Ngira was held at the mission six days after his disappearance. The following week, Mr. Senwangama and a convalescent Gordon left for Kampala to report the army brutality to the Ugandan Government and the British Embassy. They had to wait several days before obtaining an audience with Amin's private secretary. He agreed to raise the matter with the president, but would not guarantee an investigation. The British consul promised to follow up, but warned them that the chances of any satisfactory result in the current climate were almost nonexistent.

Part of her had wanted to go with them, to bear witness

and to ask Peace Corps to send her home. But gradually she had come to understand that she would not leave. This was her school, hers and Ngira's, and she would not abandon it if she had a choice. She would teach, and wait.

And of course there was also the foolish delusion, the hope that he had escaped and was in hiding, or wounded and being cared for by someone, somewhere, and would make his way back to the school when he was well, just show up one day while she was sitting on her stoop. She wanted to be there waiting for him, to tell him she was busy watching the cabbages grow.

* * *

When Theresa came to the memorial service with Ngira's family, Laurel could hardly stop looking at her. She was small, light-skinned, with the feminine version of Ngira's gracefully arched forehead. Wearing a trim white pant suit, pants being a rather radical choice for a woman here, she walked down the aisle behind Ngira's parents, coming into the church after everyone else had been seated.

The service left Laurel too enervated to move, emptied of thought and feeling, lulled by the shuffle and murmur of people leaving. Then, someone was standing in the aisle, facing her squarely: a white clad figure, a heart-shaped face against a stormcloud of black hair, dark eyes piercing. Just one look, sharp as a knife, before Theresa snapped her head away and hurried to overtake Ngira's mother, supporting the older woman with her arm.

Western Union Mailgram
FROM: Joseph H. Blatchford, Director ACTION
Washington, D.C., 9/10/72
TO: Mr. & Mrs. Arthur Bittelson, Concord, MA.

TO ALL PARENTS/GUARDIANS PC/UGANDA VOLUNTEERS AND TRAINEES:

THIS WILL ADVISE YOU OF BREAKOUT OF HOSTILITIES IN UGANDA. WE ARE IN CONSTANT CONTACT WITH STATE DEPARTMENT, AMERICAN EMBASSY AND PEACE CORPS STAFF IN UGANDA WITH EVERY INDICATION THAT ALL VOLUNTEERS AND TRAINEES ARE SAFE. FIVE VOLUNTEERS UNDER ADMINISTRATIVE DETENTION AND SAFE IN CAPITAL RECEIVING GOOD TREATMENT. THEIR FAMILIES HAVE BEEN NOTIFIED. DEEPLY REGRET DEATH OF ONE FORMER TRAINEE, LOUIS MORTON, INADVERTENTLY SHOT WHILE ON PERSONAL TRAVEL. WE WILL NOTIFY YOU SHOULD THERE BE NEED. REST ASSURED EMBASSY AND PEACE CORPS/UGANDA ASSIDUOUSLY FOLLOWING UP ALL AVENUES PROTECT SAFETY OF VOLUNTEERS. NO NEED CALL HOWEVER SHOULD YOU HAVE SPECIFIC QUERY . . .

39

Oh, Uganda

Three days before term would start on September 15th, Mr. Senwangama was bustling around as usual and students and teachers were coming back from the long summer break. Gordon insisted he was recovered enough to begin teaching, joking that his thick Brit skull had come in handy for something. Everyone knew what had happened to Ngira only a month ago, but no one talked about it, at least not in Laurel's hearing. Word was, Aiwa and his men still occupied Travellers Rest. No one talked about that, either. Everyone was determinedly focused on back-to-school preparations, as if the threat of the soldiers' presence could be neutralized or made irrelevant by refusing to speak of it. But under the façade of business as usual, everyone was tense and uneasy. Buses with teachers and students traveling back from their home villages had been stopped at roadblocks. People were taken off the buses, and sometimes they were robbed, beaten, and women were raped. Students who were already returned did not use their time before term started to engage each other in impromptu football or volleyball, or walk the school grounds in the evening talking and laughing loudly. An undercurrent of fear lived at the school, like a tremor deep inside the earth.

"Madam," Caspar called her to the living room with a note of urgency. Outside the window was a cloud of dust, a Land Rover, and two soldiers headed for her door, rifles slung over their shoulders. A thump on the door stopped her heart. For a moment she could not move or speak.

"Should I go?" Caspar asked, wide-eyed.

If no one answered the door they might just open it and walk in, and she did not want to have them inside the house. Better to answer. But Caspar could not be expected to deal with men like these.

"No, it's all right, Caspar. I'll go. But I may need you to translate."

She opened the door a few inches. One soldier was big and broad, the other smaller, thin-faced. Dirty, torn khaki uniforms, a strong smell of sweat, two dark faces blank as walls. For all she knew, one of them might be the one who had grabbed her that day. Or the one who shot – act calm. Don't show any fear. "Yes?"

"You come." The big one, his voice hard as a fist. She felt her knees go weak. They all stood silent for a moment, then Caspar said something in Kinyarwanda as casually as if he were talking to the man who came selling milk. The soldier did not reply and did not take his eyes off Laurel.

"You come Kisoro!" he shouted.

"No," she said, trying for firmness. "This is a school, and I am a teacher here. You must go see the Headmaster, Mr. Senwangama. He is the one in charge." She attempted to close the door, but the big one put his foot in the way.

Caspar objected in a flood of Kinyarwanda until Laurel stopped him with a hand on his arm. The last thing they should do was antagonize the man. She stared at the huge unlaced boot, the black ankle caked with dust, and wanted to scream.

"You come," the soldier said again, a growl this time. Over the loud hammering of her heart, Laurel realized they

256

were probably the only English words the man knew. He had not understood Kinyarwanda, either.

It would need to be Swahili. "Hapana," she said. "Utakwenda Senwangama." Sending them to the headmaster would at least buy her some time.

The two men conferred in hissed angry tones, the booted foot still firmly blocking her door. "Ha-pa-na," the big one pronounced, as if speaking to a misbehaving child.

She must stand her ground, refuse to take no for an answer. "Utakwenda Senwangama."

The big soldier looked back at her, frowning. With every muscle tense and shaking, she braced herself against the moment when he would push his huge body through the door.

To her immense relief, the big man sighed and said, "Senwangama wapi?"

Laurel pointed in the direction of Mr. Senwangama's house. The balance of power between them had shifted, if only for the moment. The man said something to his companion, who secured his rifle under one arm and took off at a trot down the road. The one in charge removed his foot from the door and Laurel quickly closed and turned the deadbolt. Trembling, she looked out the front window. The vehicle stood empty. The big soldier must be standing guard at her door. She forced her paralyzed mind to think. She might try to escape out the back, but what if he saw her? She was certain he would take the excuse to shoot her. She had little choice but to wait.

"I think it will be all right, Madam," Caspar said in a voice so consoling it almost brought her to tears. Caspar did not know what these men were capable of. Still, it was a good sign that they agreed to go to the headmaster. Don't panic, she told herself, trying to breathe normally. She was a foreigner, they would not dare hurt her. They had let Gordon go – but that Captain Aiwa, what he had done to Ngira – tears pricked her eyes. She fought them back and found her voice.

"Caspar, you should leave now by the back door. I don't think the soldier will bother with you. Just go quietly."

He grinned at her. "But Madam, it is not time for me to go home."

"Caspar, I don't want you mixed up in this. Please, leave now before the other one gets back –"

"It is all right, Madam. I will stay."

Laurel smiled at him, this overgrown teenager who owed her nothing, but did not hesitate to put himself at risk to help her. Too agitated to sit down she stood, waiting, with Caspar awkwardly shifting from foot to foot, until she heard voices on the road, then a knock on the door.

"Miss Bittelson, this man says you are wanted at Travellers Rest." It was Mr. Senwangama's voice, thank God. She opened the door. "He says someone is asking for you on the short wave." Seeing her face, he softened his somewhat annoyed tone. "I think he is telling the truth. In any event I have told this man that I must bring you in my car. I have already sent for my driver. Mr. Coopersmith is on his way to the mission to inform the priests where we have gone."

Relief flooded in. "Thank you so much, Mr. Senwangama." The soldiers were waiting on the stoop, muttering, impatient, but now at least she was not alone.

* * *

On the return from Kisoro in the Peugeot, Laurel studied the back of Mr. Senwangama's head. His sparse, graying coils of hair were hung with droplets of sweat glistening like tiny jewels. The creases on the back of his neck, crinkles next to his eyes, his pleasant voice keeping up polite conversation, as if they had just been out for a Sunday drive; looking at him, Laurel felt a surge of gratitude and affection. The Headmaster had taken a considerable risk escorting her to Kisoro. Now she had to tell this kind man that the voice crackling on the short wave had been Chip calling from Kampala, and that tomorrow she was leaving Butawanga and then, most probably, the country. Pulling you in – tomorrow – Ministry of Education car – pack light. Keep a low profile, he had said, whatever that meant. But Mr. Senwangama would accept her leaving with the equanimity of someone who was used to coping with constant change. He had to concern himself now with the very survival of his school, and to him the loss of one privileged young American girl who had played for a while at being a teacher would make only a brief ripple in the depths of Butawanga's, and Uganda's, uncertain future.

<u>40</u>

Father Matthew's Journal

5th October, 1972
Kisoro, Uganda.

I dare to hope that God has not abandoned me! He has stretched out His hand to me, the weakest of sinners, to pull me from the depths of my moral quicksand – merciful Heaven, will I ever find the strength to fully grasp that hand?

When that pathetic child came to say goodbye, I allowed her to go on believing he was dead. She punishes herself for not acknowledging her love, blames herself for not preventing his death. Her pain was there, in her eyes, in her pale suffering face. I turned away. What harm would it have done to say the few words that would have lifted the terrible burden she now carries home with her? As a priest my duty was clear, and I failed in it as I have failed in so many things to do with the heart.

Poor, deluded Rabelais. Even on his sickbed he wrote to the girl, keeping it a secret from me, as he thought. But Mtembo knows where his first loyalty must lie, so of course he brought that letter to me instead of her. The foolish man's declaration of love twisted in me like a knife. I threw it on the fire. I told Mtembo to say that it was delivered.

If she had received that letter and found out Rabelais was still alive, she might have found some way to stay on at Butawanga. Her presence would only have confused him and fueled his sad infatuation.

Were they lovers? It hardly matters, now. She is gone, and we are well rid of her. She said she loved him, but she's young and shallow, and the novelty of having an African man would have worn off quickly. Meanwhile, he was digging himself deeper in his commitment to her, worrying about complicating her life with a forbidden liaison, worrying about protecting her, when it was he who needed protecting, my poor, dear Rabelais –

A visceral memory intruded, of the thud of hard boots against flesh and bone; how he had followed that terrible rhythm into the bush, entered the clearing and saw the human form crumpled on grass matted with blood. How he saw two soldiers, one in full uniform, the other bare-chested, a shirt lying near the inert body. Two rifles were propped against nearby trees. The bare chest made a whinnying sound as he kicked, lost to his litany of abuse, while the uniformed one stood by watching with a look of fascinated horror.

"Kwisha!" the priest had shouted. "In God's name, stop!" He stood in his white vestments, reaching out in a gesture of supplication. The men stopped to stare blankly until their eyes, dazed with bloodlust, gradually registered his presence. Bare Chest lunged for his rifle and, eyes wild, aimed it at the priest. Father Matthew raised his arms to Heaven and said, "God forgive you."

The uniformed man stepped forward, put his hand on the muzzle of his companion's gun and pushed it away from its target just before the shot discharged. The two argued. Bare Chest made an angry gesture and took a step back. Uniform spoke then with haunted eyes: *Your God can never forgive me.*

Father Matthew summoned enough voice to say, "God forgives all who stand before Him in true repentance and promise to serve Him." Uniform fell on his knees and wept like a baby, while his shirtless comrade registered disbelief and then active derision. The repentant will proved stronger. They agreed to fire two rifle shots in the air so that another soldier, waiting in the Land Rover for them to "finish" the captive, would assume they had done so. They would report back to their Captain that his order had been carried out.

When the men left, crashing through the bush as if pursued by demons, Father Matthew realized he was not going to die, and the fear that had nearly paralyzed him drained away. Then he heard a groan. He forced himself to grasp a shoulder sticky with drying blood and turn the victim onto his back. He recoiled from the face, dark and swollen, a clotted black mass where an ear should have been; then, the sickening moment of recognition.

Praise God for granting Mtembo the courage to remain waiting for me on the road, even after he heard the shots. He had seen a wounded man being driven off, and his speed in finding me in the church as I prepared for vespers was surely the Hand of God. I thought to collect Phillip and Lawrence and the car, but he urged me to come immediately. We were faster on foot through the bush than we would have been by road. My shock at discovering it was Rabelais – is indescribable.

When we brought him out he was near death, but it was too risky to bring him back to the hospital. That Captain might have heard about his rescue and come to finish the job. No one could have stopped him. Mtembo's family agreed to keep him at their shamba, where Lawrence and I visit every day with antibiotics and dressings. He needed blood, which I supplied in part. Convincing Lawrence to secrecy was difficult, but the imperative of safety finally persuaded him. I think he suspects there is more to my concern, but he does not question me.

Through Your Mercy, Rabelais is better each day. When he is strong enough to be moved, we will enlist some men to help us carry him through the mountains into Rwanda, where Mtembo has relatives. When he is more fully recovered, we will see what to do then.

My blood now flows in his veins.

Elation was suddenly replaced by a sadness so heavy that Fr. Matthew could not move. Memory flooded in, of himself as a teenager in his first car, parked at one of the Lake Michigan beaches at night, fumbling over some girl, sickened by her perfume. He remembered how beacons of light from commercial vessels had seemed to have the magical power to take him out of himself to a place where life was not a prison of human weakness.

He saw himself as a child on the same shore, standing with his father on a summer Saturday and listening as he described the great Seaway under construction east of Lake Ontario, which would open all the Lakes to the Atlantic Ocean through the Saint Lawrence River. The locks were to have names, his father had explained, like the names of presidents or famous historical figures. *Moby Dick,* the 12-year-old Matthew had suggested, from his favorite book, and his father laughed and said it was a fine name for a lock and who cared about old presidents anyway. He had never been able to reconcile times like that with the other times when his father sat drinking beer in the kitchen, and all he might say was, *get out of here, damn you*; and he would hear his mother moving around upstairs like a frightened mouse, pretending nothing was wrong.

His body was overtaken by tremors, as from some great cold against which he could not warm himself. He saw himself again, a man this time, standing naked on that shore in winter, laid open to the scrutiny of God, welcoming the arctic blast that would turn him mercifully into ice.

He saw Ngira's face, dark and broken. It was all he could see, burning into his brain. Then he heard Laurel's voice: *I loved him.* The sadness again, almost unbearable, pressed down on him with such weight that he was hardly able to move his pen over the damp white paper.

He almost died. Was it not Your Hand, Holy Father, which guided me to Rabelais' side in his hour of need? I expected to die that day as well. You saved us both. When that soldier went down on his knees before me, You empowered me to grant him Your Forgiveness. I must believe I am given another chance. You have shown me the depths of Your Divine Mercy, and I would be a fool to ignore it. I will pray daily for the strength to once again approach Grace.

I will pray, yes, but I must also act to redeem myself. I must make a full confession to Lawrence and Phillip and place my penance in their hands. They will instruct my formal confession, and help me turn my face toward God again. Or perhaps they will send me away. I will abide by their decision.

When Rabelais recovers from his grievous wounds, as I trust in You that he may, he will need my help and counsel more than ever, and I will not be able to give it. No, let me begin to be truthful – it is I who need him, not the other way around. I don't know which will be the worse agony, to be sent away from him or to stay here and be forbidden to see him. Whatever my fate, I must endure. I will cast out my demons, emerge purified and able to serve God once again. As

264

Kierkegaard wrote: "...it is not the way which is narrow, but the narrowness which is the way."

<u>41</u>

Undelivered

26-8-1972

Laurel,

Though it has been some weeks since we have spoken, I am alive. At this moment I am unable to write, but Mtembo has kindly agreed to write as I dictate, adding to the many kind acts he has already done. For his sake and yours, I will be brief. Father Matthew wishes the fact of my survival to remain a secret. He does not want to put me or the mission at risk from the soldiers by making my rescue known. I think it unlikely that Aiwa would go to such trouble, now that his whim of cruelty has passed. Father Matthew saved my life, and although I do not like to go against his wishes, I must let you at least know that I am staying with Mtembo's family while I recover from some injuries. I have asked Mtembo to deliver this message without the Father's knowledge. Please keep this a secret for now. Soon I will write to Gordon and the Head, and when I am well enough I will return to Butawanga, but that may be some weeks yet. If for some reason I cannot return, I hope through this to relieve any anxiety you may have on my account.

You must have been terribly frightened that day in Kisoro, as I was. Although the Captain released you, I did not know if you made it safely away until the Father told me that you were over there at the mission. Only then did I draw a peaceful breath. Laurel, you are as precious to me as life itself. It is selfish of me to tell you this, especially now, but lying here like this I see everything clearly. I allowed myself to forget that you are an American from another life. What happened between us has caused you confusion and regret. It is because I love you that I expect nothing from you. That is what I would have explained if I had made it back that day. You must return to your true life in the States, go back to your brilliant future, without a thought for anything or anyone here. You are a star that came to shine on us for a brief time. For me, that is enough. It is much more than enough. When we meet again it will be as friends, the way it was before.

Now I will stop so Mtembo can be on his way.

IV

Finding Grace

"An old adage says that love is older than anything else."

Soren Aabye Kierkegaard, *Edifying Discourses*

42

Ghosts

Life on a college campus was familiar yet strange. Being a graduate student was different and in some ways more demanding than undergraduate life had been, but Laurel knew the strangeness was because she was not the same person she had been two years ago, dissatisfied with her life, her country, herself, and seizing on the Peace Corps as an experience she had to have.

She was back in Boston for four months now, but she failed to recognize herself in the mirror these days. Her own reflection was oddly unfamiliar, the baggy "peasant" blouses and long skirts she had taken to wearing, the new short haircut that had reduced her red mop to a frizzy cap. She had thrown away her clothes from Africa like unwanted memories, but instead of feeling relieved, she only felt emptied.

Sometimes, if she felt strong enough, she would listen to the cassette of the Kampala Shining Stars, the university choral group. She could not reconcile the memory of expansive landscapes and crystalline air, people's friendly smiles and musical greetings, with her overwhelming sense of grief and loss. That last trip to Kampala in the official Ministry car had been surreal: armed, drunken soldiers manning checkpoints along the road, at each stop tensely waiting while she and her documents were looked over, the countryside suddenly bleak and hard. Some of the volunteers living near cities had lived with sounds of continual gunfire from barracks. One girl, stationed in Mbarara, had woken up one morning to find several corpses in her garden. Butawanga had been relatively unmolested, after all; if only they had not traveled to Rwanda, Ngira would still be alive.

She was like a time traveler who dares to penetrate a time where she does not belong, cannot prosper, and only rocks the boat for those already there. Now she was back where she belonged, in a hollowed-out version of her old life, absent the spark of dreamy ambition that had made her so unsettled and impulsive. All she wanted was to sit at her piano and not think about yesterday, or tomorrow.

She played her usual repertoire, all the classics to which she would never do justice, sheltering in their beauty. Then, more and more often, she worked on her own composition, begun in her head while still at Butawanga. It was almost not a conscious labor, but a trance in which time lost all bounds, and her deep pool of sadness flowed out into the music without ever registering in thought. She did not need to write it down. The music was a constant presence, living and growing inside her, allowing her to ignore the empty core of her being.

Sometimes a thought crept in while she played, a feeling that Ngira was standing beside her or walking quietly through the room listening, hand on his chin. She would take him to concerts or the opera. He would like opera; they might start with Bohème, holding hands as the arias of love and loss swelled around them. But it was no good imagining what might have been.

In January, she started back at B.U. Here, with a graduate Music department full of young people, it was easy enough to find someone with whom to go to the opera.

There was Richard, a Music Theory major in the PhD program, who intended to go right into teaching at a university. Sue Ann was in Music Education and her fiancé, Scott, was in law school but enjoyed concert-going. Barbara, Patrick, Michelle, she was just getting to put names with faces, never letting on that for some reason she felt like she was only going through the motions of a social being, mimicking their gestures and speech like a foreigner.

They all seemed to feel infallible, invulnerable, and entitled to all the good things life had to offer. Laurel remembered feeling that way once, but she did not feel that way now.

Still, it was a secure life, learning and research a pleasure. The Music department owned six pianos, including two Steinway concert grands. Everyone was enthusiastic and determined. Laurel tried never to be idle, because that was when the sadness crept in like a poisonous fog, the memories planted an embryo of guilt for taking him to Rwanda, then for not having brought help in time. She might have been raped, killed, but Ngira had saved her. She was lucky. She was white. He was the one who died. Now she understood that parable about the unhurt soldier who limped when walking past his wounded comrades. Sometimes she felt the need to limp.

On the surface, she had merged without a ripple into the flow of American life. After coming home in September, she had lived out in Concord with her parents until just after Christmas. In January, she started graduate school at B.U. for her Master's in Music Education. Uganda, the school, her students, the guns, the soldiers, the sound of Ngira's voice, all safely tucked away in the past; unreachable, except through unbidden daydreams, or uncontrollable nightmares from which she sometimes was awakened by the sound of a scream, imagined or real, his, or her own.

She had left her parents' house and moved back into the Somerville apartment where Tessa still lived – where up until last spring, Alan had also been living. Laurel did not speak to her friend about Ngira or how she had felt, what had happened between them. She did not feel comfortable confiding in Tessa anymore; things were changed between them, no matter how they might pretend otherwise.

In fact she had confided to no one about Ngira, not Tessa and least of all her parents, who in any case were uninterested in knowing anything about Africa other than that she had been safely returned from it.

* * *

She had received two letters from Ellen, sketchy, frenetic missives about gorilla groups and treacherous bureaucrats, and scraps of news. The boys at Butawanga are on strike for better meals in the dining halls. Rajaraman had to leave the country with the rest of the Asians, and Travellers Rest is closed. There are no more sugar, coffee, or manufactured goods, and fewer tourists, that last a plus in Ellen's opinion. The Haubers send their love. Laurel was glad to receive and answer Ellen's notes, but aside from that had had no contact with the world and people she had left behind at Butawanga.

Would Ngira have agreed to come to Boston? Would she have dared to ask it of him? *Impossible, Laurelchka,* her mother would say with that lilt of lightly rounded vowels, clip of precise consonants. You are from two different worlds, her mother might say, as Ellen had.

Laurel thought her mother would have come around in the end, but she couldn't be sure. Now she would never know. Mama could content herself with commenting on her daughter's social life, how she hoped that Laurel wasn't kept too busy with her studies, and what about that Richard she had mentioned – he sounded promising. Although she told her mother that Richard was self-involved and boring, what she did not say was, anyway I'm still in love with an African man.

How could she say it, and how could it possibly be true? Still in love with a man who had died halfway across the world, who may have felt nothing more than a passing attraction for her; and what, after all, had she really felt for him? Friendship, yes, and a bond of trust strengthened by circumstance and her sense of vulnerability in a foreign land; now she was back home, and it was all as remote and inaccessible as a dream.

No. More than that. She would not lie to herself again. She had loved him, and she was still in love with the memory of him. Five months had passed since his death, but no matter how she tried, she could not bury Ngira.

43

Doris

The Kennedy Diner, formerly "The Franklin," was wedged sideways into its narrow berth on West Concord, in Boston's South End. From the street, all that was visible was the battered black kitchen door, a blot of wall, the garbage dumpster. "The rump end," owner Doris Kennedy called it. She had given the restaurant her surname, the name she went back to using after she kicked out her second husband, and liked to joke about trading on the fame of those other Boston Kennedys.

To enter, you went into an alley under the shadow of the taller buildings on either side, one a medical arts practice associated with City Hospital, the other a nineteenth century brick bowfront that looked oddly isolated, inexplicably spared from a row that had been replaced with modern apartments. It was occupied by Grindel's Bakery on the ground floor, Rasta Music and Book Shop on the second, and on the top floor, apartments where unknown shadowy people could be seen entering or leaving from time to time. Laurel sometimes glanced out across the alley to see a beam of yellow light from a third story window very late into the night, where perhaps the occupant, like her, had to go to work when most of the city was asleep.

Laurel's parents were willing to pay all her living and school expenses, but at 24 years old she wanted at least some income of her own. She almost gave up on finding a part-time job that didn't require experience and would fit in with her school schedule. Then, she found Doris. "You just show up here when you're supposed to and do what I tell you – that's experience enough for me, hon." Doris's voice was as abrasive as scouring powder. She called everyone hon, and in that single word expressed anything from anger, disapproval or indifference, to affection.

Laurel worked dinner hours 5 p.m. to 9 p.m., three days a week, and the late shift 10 p.m. to 6 a.m. on Saturday, the only day the diner stayed open 24 hours. Doris thought it was important for people to have a place to go after a movie or show, or just for some company, without having to drink alcohol or pay fancy prices. She knew her clientele of African-American, Irish, Italian working class people. "I don't like hippies, bums, drug addicts, whores, gangs, and I don't stand for no sittin' with just a glass of water."

Doris mostly left the kitchen to Charlie, a tall, wiry African-American with large hands and fingers crooked as tree roots. Charlie peeled, chopped and cooked vegetables, made dishes like his Cryin' Out Loud Chili, and worked the deep fryers for fries and onion rings. He had learned how to cook in the Army, in Korea; when she heard that, Doris said, she had hired him on the spot, certain that anyone who could cook for a crowd of lonely men out in the jungle could manage well enough in her little kitchen in South Boston. She could have hired someone to work the grill but preferred to do it herself. "I'm 42 years old, 20 pounds overweight and I look like the back end of a truck, but my cookin' is a thing of beauty." Doris was proud of her creations: plate-sized Kennedy Cakes, Bonanza Burgers (after her favorite TV western), Beefy Harvard

Hash, and in honor of the former first lady, a Jackie O-melet, miraculously light and silky.

Saturday late-night was much more relaxed than the dinner hours. Doris worked the counter as well as the grill, and Laurel tended the scattering of customers in the booths, as the outer darkness encapsulated the brightly lit room like a spaceship cruising through the timeless black universe.

Alan would have forbidden her to work that shift. She could hear him now, with his paternal tone: not in that neighborhood. She could see so clearly the life she would have had with him. The last she had heard, through her mother, he was already engaged to some lucky girl. Laurel wished him well, even though he had broken Tessa's heart.

Laurel wanted to hate Alan, and to disapprove of Tessa for falling so hard for him, but she was no longer capable of finding fault with the people she loved, or had loved. In the Somerville apartment they had spent a few evenings talking over a cup of chamomile tea, and it was beginning to feel something like their undergraduate days, especially since Tessa was back together with her former boyfriend, Jake.

She would catch the bus home in the morning and sleep until noon, then go out for her Sunday visit to her parents in Concord. Jake and Tessa were usually still asleep when she came in around 6:30 a.m., and were often just getting up along with her at noon. Tessa was not in school and working afternoons and evenings, six days a week, at a head shop in Harvard Square, selling incense, wind chimes, roach clips, and other counterculture paraphernalia. Jake, the man responsible for Tessa's three-month pregnancy, was still unemployed. He had an undergraduate degree in political science, but beyond railing against the military-industrial complex that had sent him to Vietnam, he seemed to have little direction in life.

Jake preferred sleeping in the daytime with the sunlight streaming in, he said, because there were fewer nightmares then. In Vietnam he had used amphetamines to keep himself awake, Quaaludes or Valium to get to sleep, and marijuana for the time in between. Laurel knew he still used some of these drugs, but not how much or how often. Sometimes he looked pale and shaky, and she would urge him to get some rest; how much he actually slept behind the closed door of Tessa's bedroom was not her business to ask.

To all appearances, Jake and Tessa got along well. When they had invited her to move back to the apartment, Laurel was glad for the chance to get out of her parents' house. She could get to campus easily by bus from Somerville, as they both had in their undergraduate days. The couple were glad to have her sharing rent and utilities, but Laurel knew that soon after the baby came in June she would want to leave, to give them their space. She hoped Jake succeeded in finding a job before then. Most of all, she hoped he planned to stick by Tessa after the baby came, when she would need him most.

<u>44</u>

Someone else

Her Sunday visit to Concord was the only time she got to sit down and really play. Here in her parents' living room with the afternoon sun slanting in, she could be alone with her piano as long as she wanted. Her parents understood this and did not feel slighted. They liked listening from wherever they were in the house.

Today it would be Chopin, cool and polished as ebony, allowing her to play out the busy demands of the past week. She had planned her pieces as she drove, her second-hand Ford Pinto invoking pessimistic minor keys, as if the car itself were constantly anticipating breakdown. The E minor Mazurka, one of her mother's favorites, the C minor Polonaise, finishing with the "Raindrop" Prelude, the notes flowing from her fingertips like water; she would be free, for that hour or two, from wondering why she still felt unable to connect with anyone or anything in her current life.

Then, limber and relaxed, she would take up a pencil and the manuscript sheets of her own composition, to probe a little further into the secret inner music that she had always known was there, but was only beginning to recognize.

* * *

After dinner, Laurel and her mother went in to clean up the kitchen. Margaret wore her usual Sunday dress, stockings, low-heeled pumps. The dishes were washed, dried, and put away. Her mother would be appalled to know how often she and Tessa let the dirty dishes sit in the sink overnight. But then, there was so much she did not know, and it was better for both of them to keep it that way.

Laurel's mail was lying on the kitchen table. She had not yet bothered to change her address. This week there was a letter from Ellen in the little stack. It had been a good while since she had heard from Ellen, and Laurel looked forward to her news. She generally took her mail back to the apartment unopened, to read in the privacy of her room.

"Will you sweep, please, Laurel?"

"The floor looks fine, Mother." Sometimes, Laurel liked the formality of *Mother*.

"Drop a crumb, roaches will come. Don't miss the corners."

Laurel got the broom, but couldn't help a sarcastic grin. "I'll bet there isn't a cockroach between here and Boston."

Margaret stood and looked at her, as if trying to decide whether this was really her daughter. "There were no cockroaches in our house in Warsaw, either, but there were plenty in other houses. They find their way to wherever there is food for them. As soon as you let down your guard, they come in."

Laurel had thought it best not to tell her mother about the giant roaches in the dorms at Makerere during training. In fact, she had given her parents only the briefest account of her experiences, leaving out the details that would have made them anxious in retrospect, and leaving out, for the most part, Ngira. As far as her parents were concerned, her year in Africa had been an error in judgment that was best ignored, as if it had never happened.

Laurel flipped through the rest of her mail. Something from the college Business office; an ad for an upcoming sale at the Harvard Coop; the monthly newsletter from Musical Heritage Society. She picked up Ellen's letter, a treasure she would open later, and turned it over idly, content to let it wait while she spent this time with her mother.

At forty-seven, Margaret's carefully made-up face looked almost unlined, and her blonde hair was still bright, graying only at the temples. A downward set of her mouth, some sagging skin on her neck, were the only visible hallmarks of the passage of time. Comparing herself to her mother, Laurel was the ugly swan that had failed to fulfill its inheritance. She finished sweeping and joined her mother at the kitchen table.

"You're still beautiful, you know, Mother?"

Margaret smiled. "Well, thank you, sweetheart. At one time I was. Now, you are the beautiful one."

Laurel laughed. "Do you have me confused with someone else?"

Her mother stared. "What do you mean, someone else? Sometimes I don't understand you."

"Of all the things I am, Mother, beautiful is not one of them. I always thought you disapproved of the way I look, my crazy hair, no makeup and all that."

"You are quite attractive, Laurelchka, pale and fiery at the same time, like your father. I only think you could make more of what you have, that's all. You seem to make an extra effort to look, well – plain."

Of course, even a compliment from her mother would contain a negative message. "Plain but beautiful, that's me."

"Have it your way, Laurel, as you always do. Let us not

argue the point. How is Tessa?"

This was her mother's way of asking if Jake was still in the picture. Cohabitation before marriage was not socially acceptable to her parents' generation.

"Tess is fine. She likes her job, and she still gets in some painting time." The news of Tessa's pregnancy could wait for another few months. Tonight she just wanted to sit with her mother for a little while without arguing.

"And the young man?"

"Jake is – trying. He's applied for a job with a political campaign."

"Oh? For whom?"

The candidate was running on the Socialist Worker's Party ticket, too anti-establishment to sit well with her mother. "I forget the name. But you'd be surprised at Jake, he's cleaned up, even got a haircut. Vietnam was hard on him, you know? He's really trying to get his act together."

"Yes, well, that remains to be seen. Tessa should stop coddling him and find someone more reliable."

"Someone like Alan, I suppose." Stupid, opening this old wound again. "He was with Tessa while I was gone, did you know that? She really fell for him, but he just used her and then walked out."

"Yes, Alan was self-centered. Most men are."

Laurel was dumfounded. "I can't believe you're saying that. You acted like it was the end of the world when Alan and I broke up."

Margaret shrugged. "I worry about your future, that's all. Alan would have been a good provider."

"A good provider? You wanted me to become a slave to his ego just so he could support me? Come on, Mother, give me a break."

Margaret pursed her lips. "Marriage is not a dirty word, Laurel. Even if you girls today have more opportunities than we did, it is still very hard for a woman to make her way alone." She glanced toward the kitchen door. "After losing my parents in the war, security was everything." Her voice was low, almost a whisper. "I love your father, but when I married him I had no idea even of what love was. It grew, you know, over time."

This was the first time her mother had confided something like this to her, one woman to another. Laurel felt something momentous shift between them. She felt both suddenly old and terribly young at the same time. "Yes, I know, Mama."

Margaret came up and ran her hand over the short wisps of her daughter's hair. Laurel closed her eyes at her mother's touch, both women momentarily lost to this sense of something shared, until the sudden intrusion of the front doorbell.

"On Sunday evening? We're not expecting anyone."

They listened to the muffled sounds of her father talking with someone, not anyone they knew judging from the formal tone; shortly afterward, the sound of the front door closing. Laurel's father appeared, standing in the kitchen doorway as if waiting for permission to enter this female inner sanctum.

Margaret broke the spell. "Well, Arthur? Who was it?"

Laurel's father's teeth were discolored and crooked, from his habit of sucking on sour candies all day while he worked. He had adopted a close-mouthed smile that Laurel found inscrutable, since it could be interpreted to mean anything from pain to amusement. It had always been hard enough to know what her naturally reserved father was thinking or feeling at any given moment. "It was the Western Union with a telegram. For Laurel."

Everything was suspended while this unexpected fact settled into the room.

"For me? Who could it be from?"

Her father stood, mulling over the envelope in his hand. "Well, I'm sure I don't know, but it's from London, so it could be from Auntie Jane, but why wouldn't she telephone?"

Laurel extended her hand, and after a moment her father remembered her, grinned, and handed over the coarse beige envelope. Now it was Laurel's turn to stare and try to divine its contents. It was the first time she had ever received a telegram.

"For heaven's sake, Laurel, open it," her mother said.

Laurel pried open the flap and removed the single grainy sheet. Skipping over the short message, the name of the sender struck her a jolt as electrifying as a lightning ball seeking the black earth at Butawanga: Ngira David.

<u>45</u>

Regulate

It was 5:00 a.m., near the end of her Saturday night shift, when even more coffee would not relieve the blur of fatigue. The time when Doris cleaned and restarted the grill, and Laurel swept the carpet and refilled the salt, sugar and milk containers to be ready for the first of the Sunday breakfast crowd: the elderly ladies in dingy hats and gloves, stopping for coffee and a bun, lest a growling stomach detract from the solemnity of early Mass. The quiet time when Doris, hairnet capping her orange-streaked blonde hair, liked to trade gibes with Charlie as he mopped the kitchen.

Laurel had not planned to tell Doris her news, but on this day in particular she could no longer contain her excitement. Ngira was alive. He was alive and coming to Boston. At first she had thought the telegram was a cruel joke and become angry and upset, her parents hovering in dismay. On impulse she tore open Ellen's letter and there it was, two lines in Ellen's impatient scrawl, the fold of the airmail letter intervening: "Just heard from the Haubers that your friend Ngira is alive and back at Butawanga. We weren't sure you knew." Still not quite daring to believe it, she had tried to push down the surge of hope threatening to knock the breath out of her.

That was a week ago, and since then she had crossed the line between seeing the words and believing they were true. Now, she wanted to shout it to the world.

"A friend of mine from Africa is coming to the States. I knew him when I was in the Peace Corps in Uganda. He sent me a telegram from London saying he would be coming to Boston on January twenty-first. Today." The more she said it, the more real it would become. "The thing that makes it so wonderful is that when I left, I thought he was dead."

Doris cleared her throat in a noncommital way, between scrapes of the big spatula on the grill. She wiped grease onto a rag. "You hear that, Charlie? Laurel thought her friend was dead, and now he's not. He's coming to Boston for a visit."

"Dead, huh? You don't say." A bass voice from the kitchen, over the dunk and swish of the mop.

"Sounds to me like there's a story here needs telling, wouldn't you say, Charlie?"

A story that needs telling, that only Ngira could tell. "Well, you know Idi Amin took over as president of Uganda, and ever since then he and his army were on a kind of rampage." She was speaking loudly to be heard in the kitchen, and it sounded so odd, like teaching a class again, but this time not the niceties of English grammar. "We all thought my friend had been killed by soldiers. Then I got a telegram from him. That's really all I know."

"Isn't that something. So this not-so-dead friend of yours, he was a Peace Corps?"

"No, he was a teacher there, Doris. Ngira is African. He helped me a lot when I was new in the job." More, so much more. "He was a very good friend. Is."

Doris raised her penciled-in brow lines. "But does this African have work lined up over here? I hope he's not planning to sponge off you, hon, on what you make at this place, not that it's any of my business. Some men are just out for a free ride. I told you about Barry, now, didn't I?"

At least ten times. "The second most useless man that ever lived."

"That's right. When he left, it took me the better part of a year to get my car back. Of course, the most useless was my first husband. He was a sweet man, but he didn't have any idea how to get on in life, know what I mean? When I finally kicked him out, I was flat broke with two kids to take care of." Doris shook her head. "One thing's for sure, the hard-working ones get snatched up fast, and the others ain't worth the trouble, hon, believe me. Now, take Charlie there. He's not much to look at but he's steady as a rock, hasn't missed a day on the job in the three years since I hired him. Those colored girls don't know a good thing when they see it." She winked at Laurel. "So, Charlie, when's you and me getting married?"

A laugh from the kitchen. "I guess just as soon as you ask me, Doris."

"Well, you just keep on waitin', you never know when I might get around to it." To Laurel she said, "I shouldn't even joke about such a thing. Mixing the races is a sin."

Laurel felt her face stiffen. "I'm sure Charlie doesn't take you seriously, Doris."

"One thing's for sure, this poor African will want to latch onto someone when he gets here. He needs a sponsor or something, doesn't he?"

"He's not poor, Doris, and he must have things arranged, or he wouldn't be coming. I should say they. He's coming with his fiancée. For all I know, by now she could be his wife."

"Well, maybe that's better, maybe not. Just watch out you don't get pulled into their troubles."

"You're as bad as my mother, Doris."

She smiled and shrugged her meaty shoulders. "Mothers know a thing or two sometimes, but it's none of my business. Food for thought, that's all, hon."

Laurel didn't answer. She wiped the spilt salt from the counter and went to distribute the filled shakers to the tables. Hanging over everything was a dark cloud in the otherwise brilliant sky. *Theresa and I,* the telegram had read, and now she had just said the word out loud: *Wife.*

<u>46</u>

Damages

She was unaccustomed to driving into the city, but traffic was light, and today even Storrow Drive was sane. Good thing, because she was unable to keep her thoughts on the road. She had not slept after getting off the early shift, but had gone right away out to Concord since it was Sunday, certain that he would get in touch with her there when he arrived. She could not summon the concentration to play her piano as the appointed day ticked away like a racing heartbeat. Then, the miracle, both wished for and in some indefinable way dreaded: an hour ago, at 3:30 p.m., he had called.

The Blackstone Inn was a decent-looking B&B on Washington, her father had remembered, thankfully well south of the Combat Zone. She found it without any trouble, even a parking space on the street. Her parents had been upset by her rushing off like that to meet a man she had known in Africa, an African man, but she didn't care. Urgency came with the sound of his voice, his disembodied voice on the telephone that was both wonderful and frightening, because it might fade away and be lost to her for good this time.

"I'll be right there." She heard him hesitate; was Theresa there, watching his face for a sign?

"I must warn you, I look like a devil."

She had laughed, stupidly, before remembering his ear.

"Not only my ear. Some bones that were broken did not

come quite right."

It was a miracle he was alive. How he survived, where he had been; she wanted to hear it all.

Driving toward Boston, the familiar feelings flooded back, strong and irresistible. She could picture him, laughing or thoughtful; hear him talking, or singing, feel the heat of that first kiss at Ellen's cabin. Wait, calm down, she told herself, it's been a long time. So much has changed, and maybe he was never in love with me in the first place. She had not asked on the phone if Theresa was there, couldn't think beyond the pure thrill of the sound of his voice. If they were married, Theresa surely would be there, and they would all have a formal little conversation and that would be it, she would never see him again.

She had spent the week unable to regulate between peaks of high excitement and lows of panicked confusion. How would he seem, why was he here, what did he expect of her? Did she really want to still be in love with him? That one night on elephant mountain, as she thought of it now, seemed like something from another, simpler universe. Why reopen feelings that probably never should have been opened in the first place? As Ellen had said, why set yourself up for a fall?

I don't care, Laurel thought. I have to know. She climbed the stairs and paused only for a moment before knocking on the door to room number 22.

She was careful not to stare as they touched hands, the African way. But his face – she tried not to show the shock that rippled through her. His face was changed, like a wax figure that had melted and then hardened into some illogical shape.

Shaken and confused, she walked past him into the room, asking the easy questions, how was the flight, when had he gotten in, how had he found her parents' number, avoiding being face to face with him. There was one small satchel on the chair, and no sign of Theresa.

He took the bag from the chair and asked her to sit. He sat on the bed. Without a word, he switched on the lamp on the nightstand and sat quietly while she looked at him, at the pink and gray scar tissue where an ear should have been, the misshapen discolored eyelid, the crushed cheekbone, the angry red scar on his lip. Taken in slowly, it was not as bad as she first thought, but still she couldn't quite assemble it into the face she knew.

"You see, a devil, like I told you."

"I didn't realize."

"Of course not. How could you?"

She sighed, deeply. "Gordon told us they drove you away, and then there were shots. Everyone thought you were dead."

"I know. So did I. I am like Lazarus." He grimaced. "The Captain ordered me killed. *Kalasi*, he said, which means death. I was dizzy from losing blood, but I heard it quite plainly. Gordon tried to protest, but then one of them smashed his head with a rifle. I was afraid he might be already dead. They pushed Gordon out and went on with me. The Captain stayed behind."

Laurel put her hands over her face. "But why?"

Ngira sighed. "Some old tribal prejudice, or a grudge against teachers, perhaps. Who can say? In Uganda now there is a terrible power of evil which has taken over men's minds."

She watched him, her eyes skimming over face, neck, shoulders, legs, finally resting on his hands as they gestured in the air, the limber, strong hands that had touched her so gently in that other time. She blinked back tears, took a deep breath. "How are things at Butawanga?"

292

"I was only there for a short time, but Senwangama said that by then only half the students had returned. He heard that Kizuma joined Amin's army, and perhaps some of the others. Many young men have been lured by promises of wealth and property, while others have been dragged from their homes and forced to join. My brother, too, has joined these men who now are governed only by greed – and hate." He exhaled a coarse, ragged breath. Laurel knew that sound; she had heard it from Jake, a sound like someone dragging along a dead limb. She wrapped her arms around herself to ward it off, to protect herself from the pull of this man who was both so strange, and so achingly familiar.

"There has been no word from some of our teachers. Walugembe for one, and Saliwa did not come back from his home in the north. Most probably he did not want to risk the long journey. The fathers at the mission have offered to pitch in with the teaching when they can, and even some of the fourth form boys will be giving lessons to the youngest ones."

"What about Gordon?"

"Gordon is determined to stay. I have heard of at least one British expat who was imprisoned, so I was anxious to change his mind. But he says he will not be intimidated by a madman – words to that effect, you know Gordon." They smiled easily for the first time since the visit started. "I thought of waiting until he was drunk and then kidnapping him, but I was not in a condition to do that. Anyway, I feel like a coward for leaving them."

"You had no choice. It would have been foolish to stay there with the Captain still in Kisoro."

"That is what I said to myself as well, but it is an uncertainty I will always carry with me. But all that is behind me, and anyway, I do not wish to talk of myself. I would like to know about your life now." He spoke softly, his voice and accent comforting.

"My life now." She looked into his eyes. They were the same eyes, full of feeling. He waited, but she could not speak.

"You have cut your hair," he said.

"Less trouble this way."

"It is very becoming. It looks a bit African, I think."

This flustered her. "Does it?"

"Perhaps not. Africa is behind you now, and best forgotten."

"God knows I've tried to forget. But after I got home I realized how much it all meant to me. How beautiful it all was." She watched him for a reaction, but detected nothing more than polite alertness. "I couldn't stop remembering our night at Ellen's camp."

He looked away. Her heart sank. So much had happened since then.

"Yes, we should talk about that. It is a memory which came to me very often as I lay there recovering from my wounds." He smiled. "The memory of you saved me, as well as Father Matthew."

"Father Matthew?" Somehow it made perfect sense, that Father Matthew would be the one.

"It was he who rescued me from those men. He hid me at Mtembo's shamba, and Father Lawrence doctored me as best as he could."

Now, a scrim of anger. "I wouldn't have gone if I'd known you were alive, lying wounded somewhere. I was right there at the mission. Why didn't Father Matthew tell me?"

He stopped for a long minute. "My survival was a secret,

as I explained in my letter."

"But the telegram didn't explain anything. It only said you were coming."

They looked at each other.

"No, not the telegram. I mean the letter I sent to you at Butawanga. While I was still recovering."

This brought Laurel to her feet. "I didn't get any letter. There was a memorial service for you and everything, and then, then Peace Corps sent us all home."

He stared at the floor for a moment, shook his head. "I wrote to let you know I was alive, but it seems the letter did not find its way to you."

Laurel lowered back into the chair.

"Shit. All these months –"

"Never mind. Some things happen for the best. It was a great comfort to me to hear that you had left Uganda. When I was recovered enough to travel, I went back to my home village, then to Kampala, where Theresa and I stayed with Gordon's friend, Kenneth. The city is holding its breath, a terrible fear is at its center. At Amin's headquarters at the International Hotel, people said rooms were now used for torture chambers. We were glad to have an out-of-the-way place to stay. My brother John helped me to get a passport. In Kampala now, no official dares to oppose a member of Amin's special forces, as John is now." He stroked his chin in the way she remembered so well. "Without John, I may not have succeeded. Kenneth helped with my visas for England, and the States. Theresa already had her documents, but she wanted to stay with me so we could go together."

Doing what I failed to do. "That was brave. Where is she?"

"She is not here. I saw her settled in New York, then I

flew here to Boston. She is starting law school, you know, at N.Y.U."

"That's wonderful."

"Yes."

She braced for the inevitable. "Are you and Theresa – married yet?"

"No, we will not marry."

His voice lit a bright light inside her.

"She was willing to go ahead with our marriage, despite this –" he indicated his face with a wave. "I was very grateful for the offer of such a gift, but I could not pretend that I still shared her vision of our future together – or to deny that I had developed feelings for you, which she already guessed, thanks to Gordon's meddling."

She recalled the sting of Theresa's stare at the memorial service.

"But it is all right. Theresa and I are still very good friends, and we will see each other in New York City. There are other Ugandans there who have escaped the madness, and I will join them in efforts to try to get our country back."

"You're not staying in Boston?"

"No. I must leave for New York on Tuesday. I have a job waiting for me there which Father Phillip very kindly arranged. But I wanted to see you first." His eyes were softly intense, his face healed by tenderness, and she knew him then as the same person she had carried inside her all this time. She could feel his conflict as he looked at her, his struggle to retain a polite distance, his disfigurement a wall between them. Quaking inside, she moved to sit next to him on the bed.

"I don't want you to go." She put her arms around his neck, inhaled his familiar smell, felt him shiver. He turned his face away, but she turned it back to her, traced the scars with her fingertips. "I love you, Ngira. I did then, only I never said it. I'm saying it now."

He shook his head, gently took her arms from his neck. "If this was a fairy tale like Beauty and the Beast, I would now go back to the way I was before. But that will not happen. I can never be the way I was before. I am changed, both inside and out. I am a shadow that used to be a man, and there is no good kind of life I can offer you. I see now that it was selfish of me to come."

"I don't care." A line of heat happening on her forehead, cheeks. "Remember what you said about Ellen, driving back from the mountain – you said, she is a woman who follows her heart." Trembling again, tears burning through. "You were right about her, and it made me think about how wrong it is to doubt yourself when something feels so right." She took a deep breath, looked steadily at him. "Well this time I'm following my heart. I'm not letting you go."

He turned his face full to meet her eyes. "Laurel." *Lah-rel.* "Look at me. Your eyes will tell you, it cannot be."

She kissed his words away.

<u>47</u>

Fantasy on Elephant Mountain

The car drove itself through the early morning streets out of Boston, transported to a place where only good things could happen, now that Ngira was here. She would skip her morning seminar, shower and change and go back to him, push time and plane flights away and just be with him.

They had kissed long and hard, trying to erase all that had happened, clinging to each other in that overheated hotel room. They had talked, laughed, even slept a little, but they had not made love. Everything was too new, too strange, the broken past and uncertain future between them as unyielding as the scars he bore.

What to do now? She was fired with an optimism that helped override her doubts. She could think only of today, cutting class but working her shift at the diner so Doris wouldn't be short-handed during the dinner hour. They would have time to talk and find a way to stay together.

That was all that was important now. *I am a shadow that used to be a man.* No. He loved her, he had said so, and she would breathe love into him, and he would be all right, they would be all right.

"A job's a job," she had said, trying to keep him from leaving.

He had a tutoring job waiting for him at a half-way house in New York. "New York or Boston, what's the difference?"

She wished now she felt as confident as she had sounded. He had probably used all his savings just getting over to the U.S. Still, she was not ready to part with him so soon. She could support him until he found something, of course she would. His flight was at 6 a.m. tomorrow; she had until then to convince him to stay.

* * *

"So that colored girl didn't marry him, and who'd ever blame her? Don't get me wrong, hon, he seems nice enough, but he's some kind of damaged goods." Ngira was at one of the little two-seater booths near the door, absorbed in reading today's *Globe*, while Laurel was picking up an order. Thank heaven Doris was keeping her voice low for a change. "Of all the men out there, why set yourself on that one?"

Laurel looked at him perusing the newspaper, wearing a knit cap that almost covered his missing ear, and was hit by that feeling again, inexplicable, almost frightening, of aching with love for him. She glared at Doris, filled her tray and served the couple at table three, a man with a much younger woman, both well dressed, maybe a boss and his secretary, even a father and daughter out to lunch. Ordinarily Doris would have had them chewed over and digested by now, Laurel thought, but today there was Ngira to pick on.

"I just can't see it, you and this beat-up African. You're a nice-looking girl, you'll find someone else." Doris shook her head. "I mean, why take up with a colored man?"

"Black, Doris." Walking to the diner everyone on the street had taken notice of them; some had stared boldly, others had looked and then pointedly looked away. She knew it had as much to do with his skin color as it did with his scars. It had made her angry, and this, she knew, was just the beginning.

"Whatever you call them it comes to the same. I'm the first to admit there's some good ones, like Charlie, and some of my customers – still, it's not right, a white girl and a colored man. There used to be a law against it in some states. Maybe there still is."

"No, there isn't, Doris. The Supreme Court struck down those laws a few years ago."

"Law or no law, you just wait and see, people won't let you alone."

Her hand shook as she loaded her tray. "Then to hell with them. I can't run my life by what other people think, including you, Doris."

"No need to get snippy about it. I'm just saying it's a tough row to hoe, hon, and that's no lie. Why ask for trouble?"

Laurel made a conscious effort to hold her tongue.

"Well, you don't need to take my advice. What do your parents say?"

Her parents would say everything and nothing, and her mother would probably never forgive her, for certain this time, but she couldn't worry about that now. "They haven't had a chance to say much of anything. Look, Doris, I can't help what people say or think, I just know I have to be with him. This is the first time I've felt happy since I came home." She looked at Ngira again and knew this was true, and wanted more than anything to leave this place and be alone with him. Her throat was tight, her chest constricted. "And you have no right to talk that way about him. You don't even know him."

Doris shook her head and sighed. "It's light today. You deal out those burgers, then go sit down with that boy. He looks like a lost soul. You two get it all talked out." She turned toward the opening to the kitchen. "Hey, Charlie, BP and GCP, double the fries for our lovebirds out here."

When she slipped into the seat opposite, Ngira smiled and folded the newspaper. Why couldn't Doris see him the way she saw him?

"I've been thinking, maybe I can stay, after all. I could probably find some kind of work temporarily," he nodded toward Charlie in the kitchen, "until I can get teaching certification from your state of Massachusetts."

Why couldn't Doris hear the music in his voice?

"Here you go, hon, on the house. Grilled cheese platter for our little vegetarian, and a Bonanza burger special for your friend here, Mr. –"

"Please, call me David."

"All right then, David, you eat hearty now." She shrugged in response to Ngira's thank you and walked away.

Laurel barely noticed the food, or Doris. She had been picturing Ngira in some restaurant kitchen. The most he would get was dishwashing, or busing tables. With his scarred face, the Boston schools might not want him as a teacher. Suddenly she was not hungry. "So, you're David now?"

"It is easier for Americans, I think. When in Rome, as the saying goes –" Ngira took up his knife and fork, cut a piece of meat. "This is my first burger." *Buh-guh.*

The East African accent was like a familiar tune.

He saw her smile and said, "Oh, I know, it is burr-gurr. How is that?"

"Perfect," she said. "Here, take some of this ketchup and squirt it on top. Then you take your other piece of bread, which is Doris' special sourdough, and put it on top. Then you pick up the whole mess and eat it."

301

"So then, is it a law in America, that all food must be eaten in a sandwich?"

Laurel felt suddenly overwhelmed; her smile fell and she put a hand to her head.

"Laurel, I am sorry. I was joking."

"I know, Ngira, it's not that. That job in New York – tutoring teenagers at a halfway house is something you would be very good at."

He sat back, studying her. "Then you think I should get on that plane tomorrow, after all."

"I don't think there's a choice." She felt this admission like a lead weight on her stomach. "It's hard to get by in a new country, and immigration laws about employment are very strict as I understand it. Plus, they're giving you a place to live at the mission. It seems too good to pass up." Also, Father Lawrence had given him the name of a plastic surgeon in New York who might be willing to help.

"I should have realized how difficult it would be for me to leave, once I found you again." He reached over and held her hand. "I will want to go back to Uganda, you know, when things are safe again."

She refused to let tears come, and would not meet his eyes. "Yes."

"So then, our reality is a hard one. We are from two worlds which will not easily combine. It would be very wrong of me to make any sort of promises, except to say that I will always carry you in my heart."

When the choking lump in her throat subsided, she smiled at him. He was alive, and he was here, now, sitting with her, solid, his hand warm around hers. That was what mattered. Outside, white flakes were floating down onto the gray sidewalk.

"Look. It's snowing."

He turned, watched for some moments. "Eh, but this is a beautiful thing. I am glad to see it for the first time with you."

Her mind was churning. "You know, we can visit each other on weekends. Boston to New York is not even as far as Kampala to Kisoro, and the buses are faster, most of the time." She forced a laugh. "There's always a concert somewhere in New York. We could go to some." Bohème, Chopin, let it be so.

"But please, no Gilbert and Sullivan."

They laughed.

He let go of her hand. "I will be very sorry to miss your first recital at BU. I will come to the next one. I want very much to hear you play."

"It's just a music department recital."

"But your own composition – that is a very great accomplishment."

It was not so much great as necessary. Essential. It had sprung as an elegy from the dark well of absence, but the shroud of grief over its conception had somehow failed to darken the bright spring of memory, and the unacknowledged, undreamed of hope. Ngira was alive, and now that the world had turned from darkness to light, it would be titled *Fantasy on Elephant Mountain*, her first real finished composition. It was an old keyboard form, the Fantasy, begun in the Baroque, but it had appealed to her for its room for improvisation and freedom from rigid form. Yes, she had taken liberties with structure, and she would play it less than perfectly because she was still not a great pianist, but she would play it with a depth of intimacy and knowledge because it was her creation, hers and Ngira's, the bone and blood of their union, the pain of their parting. It was her gift to him, to what they were to each other, and no matter what the future held it would always be there, shining with a life of its own.

"My first opus. Actually, it's not quite finished yet. I was searching for a tempo for the final statement. I think I've found it. *Vivacé.*"

Their eyes connected and all the words, the fears, the uncertainties passed between them, and in the strength of the moment disappeared. They would leave half their food uneaten, and Doris would be miffed. But Ngira was leaving tomorrow. They had only this night to repair the past and plan as much of the future as their two worlds could hold.

"And does it have a name yet, this unfinished composition?"

She had been waiting for him to ask.

About the Author

Linda Johnston Muhlhausen was born on Long Island, New York, and received a Bachelor's degree in English from State University of New York at Binghamton in 1971. After graduation, she joined the U.S. Peace Corps and traveled to Uganda, East Africa, where she taught English Language and Literature at an all-boys secondary school.   In fall of 1972, Peace Corps volunteers were evacuated after the shooting death of a volunteer trainee and the general breakdown of law and order under the violent regime of Ugandan President Idi Amin Dada. Linda now lives and writes in New Jersey.

About the Publisher

"A book should be a ball of light in your hands."
— Ezra Pound

This past year, **BLAST PRESS** expanded its publishing program in several new directions. We have our first anthology—which is distinct from a magazine—with representative New Jersey poets with our *Palisades, Parkways & Pinelands,* a generous almost 300 page collection of over 30 poets. Another direction is the illustrated collaboration between H. A. Maxson and Dorothy Wordsworth in a new kind of "found poetry" that is a beautiful mash-up of a living poet and his long-dead collaborator's nature notebooks. *The Changing Room* is another first for BLAST PRESS, a fully-illustrated long poem by Carrie Hudak that blends dream and reality as a child's story might, but with adult themes of death and a sophistication of tone unusual in an illustrated tale. *Surfing for Jesus* is a lively new work by Susanna Rich, exploring religious themes and impacts of growing up in a church tradition in late-twentieth-century America. Joe Weil and Emily Vogel's "responsorials," are an ongoing dialog with poem answering poem in their unusual and emotionally intimate *West of Home.* Last year, **BLAST PRESS** released the widely published author Emanuel di Pasquale's *Knowing the Moment,* a delicate paean to his life on the Jersey Shore. And **BLAST PRESS** continues its primary tradition of supporting uncollected poets with a first-time poetry book by Mathew V. Spano, *Hellgrammite.* I would like to extend a special thank you to our authors and editors, and to our enthusiastic readers, for all you do to enliven the world of poetry.

With best regards,

Gregg Glory
(Gregg G. Brown)
Publisher

Also Available

Anthologies
Palisades, Parkways & Pinelands
Jersey Shore Poets

Susanna Fry
30 Poems

James Dalton
Instead

Magdalena Alagna
The Cranky Bodhisattva

Rusty Cuffs
[Thad Rutkowski]
Sex-Fiend Monologues III

Sarah Avery
Persephone in Washington

George Holler
Erotic Logic

Jacko Monahan
One-Legged Poetry

Daniel J. Weeks
X Poems
Les Symbolistes
Self-Symphonies
Virginia

Carrie Pedersen Hudak
Yoga Notes

The Arms of Venus
Queens Arms
The Queen of Cakes
The Changing Room
Bee Loud Glade

Sharon Baller
Venus Has Gone Insane Again

Joe Weil
West of Home

Emily Vogel
West of Home

H. A. Maxson
Grasmere
Call It Sleep
A Commonplace Book

Emanuel Di Pasquale
Knowing the Moment
Poems in Sicily and America

Mathew V. Spano
Hellgrammite

Linda Johnston Muhlhausen
Elephant Mountain

Warren Cooper
What Happened at Dinner, and After

Gabor Barabas
Collected Poems

Lord Dermond
[Daniel B. Dermond]
13 Stories High
Ghosts and Princes Revised

Hourless Grail
Inner Dominion
Lords Miscellany
The Mortal Words
Sacred Blades
The Unaging Muse

John Dunfy
Spinning Wheels

Joie Ferentino
BELM

Chuck Moon
God-Speck Exhibitions

Brandi Mantha Grannett
Floaters

Mary Jane Tenerelli
'Til Death Do Us Part

Gregg Glory
[Gregg G. Brown]
Adoring Thorns
The Alarmist
American Bacchanalia
American Descants
American Songbook
Antirime
Ascent
Assembling the Earth
Autobiographies
A/voi/d/ances
Benedict Arnold
Black Champagne
Brain Cell
Burning Byzantium
The Cabana at the Equator
Constellations in December

Chaos and Stars
Contemporaries
Dear Planet Jesus
The Death of Satan
A Deepening Sea
The Departed Friend
Deus Abscondis
Digital Boy
Disappearing Acts
Divine Revolt
Dr. Kilmer's Ocean-Weed Heart Remedy
Down By Swansea
Eating the Cliffside
Evil Interludes
The Falcon Waiting
Ghosts and Princes Revised
The Giant in the Cradle
Greetings from Mt. Olympus
Hell, Darling
The Hummingbird's Apprentice
Hurry Up, Hurricane!
Hymns
The Impossible Mesa
Interregnum Scribbles
It's the Sex Pistols!!!!
Jan and Marsha
The Life of Riley
The Maybe Plagues
Mercury Astronauts
A Million Shakespeares
Naked Eloquence
Nobody Poems
Night, Night
Of Flares, Of Flowers
On Being a Human Bean
The Pilot Light
Platinum Lips [CD]
Prometheus Bound
The Queen of Cakes
A Raven's Weight

Red Bank
Repetitions on the Rappahannock
Rose Lasso
Saving Cinderella
Shreads of Verity
Seven Heavens
The Singing Well
Sipping Beer in the Shadow of God
The Sleepy Partridge
The Soft Assault
Soul-Splitter
Spotty the Spot-tacular Cat
Supposing Roses
Supreme Day
The Sword Inside
The Timid Leaper
Torturous Splendours of the Dream
Ultra
Unimagined Things
Venus and Vesuvius
Vindictive Advice
A Volcano Island
Wild Onions
XXX Sonnets
Youth Youth Youth

Made in the USA
Lexington, KY
01 April 2019